JUST A LITTLE WICKEDNESS

MERRY FARMER

JUST A LITTLE WICKEDNESS

Cover design by Erin Dameron-Hill (the miracle-worker)

ASIN: B084LRZCF6

Paperback ISBN: 9798615770449

Click here for a complete list of other works by Merry Farmer.

If you'd like to be the first to learn about when the next books in the series come out and more, please sign up for my newsletter here: http://eepurl.com/RQ-KX

❉ Created with Vellum

CHAPTER 1

LONDON – MARCH, 1890

*I*t was barely past seven in the evening, and already a headache was forming behind Alistair Bevan's eyes.

"It's terrible," his father, Lord Albert Bevan, Earl of Winslow, huffed, squirming against the back of his seat in the well-appointed carriage they traveled in. "That a man like Lord Chisolm could walk about town, holding dinner parties, and passing himself off as a genial host is simply disgraceful."

"Yes, dear, we know," Alistair's mother said with a long-suffering sigh, patting her husband's hand.

"The truth must be known," Alistair's father went on, his white mustache quivering. "Families such as the Eccles clan need to be exposed for their sins."

"I agree, Father," Alistair said in as soothing a voice as he could manage. "But perhaps it would be better to wait until some sort of concrete proof is discovered before slighting the name of one of the most influential families in London."

Alistair sent a sideways look to his brother, Darren, seated in the carriage beside him. Darren wore a pinched frown that was all too familiar to Alistair. The glance they exchanged was loaded with the unique sort of tension that could only be shared by brothers who knew their father was losing his mind.

"I thought Lord Chisolm and the rest of the Eccles family were your friends, Father," Darren said in a manner that was usually reserved for speaking to a child.

"Of course they are my friends," their father replied indignantly. "One must always keep their friends close and their enemies closer, as the adage goes."

"Is that why we rushed about the moment we arrived in London from Dorset?" Darren asked with a smirk. "To pretend that your mortal enemy is actually your bosom friend so that we can keep them close?"

Alistair didn't approve of his brother's teasing tone, but he didn't try to stop the question.

"We are behaving as any civil members of the aristocracy would," their father insisted. "We received an invitation, and so we are accepting it." It was a good enough answer, and Alistair was almost pleased by it, until his father added, "And if we're clever, we can catch those beastly slave traders at their game."

Alistair winced, raising his hands to rub his throbbing temples. There it was again, his father's dogged insistence that the Eccles family—the ones who bore the Chisolm title as well as the ones who didn't—made their money through the slave trade.

"Papa," Alistair sighed, his eyes squeezed closed. "I'll grant you that the Eccles's might very well have made their fortune on the slave trade a hundred and fifty years ago, but you do realize that it is eighteen ninety and that the slave trade has been outlawed these eighty-three years now."

"He knows what year it is," their mother said in a tight voice, offended at the very idea that her husband's sanity was being questioned.

"You only know what you studied in those dusty old books of yours, son," their father scolded Alistair. "There are more things in heaven and earth than are dreamed of in your philosophy."

Alistair opened one eye to peek at his father. The man had gone from getting lost in the past to quoting Shakespeare. It wasn't going to be a good night, and they would be out in public when the inevitable breakdown happened.

"Perhaps we should turn around and go home," he suggested, but it was already too late.

The carriage rolled to a stop in front of a stately Mayfair mansion and an attendant in fine livery rushed forward to open the door. Alistair stepped out first, followed by Darren. Darren offered a hand to their mother, escorting her on to the white marble front steps, while Alistair did the best he could to help his father out of the carriage without making him appear like the frail, old man he was. The worst of it was that Albert Bevan wasn't even that old. He hadn't yet turned sixty, and already his mind and body were failing. It could only mean one thing—that Alistair would inherit the earldom, the land and fortune, the seat in the House of Lords, and the duty and responsibility that went with it all far sooner than he was ready to.

"Now," his father said as Alistair offered his arm to support him in his struggle up the steps to where Darren and Lady Winslow were waiting in the doorway, "keep your eyes peeled for anything sinister."

"Yes, Father," Alistair sighed, squaring his shoulders and walking on with as much dignity as he could.

"There's no telling what sort of evidence could be lying about in plain sight. Men like Chisolm are clumsy when it comes to hiding their nefarious activity. They grow too proud and too self-congratulatory, and that is when we must swoop in and bring them to justice."

"Of course." Alistair nodded, but inside, his heart felt as heavy as a stone.

He could remember a time when the world revolved around his father, when the man was the epitome of strength and wisdom to him. He would have given anything to have that man back, but since that was as impossible as fetching a chunk of cheese from the moon to go with supper, the best he could do was to be the man

4

his father needed him to be, as hard as it was. There were so many things that would disappoint his father to his core if he knew, starting with the fact that Alistair enjoyed the romantic company of men the way he was supposed to enjoy that of women.

"Let me know if you need me to take a turn," Darren murmured to Alistair as they reached the magnificent front hall of the stylish mansion.

"I will," Alistair promised, then glanced around at the opulence.

The Chisolm mansion in Mayfair was new, as far as stately London homes went. It had been constructed barely twenty years before in the place of an older, Georgian building, and held all the modern conveniences a man of as much wealth as Lord Chisolm could buy. The chandeliers were gilded, the art was that of grand masters, and the furnishings in the parlor they were led to, where titled and notable guests from the most desirable families in London gathered before supper, were artworks in themselves. Alistair noted several members of the royal family in attendance. He also noticed two pairs of wide, startled eyes staring out at the guests from a Japanese screen set in front of what looked like a concealed servants' entrance to the room.

That charming detail—staff in the house peeking at the glorious guests—set Alistair a fraction more at ease. He deliberately glanced away, loath to give up the secret of whoever was spying on them.

That ease was shattered a moment later when his

father leaned closer to him while staring across the room. "You see there?" He nodded to a young woman dressed in the latest Paris fashion, her hair piled fantastically on her head. "That is Lady Alice Norton. She is one of the most eligible heiresses on the market this season."

Alistair's stomach sank. "She is quite the beauty," he said, knowing it was what he was expected to say.

"She is exactly the sort of bride you should be setting your sights on," his father went on. "Not only is she a social triumph already at her young age, she could provide you with sons who bear a connection to the royal family."

Lady Alice happened to glance in Alistair's direction at that moment. All Alistair could do was to smile tightly and nod to the woman in acknowledgement. The thought of courting Lady Alice—or any other woman, for that matter—turned his blood cold. He was no liar, and any overture he made to a woman would be a lie of astounding proportions. He knew who he was, though hardly anyone else did, certainly not his family. But he also knew his duty. He knew what was expected of him.

"My lords and ladies, supper is served," announced a butler who was dressed as elaborately as any of the guests.

For once, Alistair was glad of his father's frailty. It meant no one expected him to single out one of the ladies in the room to escort into dinner. Darren upheld that tradition for the family, and their mother was escorted in by a bishop, which she would no doubt crow about for days to come. Alistair followed behind the rest of the guests, supporting his father as a savvy footman gestured for him to bring his father to a place that had been specially arranged.

"Keep your wits about you," Alistair's father whispered as they crossed into the dining room.

"Father," Alistair sighed. "Surely a family that goes out of its way to prepare a special place for you at the table is not infiltrated with the enemy."

His father let out a humorless laugh. "You would be surprised, my boy. And besides, Lady Chisolm is a Fitzgerald, not an Eccles. I'm certain this is her doing."

Alistair opted not to answer. Partly because several guests were already staring at them. Paul Eccles, Lord Burbage, Lord Chisolm's oldest son, in particular seemed to be keeping one eye on them as Alistair helped his father into his seat.

"Do you need some help there, Farnham?" Burbage asked, addressing Alistair by his formal title in spite of the fact that they'd known each other since university. Alistair rarely bothered with formalities when it came to men near his own age who traveled in his same social circles, but he couldn't think of Burbage in any way but formally.

"No, thank you," he replied with a civil smile. As soon as his father was as comfortable in his chair as he could be, Alistair seated himself in the chair beside him.

"Only, it seems as though your father needs more assistance these days than he used to," Burbage went on, his grin a little too pointed, as he took a seat across the table.

A few of the guests seated nearby were kind enough to look startled at the comment. Lady Burbage—Paul's wife of less than a year, who was already a little too round with child for polite company—leaned closer to whisper something to him with a scowl. Burbage ignored her.

"I am still here, young man," Alistair's father said in a voice that was louder than it should have been, drawing even more attention. "So don't count me out yet."

A few of the ladies tittered with nervous laughter as footmen moved about the table, serving the first course. Alistair felt heat rise up his neck, but it was hard to tell whether it was anger or embarrassment. He would rather have died than admit his father was an embarrassment to him, but the facts were the facts.

"The situation in Mozambique is quite concerning." The titled gentleman sitting on Alistair's other side tried to strike up a conversation. "But I'm certain we'll have Portugal on the run in no time."

"Their position is untenable," Alistair agreed, although the only thing he knew about the problems in Africa was that something was going on.

"They never should have—"

"Look at that," Alistair's father hissed on the other side, dragging him away from polite conversation.

Alistair sent an apologetic glance to the man trying to talk to him—who easily turned to converse with the middle-aged woman on his other side—and turned to his father.

"Chisolm will have an heir and a spare before summer," his father went on, nodding to Lady Burbage, or rather, the portion of her stomach that was visible above the table.

If Alistair could have slumped under the table to hide from the inappropriate topic of conversation, he would have. "Father, perhaps we could discuss this later."

"You mustn't let them get too far ahead of us," his father whispered in return. "You're just as capable of marrying a socialite as Paul Eccles is."

"He's referred to as Lord Burbage, Father."

"He's a viscount," his father muttered on, either stating the obvious or on his way to making a point. "You're a viscount," he went on. "His father is an earl, your father is an earl. And I can say with relative certainty that you will be an earl before he is."

"Father, please." Alistair glanced around, trying to gauge who was listening in and who was politely ignoring his father's lack of propriety.

He caught sight of two tiny heads poking around the corner of the modest doorway at the end of the room and was certain they belonged to the same pairs of eyes he'd spotted behind the screen in the parlor. If he had to guess, by the look of them, he'd say their spies were a hall boy and scullery maid. Lord Chisolm certainly didn't have children that young and Burbage was only beginning his brood.

"Look around you, son," his father went on. "You could have your pick of a bride. And I'm quite certain you could do better than snotty little Paul Eccles."

The woman seated on his father's other side cleared her throat loudly.

Heat flooded Alistair. "You know this isn't an appropriate dinner topic," he whispered.

His father huffed. "What is the point of going out in society if not to make couples? What is the difference between flirting in a ballroom and strategizing in a dining room?"

The evening wasn't going to go well. His father was already raising his voice. Alistair was no fortune-teller, but he could predict that within ten minutes, his father would be standing and attempting to auction him off to the highest bidder. He had no choice but to act.

As soon as the footman carrying the soup course came near, Alistair sent him an apologetic look. The man frowned curiously, and as he attempted to serve his father, Alistair bumped his arm, sending just enough soup splashing onto his father's dinner jacket to disrupt proceedings.

"I'm sorry, my lord," the footman apologized.

"It's my fault entirely," Alistair murmured to him, adding an earnest look to make certain the man knew it, then standing. "Come along, Father. I'll help you tidy your jacket."

Not a soul at the table looked the least bit surprised. Darren sent Alistair a grateful nod. Their mother glanced down at her soup in sorrow as the friend seated next to her whispered something comforting to her. Across the table, Burbage was doing a poor job of hiding a snicker. His father, Lord Chisolm, seated at the head of the table, let out a dramatic moan and rolled his eyes, making it clear he thought the once great Lord Albert Winslow was a pathetic joke.

Acid churned in Alistair's gut as he closed an arm around his father's shoulders and escorted him from the room.

"There's a parlor across this way where you could rest," Chisolm's butler said, directing them across the hall. "I could see if one of the valets is available to help with the jacket."

"Thank you." Alistair nodded to the man.

"Where are we?" Alistair's father asked as soon as he was seated on a cozy settee next to a cheery fire.

"We're waiting for a valet to come along to help with your jacket," Alistair explained.

"Good, good." His father nestled back into the pillows as Alistair arranged them behind his back. "I'll wait here while you search the room for signs of foul play."

"I'm not going to snoop through Lord Chisolm's house," Alistair said, shaking his head. "You might not want to admit it, Father, but there's nothing wrong with the Eccles family. I can't say that I like them very much, but they're no more nefarious than half the other grand families in England."

"That's what they want you to think," his father insisted, closing his eyes and letting out a happy sigh. "You'll find the truth. I trust you. I rely on you."

Alistair stood helplessly by, watching as his father fell fast asleep. It was bittersweet to know he had his father's complete confidence. Every son wanted to feel their father's approval, but one false move on Alistair's part and that confidence would be blown out of the water. One tip of his hand and his father would see through the illusion Alistair presented to the world.

He wasn't going to let that happen.

He moved away from the settee, walking to the fireplace to lean against the mantel, staring into the low flames. He would do his duty by his family. If his father wanted him to court Lady Alice Norton, or any other woman, he would buck up and do it. He would push his true self aside to be who his father needed him to be. He would produce an heir, take over the running of the estate, and do whatever it took to be the best Earl of Winslow possible, no matter how quickly it all happened. He would—

"Excuse me, my lord. I was told you were in need of the services of a valet?"

Alistair turned away from the fireplace to look straight into the deep, dark eyes of the most beautiful man he'd ever seen in his life. He was tall, with broad shoulders, a narrow waist, and dark hair that was swept rakishly to one side. As soon as he saw the startled look on

Alistair's face, his perfect mouth formed into a smile that went straight to Alistair's cock.

There was only one thing Alistair could say as every resolution to do his duty blasted away from his mind.

"Fuck."

CHAPTER 2

$\mathcal{T}$ime was running out. The longer Joe remained in the employ of Lord Burbage without discovering so much as a clue as to what had happened to Lily, the less likely he was to find her. He strode through the halls of Eccles House, tempted to explore his employer's study or the library or to look for some other corner of the house that he hadn't already pored over while Burbage and his father were occupied at supper. He was clever enough to explain his presence where he wasn't meant to be—cleverness had never been his problem—but even so, he couldn't risk being dismissed. Not until he had answers about Lily.

Giddy whispers from around the corner closest to the formal dining room caught Joe's attention as he debated doubling back to search Burbage's study. He knew what he was about to find before he turned the corner and grinned. As quietly as he could, he approached the two bright-eyed children on their knees, peering into the grand dining room. They were so absorbed in ogling Lord Chisolm's guests that they didn't hear him approaching until he bent close to them and whispered, "Boo."

The children squealed and leapt up, scrambling backward, knowing they'd been caught.

"Toby, Emma, what are the two of you doing?" Joe asked, laughing.

Before the two could answer, first footman, Ned, marched around the corner looking as though he would call for the children's blood. "Get back to the kitchen or I'll tell Mr. Vine to sack you and kick you back to the gutter where you came from."

Joe reached for Toby and Emma's hands. "There's no need for that, Ned," he warned the young man.

Ned stiffened, tugging at the bottom of his livery jacket. "I think there's every need, Mr. Logan."

"I'll take them back downstairs." Joe sent the uptight footman a flat look and turned to lead the children away. "Don't mind him," he told the children as they walked. "Ned has ambitions, and you can never quite trust a man with ambitions."

The children giggled.

"Did you see how grand they all looked, Mr. Logan?" Emma asked.

"Is that woman at the end of the table the queen?" Toby added.

"No," Joe laughed. "She's just some fine lady. I'd rather spend a night playing soldiers with the two of you than sit down to eat with that lot."

"But they're ever so grand," Emma argued, looking preciously earnest as she did.

"I'm going to be a soldier when I get older," Toby insisted. "Even though I'm just a hall boy now."

"Count your blessings where you find them," Joe told them as they neared the door to the servants' quarters. "Being a hall boy and a scullery maid is a damn sight better than what you could be." He would know. The stark difference in the lives of his siblings who had gone into service versus those who had stayed on the farm as day laborers was astounding.

And then there was Lily. He couldn't shake the feeling that someone had lured her into a harlot's life, by hook or by crook. Lily was uncommonly pretty. But he'd found no evidence of her at all in any of the brothels he'd investigated. Which had led him to the theory that a guest of the Eccles family had sweet-talked her away from an upright life. He could find nothing to support his hunch, though. If he didn't find out what had happened to his sister soon, he didn't know what he would do.

"Now, don't you two have work to do?" he asked, shooing them toward the servants' door.

Before they could answer, Mr. Vine stepped out of one of the fine parlors near the front of the hall, spotted Joe, and changed direction to march toward him. Joe pushed the children on, praying they were smart enough to scurry downstairs to work before Mr. Vine questioned what they were doing upstairs.

"Ah, Mr. Logan," Mr. Vine said, ignoring Toby and Emma, much to Joe's relief.

"Mr. Vine." Joe nodded to the butler, careful to observe all the formalities that their positions in the household required. God knew he couldn't afford to land on the butler's bad side. Not with his reasons for being in the house and not with all the things Mr. Vine could discover about him if he scratched the surface.

"There is a guest in need of assistance in the Queen Charlotte parlor." Mr. Vine got straight down to business.

"Assistance?" Joe shook his head slightly. "From me?"

"Lord Winslow has spilled soup on his diner jacket and is in need of a valet's skills to set things to right."

"Ah, I understand. I'll attend to him right away." Joe bowed slightly, taking great pains to show respect, and then hurrying on without being told. He didn't care much for Mr. Vine, but a comfortable life depended on befriending everyone around him and giving them no reason at all to take notice of things they shouldn't. He hadn't made it safely through as much of his life as he had, being who and what he was, by drawing attention to himself, that much was certain. Although it meant he hadn't had as much fun as he'd wanted to either. But circumspection was necessary when a man had his sorts of tastes, and ever since Lily had disappeared, he couldn't afford distractions.

Which was why striding into the Queen Charlotte

parlor and coming face to face with a perfectly dressed gentleman staring into the fire with the most sorrowful expression Joe had ever seen felt like running headlong into a solid brick wall.

Joe drank in the sight of the man—the way his clothes fit perfectly over an obviously fit body, the slight curl of his light brown hair, and above all, the intensity of emotion shining from his devilishly handsome face—before clearing his throat and saying, "Excuse me, my lord. I was told you were in need of the services of a valet?"

The man jerked away from the fire and his eyes met Joe's. The spark that passed between the two of them was palpable. On top of that, Joe could have sworn the man muttered, "Fuck," in a deep, rich tone.

Fuck indeed.

"Mr. Vine informed me you spilled soup on your dinner jacket," Joe said, taking a step forward, clasping his hands behind his back and attempting to adopt the proper, submissive posture. He couldn't do it, though. Every fiber of his being wanted to stand tall and to move gracefully, to catch the gentleman's eye.

The gentleman watched him for a few more, captivating seconds before shaking his head and saying, "Not me, my father." He nodded toward the settee closest to the fire.

Joe hadn't noticed the sleeping man. He had a feeling someone could have fired a cannon in the parlor and he wouldn't have noticed. Not with the vision of masculine perfection drawing all of his attention. He threw caution to the wind and met the gentleman's look with a flirtatious smile. If his instincts about the man were wrong, he could make light of his overly friendly look and save face, but he doubted he was wrong.

Only when he reached the settee did he pull his gaze away from the gentleman to study his father. In an instant, pity raced through him. The father had, indeed, stained his finely tailored jacket. A jacket that must have fit him well at some point, but which was too large for his shrunken frame now. The man was obviously ill, and if Joe knew anything about anything, he wouldn't be recovering.

"May I?" he asked the gentleman, reaching for the jacket to assess the stain better.

"Go right ahead," the gentleman said with a sigh, crossing to the settee.

Joe could tell in an instant that it would take more work than he could do in the parlor to clean the stain. At the same time, he was loath to undress the older man. He was so frail that, even next to the fire, the poor dear might catch a chill. Instead, he stood. A rush of excitement coursed through him at the gentleman's proximity.

"You'll have to have your valet or his clean the jacket once you get home," he said, his voice dropping to the warm tone he usually reserved for men he wanted to become more than his friend.

The gentleman blinked once, his eyes locking with Joe's. A moment later, he took in a breath and said, "I don't have a valet." Prickles of excitement raced down Joe's back, as though the gentleman had told him he didn't currently have a lover but would like one. "Father does, though," he went on, breaking away to sit on the settee and take his father's hand.

The moment of connection evaporated, much to Joe's regret. It had been ages since he'd reacted to a man like that. "If you'd like," he said, "I can fetch some soda water to take out the worst of the stain for now. It'll be enough for you to make your way home presentably."

"Thank you," the gentleman said with a weary smile.

Joe's heart skipped a beat. What wouldn't he have done to wipe that sadness out of the gentleman's eyes. Several ideas of how he could make the man forget whatever hurt him—and everything else—popped to his mind.

"Give me just a moment," he said, bowing, then turning to leave before his body betrayed him by showing just what he thought of the gentleman.

He walked sedately out of the parlor, then broke into a run as soon as he was around the corner. He dashed downstairs, nearly knocking Toby over as the boy swept the downstairs hallway, fetched the soda water and a cloth, then darted back toward the stairs, not wanting to spend a moment more than he had to apart from the gentleman. He skittered to a stop as he passed the wine cellar, then backtracked to pluck a bottle from the shelf, then raced to find a wineglass and corkscrew as well.

Finally, he made his way back up to the parlor, his arms filled with all the things he'd fetched. He forced himself to stop just shy of the parlor and to wait for his heartbeat to slow. At last, he checked his appearance in one of the many hall mirrors, then walked calmly into the parlor as though he'd been as cool and disinterested as the North Sea the whole time.

"Here we are, my lord," he said with a friendly smile as he approached the settee. The gentleman hadn't moved, nor had the pain in his expression eased as he watched his father. "I took the liberty of bringing you something to drink as well." He hesitated, then added, "You look as though you could use a drink."

The gentleman hummed in agreement, drew in a breath, then stood to make a place for Joe. As Joe handed him the bottle and glass, their fingers touched. The effect was so electric Joe's face went hot.

"Do you think he'll mind if I work on his jacket while he sleeps?" Joe asked, just above a whisper. He prayed the gentleman would think he'd lowered his voice to avoid waking the father up.

The gentleman met his eyes, and for a moment the undeniable attraction was there again. The gentleman's eyes dropped to Joe's lips, then he let out a sigh, turned away, and said, "Not at all. He probably won't even notice."

"Understood, my lord." The moment was gone once again, so Joe sat, took the bottle of soda water from his pocket along with the cloth, and unstoppered the bottle.

The gentleman's sleeping father barely moved as Joe went to work, dabbing at the stains.

"We shouldn't have come tonight at all," the gentleman said as he took the wine bottle to a small table against the wall. He paused, then asked, "Do you have a corkscrew?"

"Oh, sorry."

Joe paused in his work to reach into his pocket for the corkscrew. When the gentleman came to take it, their hands brushed again. Joe could have sworn the man lingered before turning away and returning to the table.

It was ridiculous. Joe was a valet from a background that was barely middle class. The gentleman was obviously wealthy and titled. And yet, what made them different from normal men leveled the playing field between them. At least to a certain degree.

"Why do you say you shouldn't have come?" Joe asked, eager to keep the conversation going, as he worked on the father's jacket.

The pop of the wine bottle sounded before the gentleman spoke. "You can see that my father's health is not good."

Joe made a sympathetic sound, smiling at the slumbering gentleman.

"His mind is increasingly unsound as well," the gentleman went on. He paused, then said, "It is agony to watch the man whom I have admired and looked up to for my entire life decline into little more than a shell of what he once was. And for him to decline at so young an age." He paused again to take a drink of wine as he walked back to the settee. "He's not yet sixty."

"I'm sorry," Joe said, glancing up from his work to show him just how sympathetic he was.

The gentleman let out a long breath and shrugged. "There's nothing to be done. Every doctor money can buy has been consulted. No one knows how long it will be. Years still, in all likelihood. But that just means more years to watch...this."

"I cannot imagine," Joe said.

"I just wish I didn't feel so useless," the gentleman went on, resting his free hand on the back of the settee. "There's so little I can do."

On impulse, Joe reached up to rest a hand over his. "I'm certain you're doing the best you can."

The gentleman didn't move his hand or shake Joe off. He stared at their fingers in a way that made Joe want to thread his through the gentleman's and to hold on for dear life.

"I'll have to assume the duties of the title and all that entails," the gentleman went on. "Father seems to know it as well. He has taken to pointing out eligible brides to me every time we go out. He's desperate to see me married and to have a grandchild before he goes."

"Which must be painful for you," Joe said in a frank tone.

The gentleman's eyes jumped to meet his, suddenly fearful.

"I'm the same way," Joe rushed to confess. "But I

think you sensed that from the moment I walked in the room, as I did with you."

Color splashed onto the gentleman's face. He pulled his hand away, taking a long drink from his wineglass. Once he'd swallowed, he said, "So you understand how far I must go to be the dutiful son."

"I do." The gentleman's father's jacket was as clean as it was going to get, so Joe tucked the cloth back in his pocket, set the soda water on the floor, and stood. "I have a duty of my own," he said. "My sister has gone missing, and our family is counting on me to find her."

The gentleman's brow shot up in surprise. "I'm sorry to hear that. Is there anything I can do?"

A smile played across Joe's lips in spite of the heaviness of the situation. "That's very kind of you, my lord." He hesitated, then extended his hand. "My name is Joe. Joe Logan."

The gentleman took his hand and shook it. "Alistair Bevan." When Joe raised one eyebrow, he went on with, "Don't bother with the Lord Farnham part. I've already confessed more to you than I have to my own family, so it wouldn't feel right."

"If you say so, Alistair." Joe's grin widened. Especially since their hands were still joined.

Alistair seemed to notice and let go quickly. "Your sister is missing, you say?"

The seriousness of the situation returned, but a sense of camaraderie remained between the two of them. "For eight months now. She's fourteen and came to London to work as a kitchen maid. I fear she has been lured into a dangerous situation. She was here for six months before she vanished without a trace."

"Here?" Alistair frowned slightly. "Here as in London?"

"Here as in Eccles House." Joe lowered his voice. "Which is why I applied for the position as Lord Burbage's valet."

Alistair's frown deepened. "Were you working as a valet before?" He immediately shook his head and said, "That wasn't the question I wanted to ask."

"I was trained as a tailor first, but yes, I worked as a valet in the country, near Leeds, before," Joe told him. "It's how I know that soda water isn't enough to remove a stain from a tomato-based soup, and that your father needs all of his clothes retailored to accommodate his weight loss."

Alistair's eyes went wide for a moment before the gloom settled in on him again. He laughed humorlessly and shook his head. "Most people think the fate of the world and the empire and its colonies is the most terrifying thing we have to deal with in life, but they're wrong."

"It's the little traumas of our families that frighten us the most," Joe picked up the thought.

Alistair met his eyes. They understood each other. It was the most beautiful and true moment Joe had experienced in years. He would have given anything to stay there with Alistair, talking through their lives, their sorrows, and their joys. He would have given even more to have the freedom to walk around the settee that separated them, to take the sad gentleman in his arms, and to kiss him until his sighs of sorrow turned into moans of pleasure.

"Any suggestions about how to do what has to be done when it's the very last thing you want to do?" Alistair asked, the heat in his eyes hinting that he had the same thoughts.

Joe opened his mouth to say no, then stopped. "Actually, I might have an idea," he said. It came to him out of nowhere. "Have you ever heard of an organization here in London called The Brotherhood?"

He could see in an instant by Alistair's expression that he hadn't. "Do they find wives for men like us?" he asked with a self-deprecating smirk.

"They might," Joe answered with a shrug.

Alistair's brow pinched into a frown. "What kind of organization are they?"

"A social one," Joe said. "For men like us. Of all classes. Not a brothel or anything like that," he rushed to clarify, knowing too well that many of the clubs and groups of men like them were for the purpose of finding a warm body to pass the night with. "In fact, that sort of thing is discouraged on the premises of the club."

"They have a club?" Alistair stepped closer, his expression intrigued.

"Yes. It's on Park Lane, facing Hyde Park."

"And are you a member?" A look of hopeful curiosity lit Alistair's eyes.

"I am." Joe nodded. "But not a very active one. I've only been to the club once. It was nice," he said, feeling as though the word were entirely inaccurate for the peace and relief of a place where he didn't have to worry about what he said or how he behaved. There were precious few places in the world where men like him and Alistair could take a deep breath and be themselves.

"You believe this Brotherhood would have a solution to my problems?" Alistair took another step closer.

"At the very least, I'm certain you would be able to find someone to talk to who has been in your position and could advise you," Joe told him. "The one time I was there, I noted several married men of the aristocracy among the members. Men who have been in the position you are in now. The Brotherhood is not limited by class or wealth, though. It welcomes everyone from high to low."

"How very modern of it." Alistair's smile returned, as did the spark in his eyes. "I suppose if you recommend the place—"

His words were cut off and he jumped back, spilling some of the wine from the glass he still held, as a sudden swell of noise and conversation rose up in the hall. At the same time, his father stirred and mumbled as he awoke. Supper, and the intimate moment, had ended.

Alistair took another step back and a last swig of

wine. "Thank you, Joe," he said, keeping his voice down. As soon as he set the glass on the table with the wine bottle and glanced out into the hall as guests filtered out of the dining room, breaking into male and female groups to continue the socializing, Alistair's entire demeanor changed. It was only then that Joe realized how much tension had drained from his new friend's shoulders and how soft his voice had become. All that vanished before Joe's eyes, leaving a sharp pain in his heart.

"What's going on in here?" another gentleman, who bore a resemblance to Alistair, said as he stepped into the room with a grey-haired woman.

"Mr. Logan here has been helping tidy up Father's jacket," Alistair said, crossing to the couple. "Is it safe to assume you would rather go straight home than take tea with the ladies, Mama?" he asked the older woman, kissing her cheek.

"Yes," the woman said, looking as though she'd had a miserable time at supper.

Alistair smiled weakly at her, then turned back to Joe. "Thank you for your help, Mr. Logan."

"My pleasure, my lord." Joe snapped into a formal bow, throwing the imaginary mantle of service and deference around his shoulders to protect both him and Alistair from any hint of what they'd shared being picked up by the others. He marched to the door, back as straight as any good servant's.

"I'll have the carriage brought around," the man who must have been Alistair's brother said.

"And I'll see to Father," Alistair said with a nod.

As Joe walked past him, their eyes met one last time. Neither betrayed so much as a hint of what had clearly ignited between them. As Joe left the room, he vowed to himself that, no matter what it took, he would find a way to spend time in Alistair's company again.

CHAPTER 3

*A*listair Bevan refused to leave Joe's thoughts, even after the gentleman and his family left Eccles House, the supper party broke up, and the Eccles family parted company to go to bed. Joe's head had been turned by handsome men before, but there was more to Alistair than a pretty face. The conversation they'd had would stick with Joe for a long time. Duty was a heavy load, and it seemed to be harder to carry for men like them.

"Careful, Logan," Lord Burbage grumbled as Joe unbuttoned the starched collar of his master's shirt. "What is the point of having a valet to help me undress if you do it in such a ham-fisted way."

"Sorry, my lord." Joe took greater care with the collar, unbuttoning it in the back, then carrying it over to a side table as Burbage unbuttoned his shirt. He returned to Burbage to remove the cufflinks from his sleeves.

"What a disaster of a party," Burbage continued to complain, though it was unclear whether he was addressing Joe in particular or talking to himself. "Palmerston is an ass, no matter what the topic of conversation. If I had to listen to his self-aggrandizement for one more minute, I would have exploded like a shell on the battlefield."

Joe nodded, knowing his commentary wasn't necessary, and reached out to receive Burbage's shirt as he removed it.

"And what is the point of inviting a woman like Lady Alice Norton if she turns out to be such a cold fish?" Burbage went on.

Joe fought to keep his expression neutral. What business did Burbage have sniffing around a young woman like Lady Alice when he had a wife of his own who was in the family way?

"There's nothing worse than a blushing debutante," Burbage continued. "All that false modesty and pretend innocence. Women are three a penny, and I defy you to find even the most stalwart nun who won't part her legs for a pretty bauble or a few whispered words."

Disgust coursed through Joe, but he hid it by taking Burbage's shirt aside, then returning for his trousers once those were off. As Burbage sat on the edge of his bed to remove his socks, Joe fetched his pajamas from the wardrobe.

"At least dear Lady Alice didn't seem the least bit interested in taking Lord Winslow's bait and panting after his dreadful bore of a son," Burbage said. Joe's ears pricked up and his pulse quickened at allusion to Alistair. "As if Alistair Bevan could win the daughter of a marquess like that," Burbage sniffed.

"As I understand, my lord, Lord Farnham is a peer in his own right and may soon inherit an earldom," Joe said, taking Burbage's dirty socks in exchange for the pajamas.

Burbage snorted. "It will be a case of one embarrassment passing the torch to another embarrassment. Lord Winslow is as mad as a March hare, and his son is as incapable of catching the interest of a woman as an Amazonian frog."

The hair on the back of Joe's neck stood up at the comment. He glanced at Burbage out of the corner of his eye as the man stripped off his underclothes to put on his pajamas. Burbage couldn't possibly know Alistair's nature, could he? Men like Alistair were generally careful to a fault.

"No," Burbage went on, buttoning his pajama top, "Farnham is most likely to end up with some social-climbing young miss from the country, the daughter of a clergyman, no doubt, with dreams of being a countess. He'll be brow-beaten and harried, like any middle-class husband, and he'll deserve it."

Joe kept his lips pressed tightly shut as he fetched Burbage's underthings from the floor, where Burbage had tossed them. He hoped, for Alistair's sake, that he didn't end up in that sort of marriage hell. Though he supposed the best Alistair could hope for was a quiet, innocent woman with a sweet disposition who wouldn't question his inevitable lack of passion.

The tragedy was, Joe believed Alistair was capable of a great deal of passion. The sparks that had flown between the two of them made that much obvious. Given the right circumstances, Alistair would likely be fiery and imaginative. Images of the two of them locked in a carnal embrace, enjoying each other to the fullest, filled Joe's mind. He would show Alistair a thing or two, if given half a chance, and he had no doubt that the gorgeous nobleman would return the favor energetically.

The fantasy was so potent that Joe's prick stiffened in response. That in itself, while still in the process of helping Burbage to bed, was enough to startle Joe out of his thoughts and back to his duty.

"By the way," Burbage asked as he pulled back his bedcovers and slid into bed. "How did that old madman, Winslow, get on? Did he manage to spill anything else on his wretchedly-tailored dinner jacket after leaving the table? Vine told me you attended to him."

"Lord Winslow recovered well enough, my lord," Joe said with a bland smile that he hoped betrayed nothing of the disapproval he felt for Burbage's spiteful attitude, or the instant fondness he felt for Alistair.

"What a joke." Burbage laughed and shook his head as he sat with his back against his headboard, reaching for the novel he'd been reading for the last few nights. "Winslow should do us all a favor and die as soon as possible. As it is, I've no doubt he will continue to embarrass us all with his madness. Why my father insists on keeping company with him is beyond me."

"Your father and Lord Winslow have been friends for some time, haven't they, my lord?" Joe asked, stepping just outside of what was proper for him as he gathered Burbage's dirty clothes.

"Hardly," Burbage huffed. "Father despises the man. But he is useful for seating next to old codgers and boring dowagers at a dinner party." He paused for a moment before continuing with, "Father seems to think that old fool would be more dangerous if he were cut than by keeping him around."

Joe nodded, standing with his back straight, waiting to be dismissed.

"I suppose Father knows what he's about," Burbage sighed, opening his book but not looking at it yet. "And I suppose I shall have to keep company with that dullard son of his once the old bastard kicks up his heels."

Burbage said nothing more. He turned his attention to his book, seeming to forget Joe was still standing there. Joe tried not to seethe at his apparent insignificance in Burbage's eyes. Frustration was making him restless, and not just because of the callous things Burbage said about a pair of men he found fascinating. He was wasting his time, and not just by standing silently by while Burbage read.

Joe had been employed by Burbage for too long without finding a shred of evidence that might lead him to Lily. The first few months that he'd spent at Eccles

House had been filled with inquiries and investigations at brothels that had led nowhere. After that, he'd found a way to question every servant in Eccles House he could about Lily's disappearance without revealing to any of them that he was her brother. In any other household, he would have let everyone know immediately that Lily was his sister. But there was an undercurrent of nastiness, both upstairs and down, in Eccles House that prompted him to keep his business to himself. Enough to make him wonder if Lily had fled to escape it. But if she had simply found another, nicer position, she would have written home about it.

Whatever Lily had been thinking, in the last few months, Joe had grown complacent in his search. Comfort and a salary that he could send home to his parents had jostled Lily to the back of his mind. That and the number of dead ends he'd run into. And now Alistair had turned his head. He had no business letting a man who had problems of his own occupy so much of his thoughts. And yet, he couldn't abide the idea of never seeing Alistair again. Perhaps, if Alistair took his advice and sought the help of The Brotherhood to solve his marital problems, they would encounter each other again at The Brotherhood's club.

A new thought jumped into Joe's mind as he contemplated the idea of spending more time at the club. If someone among the membership of The Brotherhood had the experience to consult with Alistair about his problems, perhaps someone else might also have experience in tracing a missing family member. Someone there might be able to help him with Lily. It was true, The Brotherhood's concerns ran more along the lines of helping men like him out of sticky legal and financial situations. He had never heard of anyone at the club concerning themselves with missing persons. But if The Brotherhood's network was as extensive as he thought it was, help that he hadn't considered before might be right around the corner.

His thoughts were still rolling over each other when Burbage jerked his head up in surprise. "Are you still here, Logan?" he snapped, his face pinched in annoyance.

"You did not dismiss me, my lord," Joe said, rushing to soften his words with, "I was concerned you might still need something."

"I don't need anything from you," Burbage said, turning back to his book. "You may go."

"My lord." Joe nodded and turned to leave. He paused at the door, though, twisting back to say, "My lord, I have an errand to run tomorrow. There are several items I need for repairs to your winter coat. If there is a time when it would be better for me to run this errand—"

"Whenever you'd like, once I'm dressed," Burbage said without looking up at him. "I have no plans for tomorrow, other than to spend the afternoon at White's."

"Very good, my lord." Joe bowed once again, then turned to go, a smile touching his lips. After months of inactivity, he felt as though he might just have stumbled across something that could bring him closer to Lily. And if he happened to meet Alistair again in the process, he wasn't about to complain.

By the time their carriage pulled up to the front door of the Bevans' stately house deep in the heart of Mayfair, Alistair's headache had returned.

"Why did we leave the supper so early?" his father asked, irritated. "The fish course hadn't even been served yet."

"Supper ended ages ago, Father," Darren informed him, stepping out of the carriage first to help their mother down.

"You slept through most of it," Alistair told his father, climbing down next to help the man.

"I did not," his father growled, bristling as Alistair slipped his arm around his back, practically carrying him to the front door. "I would never fall asleep during a formal supper party, particularly not one hosted by that snake, Chisolm."

Alistair exchanged a flat look with Darren over their parents' heads. "I'm sorry to inform you, but you did."

"Nonsense," his father huffed.

Alistair nodded to their butler, Travers, who rushed down the stairs to take Alistair's place supporting his father as they entered the house.

"I'll see that Lord Winslow finds his way to bed, my lord," Travers said.

"Thank you," Alistair replied from the bottom of his heart.

He watched from the foot of the stairs in the front hall as Travers helped his father upstairs, his mother hovering just behind, her face lined with sorrow. There was nothing else he could do but feel stupidly helpless.

"I think this calls for a drink," Darren said, thumping his back as he moved forward, walking down the hall.

Alistair followed him to the family's private study at the back of the house and straight to the cabinet that held their father's liquor. In theory, Alistair and Darren had been forbidden from touching any of the bottles there from the time they were boys. In reality, they had been the ones to drink most of it for the last decade without their father noticing.

"It's a terrible business," Darren said, handing him a tumbler of scotch. "But what can we do?"

Alistair grunted and took a swig of the scotch. It was a damn sight more potent than the wine Joe had brought him from Lord Chisolm's cellar earlier in the evening.

That thought instantly brought Joe's dark eyes and tempting smile to Alistair's mind. There was no way to measure the danger of reacting to the young valet as he had. If Joe hadn't been of the same mind as him, there was no telling what sort of disaster would have occurred. But Joe was like him, and if Alistair was any judge of things, Joe had experienced the same instant attraction.

Which only made the situation worse.

"Father was clumsy about his methods," Darren said

after a drink of his own, eyeing Alistair seriously, "but he was right in his conclusions."

"About what?" Alistair asked, walking to one of the bookcases in the hope that movement would push the memory of Joe's fetching smile, trim waist, and long legs behind him.

"Speaking the way he did at the supper table was crass," Darren said, following him, "but he is right when he says you should marry, and soon."

Alistair winced as he glanced to his brother.

"I know you're shy." Darren approached him with one hand raised, as if Alistair would protest. "Especially around women. They don't bite, you know."

"I am not shy," Alistair protested, though he was fairly certain he blushed as he said as much, which would give Darren the wrong idea entirely.

Darren made a face of complete doubt. "You avoid social events whenever you can. You barely dance when you attend balls. And I can count on one hand the number of close friends you have."

Alistair was surprised that he could count any. Friendship was a liability when his secrets could be uncovered at any moment. "None of that means I'm shy."

"Whether it does or not," Darren went on, shaking his head, "the fact of the matter is that you need a wife and an heir. So do I, for that matter."

"You do?" A glimmer of hope lit in Alistair's chest. If Darren married and had a passel of children, perhaps he could avoid the same fate. It was all the same to him if the

Winslow title passed from him to Darren and Darren's sons once he was gone.

But no, as the eldest son, that burden fell squarely on his shoulders.

"I've already got a few ideas," Darren admitted. "And I'm not averse to the idea of a wife and babies. Every man meets his match eventually, doesn't he?"

He was close enough to thump Alistair's arm. Alistair grinned at the gesture and finished his scotch. What would it look like for him to meet his match? Was such a thing even possible?

Again, Joe's warm smile and the way he'd touched his hand in sympathy as they talked about their problems earlier jumped to his mind. Joe had listened so attentively and had offered such cogent advice. And the man had concerns of his own, so it wasn't as though he was merely humoring him. In fact, Alistair hadn't encountered anyone who made him feel so heard in years.

"Ah, I know that look," Darren said, his grin teasing. "Some fine woman has caught your eye after all, hasn't she?"

"No, no, it's nothing like that," Alistair insisted. Although, to be honest, in a way, it was.

"It wasn't Lady Alice, was it?" Darren laughed. "Knowing you, whichever woman Father would suggest for you would be the last one you would be interested in."

"Father and I have very different tastes," Alistair said carefully, walking back to the liquor cabinet to splash another gulp of scotch into his tumbler.

"There were plenty of fine ladies assembled at Eccles House this evening." Darren followed him at a slower place, setting his glass on the table in front of the cabinet. "What we really need is a ball or soiree of some sort, filled with debutantes eager to make a good match."

"I'm sure one will come around in a matter of days," Alistair said. He swallowed his scotch, then set his glass beside Darren's. "I may consult someone on the matter."

Darren's brow inched up. "A matchmaker?"

Alistair shook his head. "A consultancy, if what I was told is correct." In fact, he still wasn't entirely certain what The Brotherhood Joe had mentioned could do for him. Perhaps it was a matchmaking agency of sorts.

"Well, as long as you take action and take it soon." Darren gave his back one more slap before heading out of the room. "We could make a game of it," he said, turning to walk backwards as he neared the door. "See which one of us makes it to the altar first."

"I'm certain you'll win," Alistair laughed.

"I'm not half the prize you are," Darren said with a brotherly smile before stepping around the corner.

As soon as he was gone, Alistair's own smile dropped. He may very well have to race Darren to the altar, though if he won that prize it would be no victory.

He turned back to the liquor cabinet, contemplating another drink, but decided against it. If he turned to alcohol every time he was faced with an unpleasant task, he would be dependent in no time. And he already had enough vices to damn a man ten times over, as was evident in the way his thoughts rushed right back to the fascinating Joe Logan. What he wouldn't give to spend just one night with the man, no matter what his rank or position in life was.

He headed for the door with a sigh, knowing full well he had a night of delicious self-abuse ahead of him while remembering the touch of the handsome valet's hand and the fire in his eyes.

CHAPTER 4

*A*s it turned out, the memory didn't have to suffice him for long. Alistair ran into Joe again the very next day. As soon as his parents were downstairs and settled into their usual routine for the day and Darren had gone out to his club, Alistair donned his winter coat and hat and set out to investigate the address Joe had given him for the club belonging to The Brotherhood.

It wasn't hard for him to imagine that an organization catering to men like him existed in London without him knowing about it. As much as he'd protested to Darren that he wasn't shy, the truth was that he would rather have kept his own company or stayed at home in the safety of a place where no one would push him too far or ask too many questions. He had friends from university whom he regularly conversed with at the club that he and Darren belonged to, but when it came to embracing the world and all its charms, he had always given society a pass.

He wasn't certain what he was expecting of The Brotherhood's club, but it wasn't the plain, imposing, grey building that faced Hyde Park along Park Lane. The nondescript facade was so unimpressive that he walked past it twice before realizing that the ordinary, black door was, in fact, the entrance to a social club.

He approached the door, squinting at a small, brass plaque to one side that read "The Chameleon". A faint grin twitched on his lips. If ever there were an accurate description of the lot of men like him, that was it. But he continued to stare at the door for a moment before reaching for the handle and letting himself in.

The world on the other side of the door wasn't much different than the lobby of White's. As soon as the door shut behind Alistair, silence reigned, but for the ticking of some distant clock. A middle-aged man sat behind a desk off to one side, absorbed in the book he was reading. Tall columns of cream-colored marble rose up to gilded, Corinthian capitals where they met the painted ceiling. Part of Alistair expected lurid, homoerotic scenes to grace the canopy, but only clouds and birds looked down from above, almost as if he'd stepped outside into a world where he could breathe easily. The lobby stretched on into a long hallway with several, open doorways. A few liveried servants passed through the hall, carrying trays of tea or tobacco. In the distance, Alistair heard male laughter, but not the ribald

variety. The overall mood of the place was one of tran-
quility.

"Can I help you?" the man at the desk asked,
prompting Alistair to shake himself out of his stupor and
approach. He noticed a cloakroom of some sort behind
the man. It was neatly arranged with woolen coats that
ranged from fine and expensive to serviceable and plain.

As soon as he reached the desk and the mildly
curious look of the middle-aged man, panic poked at him.
He was in the wrong place. The club where he found
himself was too sedate, too normal to be what Joe had
described. There wasn't a hint of drunkenness or
debauchery. None of the coats he could see in the cloakroom were ostentatious or theatrical. The place wasn't
teeming with men in gowns or the velvet suits that had
been made so popular by the Aesthetic movement. No
one had made a pass at him the moment he walked
through the door or leered at him, and there wasn't a
single, desperate-looking call-boy in sight.

The man at the desk cleared his throat, snapping
Alistair out of his thoughts.

"Sorry," Alistair apologized, though he wasn't sure
what for. "I may be in the wrong place."

"Is there something you were looking for, sir?" the
man asked.

Alistair opened his mouth, hesitated, then forced
himself to push ahead. "I was directed to this club by a
friend of mine, Mr. Joe Logan?"

He expected the man to give him a snide look or a

knowing laugh. Instead, the man nodded as if there were nothing unusual about strange men wandering off the street and throwing the names of valets around. He slid his chair back, opened a drawer, and pulled out a ledger bound in red leather, then opened it and thumbed through the pages until he reached the "L" section. He scanned his finger down the page until it landed on the name "Logan, Joseph".

"Ah. I see," he said, then smiled up at Alistair. "Yes, Mr. Logan is a member." He reached for a second, smaller ledger, opening it and turning it toward Alistair. "If you could just sign in, sir."

Alistair stared down at the book, his heart beating suddenly in his throat. It was an ingenious idea, given the nature of the club. It appeared that to be granted admission, a man had to record his presence, which was as good as a declaration of who he was, written down and preserved. The method would ensure that anyone who was merely there to snoop or snicker wouldn't see it as worth the risk of being labeled. It also told Alistair that the men who spent time at the club truly wanted to be there. Anyone who signed their name in the guestbook was resigning his fate into the hands of the club. If the ledger was ever stolen, everyone who had ever signed it would go down together.

The thoughts rushed to him in an instant as he took the pen that the man behind the desk offered. Alistair stared at the book, pen poised over the last empty line. Curiosity got the better of him, and he peeked at the names above his and the dates those men had visited. He recognized none of the names, which came as a slight disappointment.

That flicker of emotion brought a grin to his face, and he chastised himself for being an old gossip as he carefully signed the ledger "Alistair Bevan", leaving off his title.

"Thank you, sir." The man behind the desk put away both ledgers. "The ground floor is open to non-members. If you should choose to pursue membership, I can provide you with the proper paperwork. We limit inquirer's visits to one hour, so if you lose track of time, a page will be sent to fetch you. Please let us know if you need any assistance or an explanation of the club's amenities."

"Oh, thank you." Alistair nodded, surprised at how easy the interaction had been. He glanced to the long hallway, then back at the man behind the desk. "So, I can just go on in?"

"Ground floor only. You may explore on your own. Unless you would prefer a guided tour." The man nodded.

Alistair's brow shot up, and he stepped back from the desk, facing the hallway. He felt as though he had been granted admittance to a curious new world, and he wasn't entirely certain how to proceed.

"I think I'll make my own way," he decided, sending the man one last smile before starting forward on what felt like the journey of a lifetime.

The club was perfectly maintained. There wasn't a

stain on the carpets or a smudge on the walls. Once he passed through the lobby and up a small set of stairs to the hallway, more of a feel for the place seeped into his bones. The whole club had a relaxed sort of feeling. The stuffiness of White's wasn't there at all.

A group of men sat around a table, playing cards and smoking in the first room Alistair passed. There was nothing unusual about any of them, other than how companionable they seemed together. The second room Alistair encountered was much larger and stretched the length of the building in that direction, like a reception hall. It held several tables, some of which were occupied by groups or individuals, and one wall was lined with bookshelves. Tall windows stood uncovered at the far end of the room, letting copious amounts of light into the vast space. Liveried footmen seemed to be keeping a table of refreshments organized to one side of the windows. The whole scene was peaceful, which felt beyond strange. Peace was not the word Alistair associated with his sort.

"Can I help you?"

Alistair nearly jumped out of his skin at the question, asked by a man about his age, with hazel eyes and a mass of dark, curly hair, a few feet behind him. His heart dropped to his gut when he turned to find a man he knew staring back at him with a polite smile.

"Lord Farnham," the man said, his smile brightening as he extended a hand. "What a surprise to see you here."

Alistair's alarm at being recognized immediately

seemed out of place. He took the man's offered hand. "Hillsboro. What a delight."

Maxwell, Lord Hillsboro, grinned back at him. "It can't be that much of a shock to find me here, all things considered." He glanced around at the room.

Alistair didn't know how to answer. He'd known Max at university. They'd had the same set of friends then, but, like all but a few friends from his university days, Alistair had barely kept up with him. He supposed he knew on some level that Max was like him, but at Oxford, he hadn't been in a hurry to dive deeper into the matter.

"I'm new to this club," Alistair said, fairly certain he looked like a complete fool. "And the entire Brotherhood organization, as it happens."

"I've been a member for years," Max said, clapping Alistair's back and gesturing for him to walk with him toward the table laid out with tea and cakes. "It's the only place in London I feel completely comfortable."

Alistair's brow rose. "That's quite an endorsement."

"Safe places are hard to come by," Max added with a lopsided smile. "Whoever came up with the idea for The Brotherhood and this club was a genius."

"Who did come up with it?" Alistair asked, glancing around at the details of the large room as they walked through. A few of the men at the tables looked up from their activities to nod in greeting to Max, sending Alistair welcoming smiles as well.

"Nobody knows," Max said with a slight laugh. "It's been in place for generations."

"And the police have never raided it? Its existence has never been exposed?"

Max shrugged. "No. My theory is that there are men in high places protecting the place. Probably members themselves. That or the fact that, since the rules strictly prohibit misbehavior, the enemy has never had reason to invade."

Alistair couldn't believe it. Why had he never heard of such a place before? It would have made so many things so much easier in his life. But he supposed that was what he got in return for his antisocial ways.

They reached the tea table, and Max poured him a cup. Alistair sipped it in silence as he took in everything around him. Joe had been right about men of all social classes belonging to The Brotherhood. He could tell from the quality of the clothing worn by the men at the tables that some were quite well off indeed and some were merely middle class. There didn't seem to be any working-class men in attendance, but as Alistair sipped his tea, he wouldn't have been surprised to see some.

"I take it when you say you're new, you're very new," Max said.

"I only learned about the club last night from...a friend," he confessed.

"So you're not fully a member yet?" Max asked.

Uneasiness filled Alistair. "Is that a bad thing?"

"Not at all. And it's something we'll take care of as soon as possible."

Wariness twisted Alistair's stomach. "There isn't

some morbid initiation ritual, is there?" A thousand disturbing, masochistic images—things he'd seen at university or heard about in the years since that had given him nightmares—jumped to his mind, filling him with the urge to run.

"No," Max laughed. "Nothing at all like that. It's mostly paperwork, nondisclosure agreements. The membership criteria are simple, and I'll vouch for you."

The surprises and the acceptance just kept coming. "We've barely spoken since university."

Max shrugged. "That doesn't change who you are. And I'm certain that whoever it was who gave you the club's address would vouch for you as well."

There was a question in Max's eyes, but Alistair didn't answer it. "To tell you the truth," he said, facing Max and lowering his voice, "this Brotherhood was recommended to me as an organization that might be able to help me with a particular conundrum I'm facing."

"That's what the organization is for," Max said, taking a small plate with a slice of cake from the table. "Is it a legal problem?"

"Not exactly." Alistair stared at his tea, then glanced to the cake Max was enjoying. The whole situation was beyond surreal. By all outside appearances, he and Max could have been at a garden party hosted by one of society's most upstanding dowagers. Which was, perhaps, why it didn't feel as bizarre as it could have for him to blurt out, "My father is anxious for me to marry."

Blessedly, he didn't have to say anything else. Max

hummed and nodded. "Aren't they all," he said in a wry voice. He ate another bite of cake and went on with, "I assume you're hoping The Brotherhood might have some ideas about suitable ladies, all things considered."

He couldn't help himself. Alistair laughed and shook his head. "This is all so much to take in," he said. "I feel as though I've gone through the looking glass to a world where some formal organization keeps a stable filled with women who wouldn't mind marrying a man like me."

"Yes, well, we are rather in a fantasy world at the moment, and thank God for it," Max replied. "I never did care much for reality."

Alistair couldn't stop laughing. Everything around him was utterly improbable and completely beautiful. A world simply didn't exist in which he was safe to be himself and discuss the problems of his life openly. Except that now he knew it did. He couldn't quite fit the pieces together in his mind.

It was at that moment, when his defenses were at their lowest and his head was spinning, that Joe Logan walked into the room. Immediately, his laughter switched from verging on hysterical to drying up completely. Joe caught sight of him, and it was as though an electric current shot across the room.

"So that must be your friend," Max said wryly, though Alistair barely heard him.

Joe seemed as surprised as Alistair was to see him. He picked up his pace, his smile growing as he crossed the room. "I had hoped to see you here, but I didn't think I could possibly be that lucky," he said as he reached the table.

"You referred me to The Brotherhood, and I figured there was no point in waiting," Alistair answered.

"Any luck so far?" Joe asked, his casual manner making Alistair feel more at home by the second.

"I've only just started to explain my problem to Hillsboro here," Alistair said, then remembered his manners. "Joe Logan, meet an old friend of mine from Oxford, Maxwell Preston, Lord Hillsboro. Maxwell, this is Joe Logan."

The two shook hands and exchanged pleasantries. Max sent Alistair a knowing look and a teasing grin, but blessedly kept his thoughts to himself.

"I'm glad I brought up The Brotherhood last night," Joe said, clearly better at conversation than Alistair ever would be. "After you left Eccles House, it occurred to me that they might be able to help with my search for my sister."

Max's smile changed to a look of concern. "You have a sister that needs searching for?"

"She's been missing for eight months now," Joe said. "She came to London to work in service and vanished soon after."

"That's terrible," Max said.

Joe gave Max a sad but grateful look, then turned back to Alistair. "I don't know why I haven't consulted The Brotherhood about her disappearance already, though I suspect a little bit of pride and self-reliance has something to do with it. That and the fact that I've always considered this more of a social club than anything else."

Alistair glanced from Joe to Max. "Are missing person investigations the sort of thing The Brotherhood does?"

"Not really," Max confessed, sending Joe an apologetic look. A moment later, he stood straighter and blinked. "Actually, there may be someone who can help you."

Alistair felt as excited as Joe looked at the statement.

"I'm all ears," Joe said.

"Have you heard of Dandie & Wirth?" Max asked Joe.

"Heard of them, yes." Joe nodded. "We've all heard of them."

"Dandie & Wirth?" Alistair asked, indicating he hadn't.

"They're solicitors," Max explained. "In truth, they are the unofficial solicitors for The Brotherhood. If we have a legal problem, that's where we go."

"A missing sister isn't exactly a legal problem," Alistair said, inching closer to Joe.

"Their connections extend beyond court cases and wills," Max went on. "They are so much more than simple men of the law. David Wirth is extraordinarily well-connected. He knows almost everything going on in this city, and if he doesn't know it, he knows someone who does. He charges a small fee for his services, of course, but I've also heard that he has a passion for helping those whom the law routinely ignores and casts aside. Something having to do with an event in his past, I believe."

"Then we should speak to him at once to see if he has any leads on your sister," Alistair said, not even questioning that he would be involved in helping Joe in every way.

Joe met his enthusiasm with a smile.

"They can help with your little problem too," Max said, drawing Alistair's attention again. When Alistair raised a questioning eyebrow, Max said, "You need to speak to Mr. Lionel Mercer. He's the clerk at Dandie & Wirth. Although, if you ask me, he's much more than that." A mischievous look lit Max's expression.

"He sounds like an interesting chap," Alistair said.

Max laughed. "You don't know the half of it. David Wirth might know everything that's going on in this city, but Lionel knows everyone. And I mean *everyone*. He doesn't just know them, he knows their stories and their secrets. He's the cleverest man I've ever met. Beyond clever. The man is supernatural." Max thumped Alistair's arm. "If you want advice about what suitable lady to court and how to convince her to take the plunge, ask Lionel. You won't be sorry."

Alistair was both intrigued by the prospect and worried that this Lionel Mercer might do too good a job. And at precisely the time when Alistair had met someone he wanted to get to know much better.

But Joe said, "We should go see them at once."

"You should," Max agreed.

Both of them looked to Alistair. Joe's eyes in particular were filled with hope. It was as obvious as day to him that Joe Logan could ask him for just about anything and he would give it freely.

"All right," he said. "We'll visit Dandie & Wirth. And with any luck, our problems will be solved in no time."

Either that or they'd trade one set of problems for another.

CHAPTER 5

*A*listair was nervous. It was the most charming thing Joe had seen in weeks. Alistair was trying to hide his feelings, as most noblemen did, but it didn't take much for Joe to see right through him as they left The Chameleon Club together and headed east.

"What do you think of the club?" Joe asked as they strode on, side-by-side but without touching.

"It's remarkable," Alistair said, his expression conveying surprise. "And not at all like I would have imagined."

"What would you have imagined?" Joe laughed.

Alistair shrugged. "Generally, establishments catering to our sort—" He glanced around as if checking to see whether they might be overheard. "—have a reputation for being seedy. In which case, they make me uncomfortable."

"You've been to the wrong places, then," Joe said. "But I understand what you mean."

Alistair sent him a grateful smile. "Yes, I believe you do understand me."

Joe smiled back at him with a feeling like his chest had filled with songbirds. It was quaint and ridiculous, like the first time he'd ever felt as though he wanted to be more than friends with one of the boys back home. He held the feeling close, but didn't take it seriously. There were too many reasons indulging in sweet fantasies with a nobleman wouldn't work.

"What made you decide to consult The Brotherhood about your sister?" Alistair asked as they crossed a street and continued through the relatively quiet streets of Mayfair, dampening Joe's sweet feelings a bit as he was reminded where his thoughts should have been. "I had the impression that you intended to search for her on your own when we spoke last night."

Joe shrugged, thrusting his hands into his pockets to keep himself from doing something foolish, like reaching for Alistair's hand. "I haven't had much luck on my own. When I suggested The Brotherhood as a solution for your problems it made me realize they could be the solution to mine as well. After all, if there are members with experience finding wives who will look the other way, there might be men who know what to do about my problem. And it appears I was right."

Alistair nodded, an air of shy uncertainty still hovering over him. "Tell me about your sister. Is she the sort who would see London as an adventure worthy of leaving a stable job to explore?"

Joe frowned. "No. Not at all. Which is precisely why I suspect foul play in her disappearance." Alistair nodded but said nothing as they strode on, passing maids running errands, nannies taking their young charges to Hyde Park, and carriages containing London society's finest, on their way to and from calls or clubs. "Lily was always very industrious at home. She talked of nothing but her excitement about coming to London to work. She dreamed of sending money back home so that our younger siblings could live a better life."

"I'm surprised you didn't precede her to London," Alistair said, studying him closely, as if he were genuinely interested in the life and history of a simple valet.

Joe sent him a self-effacing smile. "I already had a position as an assistant tailor in Leeds. I'd been sending money back for years."

Alistair let out a short laugh that ended with a lopsided grin.

"Do you find something amusing in that?" Joe asked, suddenly wary that he wasn't being taken seriously.

"No, not at all. I mean, not in that way." When Joe arched an eyebrow at him, he went on with, "I've lived the sort of life where money was never an object."

"So I see." Joe raked him from head to toe with a look, intending to convey that Alistair's expensive clothing gave his financial state away. He enjoyed what he was seeing for entirely different reasons, though, and risked sending Alistair a rakish grin.

He was rewarded by a flush of pink that spread up Alistair's neck to his cheeks. "What I mean is that my family has never been in a position to worry about money. We worry about other things."

"Such as?" Joe prompted him.

Alistair laughed again, but there was far less humor in it. "We worry about status and propriety. We worry about carrying the weight of the nation's history and traditions on our shoulders. We worry about leading the nation so that we maintain our place in the world."

"A heavy load indeed." Joe didn't mean to belittle Alistair's concerns, but his words came out with a certain level of dismissiveness.

Alistair looked a little hurt. He pulled the collar of his coat up against the chilly morning as they walked on. "It may not be anything to you. You may think we're all a bunch of snobbish toffs. But I can assure you, we take our responsibilities seriously."

"I know." Joe winced to show he was sorry. "We all have our place in the grander scheme of things, and each place has its own challenges."

"I hate that word, 'place'," Alistair said, hunching his shoulders slightly. "It excuses all manner of evils."

Joe's brow shot up. He was so interested in the earnestness of Alistair's expression as he spoke that he nearly stepped out into the street before the carriage crossing in front of them had moved past. He had to jump back, nearly slamming into Alistair as he did. It was a shame that he didn't run fully into the man. It would have been nice to have that contact, if only for a moment. Though if he had even the slightest excuse to grab hold of Alistair's body, he wasn't sure he would be willing to let go.

"Do you really think that?" Joe asked once he and Alistair made it to the other side and walked on.

"That hierarchy has become more of a hindrance than a help?" Alistair asked in return, then answered his question with a nod. "Perhaps the trappings of feudalism were useful in the days of knights and marauders, when famine was a yearly worry and life depended on a strong leader shepherding his people. But I cannot help but think we're outgrowing that at a fast pace."

Joe watched his face sink into a frown, and then melt into an expression of helplessness. His heart squeezed in sympathy. "Are you saying that because you're a true progressive, or is it because you feel the burden of continuing the title and all that it means a little more keenly than most?"

Alistair glanced his way, looking as though he'd been caught expressing revolutionary opinions. "I suppose I might feel differently if I were...different. Or rather, if I weren't different."

Joe hummed, needing no further explanation. "I must confess, my experience of the titled class so far has not endeared me to any of you or your sense of responsibility."

"Oh?" Alistair's brow lifted with curiosity as they prepared to cross another street. They'd made it halfway across Mayfair, barely breaking stride. All manner of people walked around them, but it was as though the two of them were traipsing through their own, private world.

"I believe it's considered inappropriate to speak ill of one's employer," Joe said with an arched brow.

"You can say whatever you'd like." Alistair grinned. "I've never been overly fond of Burbage."

That came as a mild surprise to Joe. "Really? Last night, you and your family were part of what I was given to understand was a dinner among valued friends."

"That's my father's doing," Alistair explained, shaking his head. "Though Father doesn't care much for Lord Chisolm either. But he does believe in the old adage of keeping your friends close and your enemies closer."

For some reason, the statement made Joe feel as though he were on the edge of a far greater discovery. It also made him uncommonly sad. No one should be forced to associate with friends who weren't friends at all. "If you don't mind my asking, why doesn't your father like Lord Chisolm?"

Alistair shrugged, glancing around to be certain that none of the inhabitants of Mayfair—most of whom were probably well acquainted with the subjects of the discussion—were listening in. "Father has never liked anyone in the Eccles family, even though the Bevanses and the Eccleses have been associated going back generations. That is another drawback to class," he added in a slightly more casual aside. "We're expected to maintain friendships with the right people, even if we can't stand them."

"Has Burbage ever done anything against you personally?" Joe asked. He could certainly see Burbage being an utter ass to someone like Alistair. Burbage was aggressive and brass and preferred the company of men like him, bounders and rakes. Alistair was certainly masculine enough to run in Burbage's circles, but Joe was beginning to see that Alistair was more of the sort to be at home in a library in the country than staying up all night in a gambling hell, winning and losing fortunes, and bedding whoever happened to be willing. Those facts made him admire Alistair all the more.

"I'm not Burbage's sort," Alistair said, confirming Joe's suspicions. "Not that he didn't try to convert me to his cause at university, so to speak. I believe he found me a waste of time. Burbage liked whiskey and women, and I've never been fond of either. And his taste in both was cheap."

Joe frowned, once again feeling as though he were on the edge of something. "What do you mean by that? Did he frequent brothels?"

"Yes," Alistair nodded, his expression turning thoughtful as they rounded a corner and headed into a busier section of town. "But he also prided himself on seducing the otherwise modest and virtuous daughters of the tradesmen that did business with the university."

A twist of anger pinched Joe's gut. "Like young

maids, fresh from the country, eager to impress their employers?"

Alistair nearly missed a step. He glanced to Joe with suddenly wide eyes. "You don't think that Burbage has something to do with your sister's disappearance, do you?"

Joe paused, blowing out a breath and rubbing a hand over his face. "The thought has crossed my mind, but I have no evidence of it and no proof at all. Just a thorough dislike of the man. Besides, anyone lower than his own class is completely insignificant to him. I don't believe he would have noticed Lily's existence, let alone set his sights on her."

"Have you approached him about it?" Alistair took a step closer to him.

The proximity went straight to Joe's head. Alistair's movement brought a hint of his cologne with it. The rich scent swirled through Joe, filling his mind with fantasies of loosening Alistair's collar and bringing his lips to the man's neck so that he could breathe him in more fully and taste his skin. He might even leave a mark where only Alistair could see it. The idea thrilled him.

He had to blink and take a step back to say, "I wouldn't dare," meaning the words both in answer to Alistair's question and in response to his own desires.

"Perhaps I could ask for you?" Alistair inched back as well, color rising on his face, hinting that he'd had a similar reaction to Joe.

Joe's lips twitched into a doubtful grin. "What would

you ask him? 'Pardon me, Lord Burbage, you wouldn't happen to have seduced and disposed of any young maids recently, would you?'"

Alistair lowered his head slightly. "You have a point." They walked on. "But perhaps there is a way I can discover pertinent information without addressing the matter outright." When Joe peeked sideways at him, Alistair said, "My father may just be right about keeping your friends close and your enemies closer."

"I wouldn't wish proximity to Burbage on anyone as lovely as you," Joe said before he could fully think through his words. They crossed the street to cut through a park-like square.

When Alistair remained silent, Joe glanced at him and found him grinning and pink-faced.

"I think you're rather wonderful as well," he said in a soft voice.

Joe would have shaken his head if he hadn't thought the gesture might offend Alistair. The two of them were as preposterous as children learning to flirt, and yet, there was something completely joyful about it, something so much better than the hard-edged lust his flirtations with other men always seemed to be. In those instances, the goal had been clear and short-term. With Alistair, he wasn't sure. He absolutely wanted the man naked and underneath him—or on top of him, he wasn't picky—as soon as possible, but more than that, he wanted to talk with him, laugh with him, and make him smile.

"I'm sure your family—" he started, but was cut off by

a loud bark and a mass of grey fur hurling toward the two of them from the square they walked through.

"Stop, Barkley, stop!" A small boy in a sailor suit with his hair slicked back charged after the dog.

Barkley looked as though he had no intention of stopping. He was some sort of wolf hound and bounded across the park as fast as a horse, his pink tongue flapping to one side, his eyes bright with the light of freedom. Joe thought fast, dodging out of the dog's way, but Alistair wasn't as quick.

"Whoa, boy," Alistair called, holding out his hands in an attempt to stop the charging beast. Barkley leapt right into his arms as if he believed himself to be a corgi or a terrier, which sent both man and dog toppling backward into the grass with a thud.

"Barkley, no!" the boy shouted, skittering to a halt just in front of the pile that was Alistair and dog.

"Alistair." Joe rushed forward, ready to drop to his knees and wrestle the dog away from Alistair if he had to.

But after a tense moment of stillness, Alistair began to laugh. "That's enough, boy, that's enough," he carried on, twisting this way and that as Barkley licked his face, pinning him to the ground.

Joe had never envied a dog so much in his life. "Are you all right?" he asked, laughing himself once he was certain Alistair wasn't hurt or in danger. He moved in closer, hooking a hand under Barkley's collar to pull him off.

Barkley barked once, then shifted his focus to Joe,

jumping up and putting his paws on Joe's shoulders. The shock of having a dog stare him straight in the eyes was nearly enough to knock Joe over as well.

"He really is a good dog, sir," the boy said, dodging between Barkley and Joe in an attempt to grab a leash that flapped freely from its clasp on Barkley's collar. "Really, he is."

"He certainly is friendly," Alistair said as he dragged himself to his feet. He wiped his face gingerly on the sleeve of his jacket, alternating between laughter and grimacing.

"Would that we all could be so friendly," Joe said, shrugging Barkley's paws off his shoulders.

"I'm sorry, sir," the boy said, catching the leash at last as the dog danced around him. "Barkley, sit."

To Joe's astonishment, the dog—who was twice as big as the boy—sat.

"No harm done," Joe said, then turned to Alistair. "At least, I think no harm done."

"None," Alistair agreed.

Joe reached into his jacket pocket to take out a handkerchief. He stepped closer to Alistair, but instead of simply offering Alistair the square of cotton, he went ahead and wiped Alistair's face. Alistair froze as Joe's utilitarian gesture turned tender. Joe took his time, brushing away dirt as an excuse to learn the lines of Alistair's jaw and the curves of his cheeks. They both held their breath as Joe brushed his thumb over Alistair's lips, the corner of the handkerchief the only thing keeping their skin from touching.

Alistair's eyes met Joe's. The strength of the heat there could have lit a bonfire in the middle of the park. Joe leaned closer, good sense leaving him so fast he could feel himself lifted up as though he'd suddenly lost twenty pounds. His lips were only inches away from Alistair's and the distance was closing fast.

"He's a good dog, I swear," the boy said, reminding Joe that they weren't alone.

Joe cleared his throat and moved his hands from Alistair's face to brush dirt and grass off his shoulders. "I can see that," he said as he circled around Alistair, continuing to swipe at Alistair's jacket from the back, like he would have when caring for the clothing of any gentleman he was responsible for. It took everything he had to resist brushing his hand over Alistair's backside.

"Is someone else with you, minding the dog?" Alistair asked with what sounded like an attempt to remain casual, though his voice was pitched half an octave too high.

"Nanny is just seeing to Lucy down there," the boy said, pointing to the other end of the park, where a harried woman in black was chasing a girl who couldn't have been more than four as she dashed from bush to bush, screaming for no apparent reason. At least the girl wore a smile as big and bright as her pink hair bow.

"Perhaps you and Barkley should help Nanny out," Alistair suggested with a smile.

"All right," the boy said. He stared at Alistair and Joe for a moment, but instead of the question Joe was certain would be asked, he shrugged and turned to run back across the park, Barkley loping along beside him.

"That was...interesting," Alistair said, then cleared his throat.

Joe moved around to Alistair's front, brushing him a few more, unnecessary times. It was physically painful for him to pull his hands back to his sides, breaking contact. Although he might as well still be touching Alistair with the amount of emotion that filled Alistair's eyes.

Joe offered him the handkerchief the way he should have to begin with. "You never know what's going to happen on an innocent walk through Mayfair," he said in a low, teasing voice.

The corner of Alistair's mouth twitched up and mirth danced in his eyes. "Do I look all right?" he asked in a quiet voice. "I don't look...guilty, do I?" He glanced down at his front.

If the man were any more endearing, Joe would have expired on the spot. He peeked deliberately down to the level of Alistair's hips. Of course, with his thick winter coat, the man could have had an erection the size of the Rock of Gibraltar and no one would have been able to tell.

"Everything looks fine from where I'm standing," he said with a grin. "And as a valet, I would know." He ended his comment with a wink as the two of them continued to walk on.

"I trust the offices of Dandie & Wirth aren't that much farther," Alistair said, then shot a sidelong look to Joe. "I'm not sure that I trust myself any longer than necessary in your company."

Joe couldn't have contained his grin if he'd tried. "I do believe I know exactly what you mean."

CHAPTER 6

*I*t was preposterous to think that a walk across Mayfair could turn the world on its head, but as Alistair strode purposefully onward with Joe at his side, he felt as though he was treading on new and magnificent ground. He could still feel the touch of Joe's hand on his face, the brush of his thumb across his lips. The part of him that constantly sought excuses to explain things away tried to tell him Joe was only doing his job as a valet and he'd just been ticklish, but tickling did not leave one with an erection the size of an obelisk.

Well, perhaps if it was done right.

He tried not to imagine him and Joe tumbling across a bed, wrestling and tickling each other and getting hot and hard as they tussled. He tried not to blush as they crossed onto the street where the offices of Dandie & Wirth were located. Most of all, he tried to not to let his heart throb within him or to entertain the idea that there was such a thing as love at first sight. The notion was ridiculous, meant to soften the minds of schoolgirls or trick them into what their parents considered a suitable marriage before they woke up to the binding realities of class and marriage.

But it was no use. Joe was like a fever Alistair had caught fast and couldn't shake.

"This looks like it," Joe said, the flash of a knowing smile in his eyes as he mounted the stairs and opened the door for Alistair.

"Thanks," Alistair told him as he crossed into the front hallway of the stately building.

There was more than one business with an office on the ground floor of the building. To one side, a placard on the door simply read "The False Chronicle". Alistair blinked at that, wondering what sort of a business that could be, before turning to the opposite door. Its stylish, brass doorplate read, "Dandie & Wirth, Solicitors".

"Looks like we found it," Alistair said, reaching for the door handle to let himself and Joe in.

It took half a second for Alistair to know both he and Joe had come to the right place. The offices of Dandie & Wirth, by all appearances, were no different from any other solicitor's office. The front room itself was slightly bigger than Alistair had expected, with tall windows on two sides that let in a copious amount of light. Book-shelves lined the spaces between the windows, but in addition to holding just books, they were loaded with ledgers, piles of loose paper, statuettes in marble and porcelain, trinket boxes in a dozen exotic styles, and artifacts from ancient civilizations, all arranged in an order that made perfect, stylish sense.

A pair of leather sofas were arranged facing each other in the center of the room, as though they graced a drawing room, not a solicitor's office. A few, elegant side tables complimented the sofas. One held a vase of fresh flowers in colors that matched the muted tones of the wallpaper exquisitely. A squat stove stood in one corner of the room, providing warmth and heating a kettle on its top. An open doorway stood off to the left, through which Alistair could see a second office, equally as beautiful as the front room. But the most dominant feature of the office was a large, mahogany desk, set in front of one of the windows in such a way that the man sitting behind the desk appeared otherworldly.

Alistair instantly corrected his assessment. The desk wasn't the dominant feature of the room, the man sitting behind it was. The more Alistair took in, the more he realized every tiny detail in the room was designed to draw attention to the man. He was by far the most beautiful creature Alistair had ever laid eyes on, and he radiated an aura as if he knew it. Even seated, it was clear the man was lean and graceful. His suit was the epitome of style, though he didn't wear a jacket, and his waistcoat matched the flowers. He had the most arresting face imaginable, with luminous, blue eyes, flawless, pale skin, strong cheekbones, and a sensual mouth that made Alistair's mind jump immediately to sin, in spite of everything he felt for Joe. The man didn't have a hair out of place, his clothes fit a little too well, and the way he stared at Alistair and Joe as they entered the office made Alistair feel as though he'd come to seek an audience with an oracle.

There was absolutely no doubt whatsoever, within a split-second of being in the man's presence, that he was a homosexual. He couldn't have hidden who he was if his life depended on it, a truth that was underscored when he sat a bit straighter and asked, "Can I help you?" His voice was sweet, soft, and high-pitched.

Alistair swallowed, confused by how intimidating such a delicate, androgynous man could be. "We were directed here from The Chameleon Club," he said. "I was told that a Mr. Lionel Mercer might be able to help with a problem I've encountered, and my friend here was instructed to speak to Mr. David Wirth about a separate problem."

The man behind the desk stood, his every movement as controlled as a dancer. "I'm Lionel Mercer," he said, stepping out from behind the desk and coming to meet them.

He extended a hand toward Alistair, who shook it. Alistair's assessment of him shifted again, as the handshake was firm and commanding. And unsettling. Men as beautiful and sylph-like as Lionel Mercer should have come off as effeminate, but somehow, he didn't. He radiated power.

Alistair was saved from the unnerving feeling Mercer gave him as a second man strode into the room from the other office, studying a ledger in his hands as he walked, with a far more ordinary presence.

"Who do we have here?" the man asked, looking up from his work only when he was several steps into the room. He was tall with broad shoulders, dark hair, and a serious frown that lent him an air of intelligence and grounding.

Mercer glanced to Alistair, lifting one eyebrow slightly, as if demanding he answer.

"Alistair Bevan," Alistair answered, letting go of Mercer's smooth hand to nod to the newcomer. Only as an afterthought did he add, "Lord Farnham." It seemed odd, somehow, to lead with his title when he was clearly still part of the classless world of The Brotherhood.

Disconcertingly, Mercer's expression lit with recognition and excitement. "The reclusive viscount emerges at last."

"I'm not a recluse," Alistair said, not quite able to meet Mercer's smile.

"But you aren't one for society," Mercer told him, as if he'd read the book of Alistair's life and was recounting the story. "Not that I or anyone else blames you. I understand you have quite a lot on your plate, what with your father's health. How does Lord Winslow fare these days, by the way?"

Alistair's mouth dropped open at Mercer's sudden concern and familiarity, as though they were and always had been friends. "I...I don't—" he fumbled.

"Lionel, stop scaring our clients," the other man said. He deposited his ledger on the corner of the desk, then moved to shake Alistair's hand. "David Wirth," he introduced himself, then shook Joe's hand with the same openness and respect that he presented to Alistair.

"Joseph Logan," Joe said, shaking Mercer's hand as well.

"Don't mind Lionel," Wirth went on with a sideways smirk for Mercer. "He's rather too proud of the fact that he knows everyone in England."

"Not everyone," Mercer said, glancing between Alistair and Joe, narrowing his eyes slightly at Joe, as if trying to place him. "Most people," he continued, shifting his weight to one leg. "I'm not placing the name Joseph Logan, though."

"You wouldn't know me," Joe said, sending a sideways grin to Alistair, as though they were at some sort of brilliant, theatrical entertainment. "I'm valet to Lord Burbage."

"Oh." Mercer took in a breath, and his expression lightened. "The tailor from Leeds."

Alistair gaped harder at the man. "I was informed that you knew everyone, as Mr. Wirth said, but I had no idea...." He didn't know how to finish the sentence.

Mercer brushed his stunned silence away with a wave of his hand. "When you've been in the professions I have, you learn who everyone is and every aspect of their business as a survival mechanism."

Alistair had no idea what to say to that.

Wirth chuckled and shook his head. "Ignore him. He's in high spirits today. He's even more insufferable when he's in a bad mood. You say The Brotherhood sent you here to help with certain problems?"

"Yes," Joe answered. "I was told you might be able to help me search for my sister who has gone missing."

"And it was suggested to me that Mr. Mercer might know a woman who could satisfy my father's wishes that I marry," Alistair blurted out before he lost his nerve, feeling himself turn bright red as he did.

"Call me Lionel," Mercer said. "Mr. Mercer is my father, God damn his soul."

Wirth chuckled, shook his head, then gestured for Joe to follow him to his office. "We can speak in here."

"If you don't mind," Joe said, holding his ground and glancing to Alistair, "I'd like Alistair to be part of the discussion about my sister, since he offered to help me find her in any way he can."

"And I have nothing to hide from Joe," Alistair added, continuing to feel as though every word that came out of his mouth made him sound like a soft-headed moron.

Lionel and Wirth glanced between Alistair and Joe, then exchanged a look with each other. Alistair's embarrassment deepened. He was as transparent as glass, and both men knew it.

"All right, then," Wirth said, extending a hand to the sofas. "We'll talk here. Please, have a seat."

Lionel surged forward, taking Alistair and Joe's coats as though he were a butler at Buckingham Palace and hanging them on a stand near the door. Alistair and Joe moved to sit on one of the sofas, Alistair uncomfortably. He might as well be sitting there naked, the way his personal business was on display for the others. Wirth took a seat opposite them, leaning forward and resting his elbows on his knees, his darkly handsome face knit in a frown of thought. Lionel, however, finished with the coats and perched on the arm of the sofa like an exotic bird, a phoenix who might burst into brilliance at any moment. The stare he fixed Alistair with was unnerving in its keenness.

"You need a bride who will suit your family's importance without demanding too much," he said, stating Alistair's dilemma concisely.

"Yes." Alistair nodded.

Lionel narrowed his eyes, gazing so hard that Alistair was certain the man could see into his soul. "Let me think on it." He glanced to Wirth.

Wirth raised his dark eyebrows at Lionel, his mouth pulling into a lopsided smile, then turned to Joe and cleared his throat. "Tell me about your sister," he said. "Who is she and how long has she been missing?"

"Her name is Lily, and she's only fourteen," Joe began.

Alistair leaned back slightly against the sofa as Joe told the rest of the story. Hearing it again only made Alistair's nerves bristle. He hated the idea that a young woman could simply disappear, and he couldn't shake the feeling his earlier conversation with Joe had given him that Burbage was somehow involved. But even that uneasy feeling was eclipsed by the way Lionel continued to stare at him, his brow knit into a frown.

"And you say she isn't the type to run off with whatever money she'd earned to pursue some fancy, or even a young man," Wirth said as Joe reached the end of his story.

"Not at all." Joe shook his head. "Lily is a good girl."

Alistair resisted the urge to reach for his hand in comfort. Even in present company, it would have been too great a risk.

"Did she have any other friends in London?" Wirth asked on. "Anyone she knew from home or had befriended since arriving in London?"

"No one from home," Joe said. "She may have made a friend or two since taking the position in Eccles House, but if so, she didn't write home about them."

The information seemed to weigh heavily on Wirth, giving Alistair the impression that he had an idea about what could have happened.

"You don't seem surprised," Alistair said, voicing his thoughts.

Wirth blew out a breath and sat straighter, rubbing a hand over his face. "I wish I were," he said. "But this isn't the first case of a young person disappearing that I've heard of recently."

Joe's eyes snapped wide and color splashed his face. Alistair's heart thumped harder in his chest at his friend's reaction. "What have you heard?" Joe asked.

Wirth's expression grew hard. "Rumors only, at this point. Young people and children who are otherwise models of good behavior and hard work simply vanishing. And yes, there are always the stories about naughty or ambitious young people disappearing. Those stories may be connected. It's the fact that children who shouldn't go missing have vanished, and from situations where they should have been safe, that concerns me."

"Who has gone missing?" Alistair demanded, sitting forward. "How many are we talking about?"

"It's only whispers and casual mentions in passing so far," Wirth said. "Friends saying that they've heard something or buried items in one newspaper or another that seem unconnected. Your story, Mr. Logan, seems to confirm, at least for me, that there is something else at work here."

"Lady Matilda Fairbanks," Lionel blurted suddenly.

His interruption came so fast and seemed so out of the blue that Alistair felt like he'd been punched in the gut. "I beg your pardon?" he asked.

"Lady Matilda Fairbanks," Lionel repeated. "She's who you need to pursue." When Alistair—and Joe, and even Wirth—merely stared at him, he went on with, "Unless I am mistaken, your father has a curious friendship with Lord Chisolm."

Alistair blinked, completely thrown for a loop. "He does. They don't get along, but they remain friends."

"And they like to upstage one another," Lionel continued with a nod. "Chisolm's son is Burbage. Burbage is married to the former Lady Katherine Fairbanks, Lady Matilda's sister."

Alistair's expression tightened. "You would have me court the sister of my father's worst enemy's daughter-in-law?"

"It would be a perfect match," Lionel said, tilting his chin up and grinning as though he'd written the latest drama to grace London's stage. "Provided you are looking for a wife and not a friend. Lady Matilda despises her sister, and nearly everyone else in society, and would go to any lengths to upstage her. She is not a warm woman. Considering your father's poor health, she would see a match with you as her means to become a countess before her sister, since Lord Chisolm isn't going to give up the ghost any time soon. As such, she would be willing to put up with a man who doesn't want her in bed. Knowing her, she'd probably prefer it, as long as her place was secure. And really, she's not as much of a shrew as most people believe, she just doesn't suffer fools wisely. You may be able to form an agreeable alliance with her after all. Just don't expect affection." He sat straighter, a smile spreading across his cunning face. "Yes, Lady Matilda Fairbanks will do nicely."

Alistair and the others could do nothing but stare at him. Lionel seemed absolutely certain of everything he said.

"That was quick," Wirth told him with an arch of one brow, as if outbursts like that happened frequently. "You have outdone yourself."

Lionel shrugged. "It wasn't a difficult riddle. Nothing puts a woman in the mood for marriage, or makes her less particular about who with, than sisterly rivalry."

"And you would know?" Wirth teased him.

"My sisters fight like cats," he drawled, returning Wirth's grin with a pointed look.

Alistair was surprised that a man like Lionel had sisters, that he had a family at all. He seemed more like the sort who had once been a marble statue enchanted to transform into a flesh and blood man.

Wirth didn't appear entirely convinced. "You cannot just assume sisters don't get along. Where did you get your information?"

Lionel stood and walked between the two sofas to the stove in the corner, where a kettle sat steaming. "Their father, Lord Yardley, gets extraordinarily talkative post-coitus," he said over his shoulder with a look that could only be called devilish.

Alistair's jaw slipped open as the implication of Lionel's words hit him. Joe sputtered into laughter, which he tried and failed to hold in. Wirth seemed entirely nonplussed.

"Don't worry," Lionel continued speaking over his shoulder as he poured hot water into a teapot he'd taken from the closest bookcase, adding tea leaves as he did. "I haven't been in the game for years now. But it paid my way through university and beyond." He finished with the tea leaves, then carried the teapot over to the table closest to the sofas. "It's amazing what being agreeable can do for a man. I made many friends and I kept them. I gave them what they wanted, and they continue to give me what I want."

"Understood," Alistair said, or rather croaked, mostly because he wasn't certain he wanted an explanation that was any more detailed. "I'll investigate Lady Matilda as soon as possible."

"Don't bother with that," Lionel moved to another of the bookcases to retrieve a small tray with teacups, sugar, and cream. "You'd only waste time. I'll let Yardley know you're interested, and I'm certain he'll make the proper introductions."

"You...you will?" Alistair blinked.

"Darling, it's what I do," Lionel said, bringing the tray to the table and beginning the work of making tea for them all.

Wirth cleared his throat. "Yes, well, if you're finished playing matchmaker."

"I am," Lionel said as though he were the queen dismissing Parliament.

"Then back to the matter of Lily Logan and the other missing young people." Wirth grew serious again.

Joe's laughter dried up and his expression hardened. "Anything at all that you can do to help locate her would mean everything to me. I'll pay whatever you ask."

"Don't worry about payment until I produce results. In the meantime, I'll make inquiries," Wirth promised. "One of the men who mentioned the other missing young people to me was a police officer, Patrick Wrexham. He's a friend whom I'd trust with my life and a fellow member of The Brotherhood. He can absolutely be trusted to investigate thoroughly and discreetly."

"What should we do until you're able to speak to him?" Joe asked. "Or until he's able to find anything about Lily?"

"You should drink your tea," Lionel answered, handing both Joe and Alistair teacups. "And tell us how the two of you met."

Wirth rolled his eyes but didn't contradict him. "Unfortunately, investigations like this don't move quickly," he said. "Especially since you say your sister has been missing for months."

"As long as we find her, I don't care how long it takes," Joe said with a sigh, then added, "We met at Eccles House. Alistair's father needed the services of a valet. Conversation happened."

Lionel hummed sagely, handed Wirth a cup of tea, then took his own cup back to the arm of the sofa he'd perched on before. "It always begins with a conversation," he said in a sentimental voice.

Alistair nearly choked on his tea.

"We're just friends," Joe said, handling the situation far smoother than Alistair ever could.

"A valet and a viscount?" Lionel asked, raising one eyebrow as he raised his teacup to take a sip. "Seems rather like an all or nothing class division to me."

"Lionel," Wirth warned him. "Do save your opinions until they're asked for."

"Yes, but my opinions are always right, so I don't see any reason to deny them to the world," Lionel answered with perfect sincerity.

Alistair wondered if he were joking. He wondered if there was more to the relationship between the two men than a working one. But as they finished their tea, chatting about inconsequential things, then stood to leave, he found himself wondering about far more important things.

"I have a good feeling about this," Joe said as they walked out of the building and back onto the chilly street, buttoning their coats as they went. "I haven't had any sort of confidence that I might track down my sister for weeks now."

"I'm glad," Alistair said, distracted by his own thoughts. He pulled his collar up around his neck, glanced around to be sure no one was close enough to them to listen in, then went on with, "I'd like to see you again," as they strode down the street.

He caught the smile that lit Joe's face out of the corner of his eye but didn't risk looking directly at him for fear that everything in his heart would show on his face.

"I'd like that too," Joe said after a few steps, darting a sideways glance toward Alistair.

Alistair's moment of elation fell instantly flat. "I've no idea how to orchestrate a meeting, though. Lionel is right —a viscount and a valet cannot socialize easily."

"That's not what Lionel said," Joe told him with a laugh. They paused at an intersection and Joe looked straight at him. "I'll see what I can arrange, though."

"What you can arrange?" Alistair's brow flew up. Since when did valets have the ability to arrange clandestine meetings with men of his station?

"I'll think of something." Joe winked at him.

It was all Alistair could do not to check around them to make certain the flirtation hadn't been seen.

They crossed the street, but another pause followed. "Eccles House is this way," Joe said, pointing down the cross street.

"And my father's house is in that direction," Alistair sighed, nodding forward. He hated the idea of walking away from Joe, but didn't see how it could be avoided. "Thank you for referring me to The Brotherhood," he said.

"And thank you for coming with me on this errand. It might not look like it, but it was more difficult than it appeared."

They stood where they were, simply looking at each

other for far longer than they should have. In the space of less than twenty-four hours, Alistair's world had altered beyond recognition, and he had a feeling it would never be the same.

"Until we meet again, then," Joe said, touching the brim of his hat.

It was a poor way for friends like them—if friendship was the word for it—to part, but it was the best they could do. Alistair nodded, then marched on, feeling as though he'd left his heart behind him.

CHAPTER 7

*D*ays passed, and nothing happened. The strain of it wore on Alistair's nerves as though he were in the middle of life-or-death combat. His brief visit to The Chameleon Club and the trip to Dandie & Wirth seemed like a dream he'd woken up from, only to face a cold, hard reality.

"We shouldn't be taking Father out in his current condition," Darren whispered to him as the entire family jostled through the streets of London in a cramped carriage on their way to the theater. "He should be in bed, resting."

"Nonsense," their father grumbled from the forward-facing seat across from them. "I'm perfectly well. Well enough for the theater."

Alistair and Darren exchanged a look. The two of them were squeezed into the rear-facing seat, their broad shoulders wedged uncomfortably into the narrow space.

But their father had grown frail enough that he didn't seem fussed at all to be seated between their mother and younger sister, Beth, who had just returned from a jaunt to the country with her friends.

"You do need to take care, Father," Alistair said, hoping his smile came off as compassionate and not condescending. He couldn't shake what Lionel Mercer had mentioned in passing the other day—that Lady Matilda Fairbanks would jump at the chance to marry him because he would likely inherit the earldom soon. The only way that would happen was through the death of the man sitting across from him, a man he had adored since boyhood. It was a bitter pill to swallow.

"Your father does not want to miss Everett Jewel's performance," their mother said in a disapproving voice, though whether it was their concern or their father's recklessness that she didn't approve of was hard to tell.

"He is supposedly the most talented actor to take the stage since Edmund Kean," their father said, his face lighting up. "Everyone is talking about his Hamlet. And rumor has it that he has the voice of an angel in addition to dramatic gravity."

"We're seeing a comedy, are we not? *The Cabinet Minister?*" their mother asked.

"Yes, Mama," Beth answered, glancing past their father to her. "But that's part of what makes Jewel so sensational. He's versatile. I've heard that, if the applause is grand enough, he'll sing after his curtain call."

"We must all be certain to applaud with gusto," their father said.

Alistair exchanged another look with Darren. He doubted his father was capable of doing anything with gusto anymore, but if a sensational actor could put some life back into him, he would hire the man to come serenade his father during tea.

That fancy brought thoughts of Joe rushing in with it. How exciting would it be to have Joe serenade him? Though really, it was a ridiculous notion. He didn't even know whether Joe could sing, and it was horribly classist of him to assume Joe would be the one to do the singing. Why shouldn't he creep over to Eccles House and find a way to stand outside the servant's hall, putting on a romantic performance himself?

Because the idea was ludicrous in every way, that was why. He couldn't even call on Joe the way he would on his normal friends. He'd lost patience with the whole thing and gone to The Chameleon Club twice in the last week, completing his application and becoming a full-fledged member when he did. But all he'd encountered there was friendly conversation with men he didn't know well. Though Hillsboro had been there, telling him all about his new endeavor patronizing an orphanage. Hillsboro had helped Alistair with his official application to become a member of the club as well.

It wasn't enough, though. If he didn't find a way to see Joe again soon, he wasn't certain what he'd do. Something drastic that would end in disaster, no doubt.

"You seem more than usually agitated," Darren muttered to him once they reached the theater and stepped out to help Beth and their mother down. "Something wrong?"

Darren was the absolute last person on earth Alistair could confide in, so he settled for a benign, "I still think this is a bad idea and Father should be at home."

Darren hummed in agreement, then leaned back into the carriage to help their father out.

The prickles that raced down Alistair's back only got worse as he offered his arms to his mother and sister and proceeded up the stairs and into the grand theater. The crowd of theatergoers was already thick and loud. Half of London society seemed to be present for the performance, even though it wasn't the show's opening. Two, gigantic posters of Everett Jewell looked down on the crowded lobby. If the likeness was at all like the man, he was outrageously handsome, with dark hair, piercing blue eyes, and the look of the devil about him. Clusters of ladies stood under each of the posters, glancing up at the man as though observing the stations of the cross in a cathedral, ready to prostrate themselves in worship.

"Good heavens." Beth shook her head as she spotted the groups of admirers. "Do they think the man is going to step down from those posters and propose to them?"

"I don't believe it's a proposal they're after," Alistair commented with a wicked grin.

Beth laughed, her cheeks going pink as she understood exactly what he meant.

"He's an actor," their mother said with a sniff, completely missing the ribald undertone. "He certainly isn't suitable for any of them. Why, that's Lady Hyacinth Gimble and Lady Eleanor Haverbrook. Her father is a duke. She shouldn't be gazing at a portrait of an actor like that. It's obscene."

Alistair and Beth both made choking sounds as they tried to hide their laughter. After the intensity of the past week, it was something of a relief, and it made Alistair wonder if he should spend more time with his sister. She was barely out of the schoolroom, but he had to admit that she'd blossomed into a woman while he wasn't looking. Women were always more understanding about certain things, especially when it came to matters of the heart, so perhaps it wouldn't be as much of a risk if he—

"Lord Farnham, I believe?"

Alistair was taken completely off-guard by the stately, older gentleman who approached him and nodded slightly in greeting.

Tension immediately gripped him, as though an iron band had been clamped around his chest. "Lord Templeton." He nodded back to George Fairbanks, Lord Templeton, then acknowledged the young woman on his arm, his daughter, Lady Matilda Fairbanks, with the same gallantry, even though his heart was instantly racing. "Lady Matilda. What a pleasure to see you this evening."

"The pleasure is all ours," Lady Matilda answered for

her father, extending an elegant, gloved hand toward him.

Alistair took her hand and performed the requisite bow over it. Was the meeting a coincidence or had Lionel pulled his strings already?

"This is a surprise," Alistair's mother said as Lord Templeton greeted her. "I don't believe we've spoken in a decade at least, Lord Templeton."

"An oversight on my part, I can assure you," Lord Templeton said. "I was just reminded the other day of how delightful the entire Bevan family has always been and how our family and yours should renew our acquaintance." His gaze slipped sideways to meet Alistair's with frankness.

Yes, Lionel was most certainly behind the chance meeting.

"Are you a theater aficionado, Lord Farnham?" Lady Matilda asked, raking Alistair with an assessing look as she did.

"My father certainly is," Alistair answered, unnerved by the sharpness of her look. She was sizing him up the way he'd seen breeders size up horses. But then, if he were honest, his reasons for potentially courting her wouldn't be that much different than her reasons for allowing him to. "I haven't attended nearly as much as I should. Perhaps if I had a regular companion who enjoyed it I would," he went on.

Inside, Alistair heated with discomfort at what

sounded like too obvious a line, but Lady Matilda's smile widened.

"I should attend more myself," she said. "But you are right. It is so difficult to find a suitable companion these days."

She tilted her head down slightly and glanced up at him through thick lashes. The gesture was coy, but the calculated interest in her eyes was unmistakable. It was also disconcerting. Lady Matilda Fairbanks was a woman who knew what she wanted. Of course, the only reason that unsettled Alistair was because he knew exactly what he wanted too, and it wasn't her. But life wasn't always about what one wanted.

"Lord Templeton," his father said in a voice that was both pleased and frail as he and Darren joined the group. "What a surprise. It's been ages."

"It's been too long, sir." Lord Templeton shook Alistair's father's hand, poorly disguised pity in his eyes. At least the emotion was sympathetic. If the man had sneered or scoffed at his father, Alistair would have abandoned the entire charade, no matter how good a match Lionel Mercer thought he and Lady Matilda would be. "You must forgive me for failing to call on you for so long. Duty calls, of course."

"Of course," Alistair's father agreed. "How is your brother, Reginald?"

As the two older men launched into a conversation of old times, Alistair stole another glance at Lady Matilda. She watched him with a smile of her own. More than that, she let go of her father's arm and stepped closer to Alistair's side.

"I don't know why my father was so intent on making certain the two of us met this evening," she said in a sultry alto, "but I'm glad he did."

"You are?" Flirt. Alistair knew he had to flirt. It was a damn shame he was so bad at it.

"Apparently, Papa heard whispers that you might be on the marriage market," Lady Matilda went on, her smile warming.

Alistair hated himself for taking the bait, for playing the game he'd been forced into, but all the same, he said, "My father's health isn't what it used to be," and inched closer to Lady Matilda. "I have a duty."

Lady Matilda nodded subtly, her eyes sparkling. "Fortunately, I have been trained my whole life to assume exactly the sort of duties a man in your position might need help with."

She met his eyes with stark understanding. So much so that Alistair wondered how fully she comprehended who he was and how she might fit into his life.

He was spared having to find out as a chime sounded, indicating the heart of the theater was now open and patrons could take their seats. The women who had been gazing adoringly at Everett Jewel's posters rushed to the front of the crowd, causing a stir as they pushed on, trying to be the first in the theater. The rest of the crowd in the lobby began to stream toward the open theater doors as well, making Alistair feel as though standing still were swimming against the current.

"We should probably take our seats," he said, relieved that he wouldn't have to figure out how to entice Lady Matilda into marriage right then and there.

"You're right," she said, taking her father's arm once more. "But we must have you to supper. Soon."

"Quite right," Lord Templeton said, turning from his conversation with Alistair's father. "How does this Tuesday suit you?"

Alistair's brow shot up. The whole thing had been easy. Too easy. He could already see how it would progress. Supper on Tuesday, a few more jaunts to the theater in the coming weeks, teas, family get-togethers, and by June he and Lady Matilda would be standing at the front of a chapel together. And then he'd have to figure out how to summon up the courage to do the rest of his duty and produce an heir. The thought was enough to make him instinctively search the lobby for a way out.

As he glanced toward one of the doors to the street, he discovered Joe standing there, leaning against the doorframe, arms crossed, watching him with an expression of amusement and fondness. Every fiber in Alistair's body reacted to that saucy look, raising his temperature by several degrees.

He whipped back to smile tensely at Lady Matilda, then nodded to Lord Templeton. "Tuesday would be perfect," he said.

"Good." Lord Templeton nodded. "I'll send you more

details once I make arrangements." He arched one eyebrow slightly, as though speaking a hidden language to let Alistair know he'd carried out the favor that was asked of him, then offered his arm to Lady Matilda. "Shall we battle this crowd of sycophantic ninnies to find our box, my dear?"

"Yes, Papa," Lady Matilda laughed. "Until Tuesday, Lord Farnham." She sent Alistair a victorious look, then walked on with her father.

"Well done, son, well done," Alistair's father congratulated him with a weak slap on his back. "Lady Matilda seemed utterly taken with you."

"Yes, I think you've found yourself an admirer," Beth added with an excited grin.

"It's about time," his mother sighed, clasping his father's arm to help him shuffle along toward the stairs leading to the boxes.

Once his family had moved a few steps ahead, Alistair glanced back to Joe. Joe straightened and jerked his head out toward the street, questioning in his eyes. Alistair opened his mouth before realizing the ridiculousness of trying to reply over so much distance packed with so many people. Instead, he nodded, then held up a finger, asking Joe to wait one moment. Joe nodded, then Alistair turned back to his family.

"I've just spotted someone I know," he told Darren in a clandestine voice.

"You know people?" Darren joked in return.

"Believe it or not, I do." Alistair pretended to joke as

well. "Would you mind taking Father and Mother and Beth in? I'll just be a moment." He hesitated, then said, "I desperately need to speak to this friend."

Darren laughed. "I'm still surprised you have friends. You need more of them. Go ahead. We'll stop any of the rabid ladies in love with Jewell from taking your seat."

Alistair thanked his brother with a slap on his shoulder, then turned to make his way against the crowd, heading out of the theater.

He found Joe standing on the street, a few yards down from the theater's entrance, looking as tempting as a treacle tart in the lamplight. His clothes and coat weren't of high quality, but he wore them so well and stood with such confidence that he could have been a member of the royal family.

"I told you I'd find a way for us to meet," he said in a low voice as Alistair drew near. "I heard Lady Burbage mention something in passing about who might be attending this premier."

Self-consciousness rolled off of Alistair as he moved to stand as close to Joe as he dared. "You aren't needed at Eccles House tonight?"

Joe shook his head. "Burbage is off causing some sort of trouble with his less reputable friends. He won't be home until well after midnight, if he comes home before dawn at all."

Alistair wasn't surprised in the least. He glanced over his shoulder at the theater, then inched closer to Joe. "I'm here with my family," he said, as though it were both an explanation and an apology.

"Oh." Joe's inviting grin dropped. "I'm sorry to interrupt."

"It's no trouble at all," he said, his heart feeling strangely as though it were magnetic and being drawn out of his body toward Joe. "Only, what with my father's poor health, and because my sister is here with us as well...."

"I understand," Joe said, reaching for Alistair's hand in the shadows cast by the streetlamp. "I shouldn't have assumed anything."

Alistair was fairly certain he would die on the spot at the brush of Joe's hand against his. He suddenly wished he were an orphan. "The show shouldn't be that long," he said, glancing hopefully into Joe's eyes. "Our family never goes out afterwards for anything. Father and Mother always just want to go home. But I don't have to."

Joe's suggestive grin returned. "You don't have to rush home to be tucked into bed?"

He shouldn't take the bait. They were on a crowded street, for Christ's sake. Anyone who happened to over-hear could send the police after the both of them. But he couldn't resist saying, "Not unless you're doing the tucking."

Fire lit Joe's eyes. He slipped his fingers between Alistair's with friction that sent Alistair's imagination soaring and blood rushing to his cock. The sensation was so intense that Alistair had to take a half step back to stop himself from crashing against Joe and kissing him in the middle of the crowd of theatergoers.

"I'll wait," Joe murmured, tucking his hands into his coat pocket. He nodded across the street to a pub that catered to theatergoers. "I'll just have a pint or something in there and watch for you."

"I won't be long," Alistair promised, his voice hoarse with desire.

Joe took another step back and winked, then turned to stroll across the street. Alistair watched him cross to the pub, his heart beating furiously and his cock growing harder by the second. It took a monumental effort of will to pull himself together and head back into the theater for what was certain to feel like the longest theatrical event of his life.

CHAPTER 8

*J*oe sat at a table in the window of the pub across from the theater, watching the doors as though they were the stage and waiting for Alistair to come out. Every time the doors opened and a gentleman stepped onto the street, his heart sped up. And every time that happened, he laughed at himself. He hadn't been so eager to meet up with a man since he'd been fresh out of the schoolhouse and discovered that the cobbler's apprentice wasn't averse to letting him suck his cock. Even if he never returned the favor.

As the evening wore on, he drew more stares for sitting by himself, fixated on the theater.

"You aren't thinking of causing any trouble, are you?" one of the barmaids asked him with a saucy grin as she came to take away the pint he'd finished.

Joe laughed. "I aim to cause all sorts of trouble," he told her. "But not the kind you think."

She gratified him with a suggestive smile and a flirtatious glance over her shoulder as she walked away. Let her—or any woman—think what they wanted about him. There was safety in appearing like any other man.

When the theater doors flew open, disgorging patrons at last, Joe shot to his feet. The sudden burst of color, light, and sound as chattering upper-class ladies and gentlemen and smiling middle-class theatergoers mingled on their way to the sidewalk and the carriages waiting to whisk them home echoed the lift in Joe's heart as he stepped out into the chilly evening. He strolled casually to the end of the street, hands tucked in the pockets of his coat, waiting for the familiar sight of Alistair's blond head.

The excitement that filled him when he spotted Alistair helping his father through the door and down the theater's steps had him laughing at himself once more. But there was something gratifying about the blossoming feelings he had for Alistair, foolish as they were. Life was too full of sorrow and misery not to nurture the tender shoots of affection when they sprouted up. He would save worrying about the consequences for another day.

Alistair spotted him from the top of the stairs and nodded briefly before focusing all his efforts on his family. For a moment, Joe thought Alistair's brother caught the gesture. He checked to see what Alistair had nodded at, which prompted Joe to hunker down in his coat. Alistair's brother gave up his search almost as quickly as he'd started it.

At last, Alistair secured his father, mother, and sister in one of the carriages lining the street in front of the theater, had a word with his brother, then broke away from his family and started briskly down the street. There were still too many theatergoers around for Joe's liking, so he crossed to the side of the street where Alistair stood, walked right past him with a quick sideways look, and headed on as though he had an errand elsewhere.

Alistair followed him a few paces behind until Joe reached an alley that ran in back of the theater. A small crowd of ladies, as well as a few starry-eyed gentlemen, hovered around the stage door, waiting. If Joe's calculations were correct, the sort of people who would be waiting at the stage door for whichever acclaimed actors might come out to greet them would be the kind to ignore, or even sanction, whatever he and Alistair might say.

"Are you sure we're safe here?" Alistair asked in a near whisper as they hovered around the edge of the cluster of admirers.

Joe grinned, inching closer to Alistair and facing him. "I love how concerned with safety you are," he said, letting his heart run riot in his chest. "And for the record, I adore how considerate of your family you are as well."

"Do you?" Alistair's brow shot up. "You aren't...irritated that I chose to watch the show with them instead of...."

"No, not at all," Joe said when it was clear Alistair

wouldn't finish his sentence. "I'd do the same myself. Family is important."

Alistair hummed and nodded. "Of course." He paused before asking, "Have you heard anything from Wirth about your sister?"

Joe's grin dropped. "Not yet. Wirth sent me a letter the other day to say he's made contact with that police officer he mentioned and that the investigation is ongoing, but that's it."

Alistair hummed again, then huddled into his coat to fight the cold. Or perhaps to make himself as unnoticeable as possible. He darted wary looks at the restless crowd around the stage door for a minute before sending Joe a sideways glance. "Why are we standing here?"

"So I can admire the way you look in the lamplight when you're nervous," Joe replied, his grin returning.

Alistair let out a breath and dropped his shoulders. He faced Joe with a wry roll of his eyes. "I'm certain there are far more places the two of us could go where you could admire me."

"St. James's Park?" Joe asked, half joking. St. James's Park was notorious for quick, clandestine meetings between men like them where money often changed hands for five minutes of pleasure.

The shock of pink that flooded Alistair's face was apparent even in the dim light.

"I'm joking," Joe laughed and shook his head. He let a beat pass before continuing with, "For that, nothing less than a room at the Savoy would do."

Alistair blew out a breath, then laughed himself, still red-faced. "You have expensive tastes for a country boy."

"I'm standing next to you, aren't I?" Joe countered.

The stage door burst open a moment later, interrupting their flirtation. The crowd of hangers-on burst into energetic applause as a tall man with dark hair, blue eyes, and magnetic presence stepped out to greet them. Joe recognized him from the posters hung around the theater, Everett Jewel, and was immediately impressed.

"What a delight this is," Jewel said as though he were still on the stage. "You all do me a great honor by waiting here for me."

"I would fly to the ends of the earth for you," one of the ladies said, surging toward him. She was held off by a burly man in a dark suit who stepped forward to protect Jewel.

"Just say the word, and I will be yours," another of the ladies said, equally eager.

"And so will I," one of the gentlemen said, sighing dramatically.

Joe exchanged a wide-eyed look with Alistair that nearly had both of them bursting with laughter at the man.

"That's a bit obvious," Alistair muttered, sending Joe over the edge.

To their surprise, Jewel sent the man a rakish wink and said, "You flatter me."

Joe and Alistair shared another, even more surprised look, and it was all Joe could do not to double over with laughter. Jewel went on to flirt with the ladies surrounding him as well as he signed programs and doled out kisses to their cheeks, but surprisingly, he treated his gentlemen admirers with the same teasing flirtation, seeming not to care who was watching him do it.

The spectacle was a distraction, and as the almost hysterical fervor around Jewel grew, Joe grabbed Alistair's sleeve to tug him away from the noise. "The night is young," he said once he was sure he'd be heard. "Let's enjoy it."

Alistair glanced from the crowd around Jewel to the passersby on the street to Joe. "It's a shame there isn't someplace we can go for a pint in peace."

"Actually," Joe began, brightening, "I believe there is."

He started out of the alley, gesturing for Alistair to follow him. The Chameleon Club wasn't the only establishment frequented by members of The Brotherhood. The network had several safe spots, although the pub Joe had heard of wasn't strictly sanctioned by The Brotherhood. The Brotherhood prided itself on rules of propriety and restraint, but from everything Joe had heard, The Cock and Bear had no such rules.

The Cock and Bear was still within the boundaries of London's theater district, and the moment Joe stepped inside it's rowdy, raucous atmosphere, he knew the rumors were true.

"It's louder than the theater in here," Alistair said,

forced to raise his voice above the clamor of conversation and song.

The place was packed. Even though the main room was larger than most of the pubs Joe had been in, it seemed cramped. There were few empty places at the tables crowded into the room, but it was the small stage at one end of the room and the piano that stood on it that seemed to draw the most attention from the patrons. A man in a red velvet jacket sat at the piano, banging away at a popular song, while at least a dozen men and a handful of women sang along. Half of the patrons of the pub sang with them from wherever they sat. The mood of the place was jolly, wild, and excited.

"Do you want a drink?" Joe asked, almost having to shout over the song, as he led Alistair through the crowd to the bar.

"I think I'll need one if I'm going to make it through this," Alistair answered, his eyes bright with wonder.

They found spots at the bar and were able to order. Joe laughed at the speed with which Alistair downed his whiskey, then asked for another.

"I don't usually like crowds," he explained, his voice rough from swallowing the alcohol, as he traded his empty glass for a full one.

Joe slapped him on the back, then nudged him away from the bar to a space that had just opened along one of the walls, where they could see the stage and observe the entire pub. It was obvious Alistair wasn't used to the sort of crowd that took up space and made so much noise, but everyone around them was enjoying themselves. The mood was merry, the song was fun, and smiling faces abounded. Not just smiling faces. As Joe claimed a spot for them against the wall and leaned back, rubbing shoulders with Alistair as he did, he spotted a couple in the corner going at each other with abandon. A male couple. Their mouths seemed fused together, and their hands fumbled where they shouldn't have in public.

"I'd give the two of them a standing ovation, if I weren't so jealous," a familiar voice said at Joe's side.

He turned to find Lionel Mercer—pale face pink and blue eyes bright with alcohol, dressed in a lavender waistcoat and rose cravat—sliding up to him. Lionel wedged his way between them, throwing his arms around Joe's and Alistair's shoulders, and proving he was taller than he'd seemed in the office as he did so. Lionel wore a drunken grin as he stared at the entwined couple in the corner.

"Fucking vow of celibacy," he grumbled, if it was possible to grumble in a voice that would make a soprano green with envy.

"What, you?" Joe asked, blinking. He'd barely met the man, but Lionel Mercer was the last person he would have pegged to have taken a vow of celibacy.

"Long story," Lionel told Joe before rolling his head to the other side to smile at Alistair. "D'you meet Lady Matilda tonight?" he asked, words slightly slurred.

Alistair stood a bit straighter. "I did." He nodded. "I assume I have you to thank for that."

"You do." Lionel's smile turned triumphant. "George was delighted at the prospect of a match when I suggested it."

A twist of jealousy pinched Joe's gut. He had no claim on Alistair and certainly no right to prevent him from doing what gentlemen of his class did and marrying a titled lady, but the flare of possessiveness that shot through him was unmistakable. He ducked away from Lionel's arm around his shoulder and executed a quick turn around the man to Alistair's other side, then proceeded to circle his arm around Alistair's waist and tug him close.

"Ooh. Lady Matilda has competition, I see," Lionel said, spinning away from Alistair as though he and Joe were part of some sort of choreographed dance around him. "I know which prize I'd choose," Lionel went on before swaying forward and planting a sloppy kiss square on Joe's lips.

A second later, Lionel stepped away, winked at Alistair, then sauntered back into the singing crowd, joining in with the song.

"He's drunk," Alistair said, eyes wide with astonishment, not just for Lionel, but for everything around them.

"He's not," Joe said, his tingling lips pulling into a lopsided grin. "I didn't taste a drop of the stuff on him."

Alistair shot a narrow-eyed look Joe's way. "High, then?"

Joe shook his head. "Unless I'm mistaken, Lionel Mercer is as in control of himself as anyone, and he's just toying with us for sport."

Indeed, before Joe could finish his assessment, a man he didn't recognize stepped up to Lionel's side and said something with a grim expression. Lionel's inebriated smile immediately dropped to deadly seriousness as the two exchanged a few words of what Joe was certain was business. Lionel said something to the man in return, then nodded straight to Joe.

For a moment, Joe was certain he was about to be exposed and punished for every sin he'd ever committed. Lionel resumed his false drunkenness as the other man pushed his way through the rowdy crowd to reach Joe and Alistair. Joe suddenly wished he hadn't had even a single drink. He straightened and pulled his arm away from Alistair's waist.

"Joseph Logan?" the man asked.

"Yes?" Joe asked hesitantly.

The man extended his hand. "Officer Patrick Wrexham."

Alistair tensed by Joe's side.

Joe held his breath and took Wrexham's hand, certain he was about to be arrested for indecency, in spite of the crowd around him and the politeness of the handshake.

"I'd like to talk to you about your sister," Wrexham said, letting Joe's hand go. Only then did Joe remember Wirth had mentioned Wrexham was also a member of

The Brotherhood. He was handsome, with a stocky build with muscular arms, and he had the sort of round face that made him appear younger than he probably was.

Joe glanced to Alistair, his heart racing, then back to Wrexham. "What do you need to know?"

Wrexham crossed his arms and frowned as if they were in a police station instead of a hot, noisy pub full of singing and carousing. "Did she know a man named Adler?"

Joe blinked and shook his head. "I have no idea. She never wrote anything home about anyone named Adler, but that doesn't mean she didn't know him."

"Who is this Adler anyhow?" Alistair asked, pushing away from the wall to take an active role in the conversation.

"I'm not entirely certain yet," Wrexham answered. "I've heard reports he's a toymaker, a haberdasher, and a sweets seller. I've even heard he is a she. But frankly, all of those things sound like lies a criminal would tell a child to lure them away from where they should be."

"So you think this man lured Lily away from her position at Eccles House?" Joe asked, in the mood to storm through London looking for the man so that he could strangle the life out of him.

Wrexham nodded. "It appears so. Unfortunately, that's all I know right now."

"You'll let us know if you discover anything else," Alistair said.

Wrexham seemed to notice him for the first time. "I'm sorry, but how are you involved?"

Alistair flushed in the way that Joe would have found charming, if his every nerve wasn't on edge, thanks to the new information Wrexham had. "I'm a friend," Alistair said, his jaw clenched tightly.

Wrexham hesitated for a moment then nodded. "Investigations like these are tricky. Children go missing all the time, unfortunately. But if we can—"

He was cut short as the pub's door banged open and the larger than life figure of Everett Jewel marched in as though making a grand entrance on stage.

"Ladies, gentlemen, and those who have yet to decide, I have arrived," he announced.

The pub immediately erupted into applause that was so loud Joe could barely hear himself think. A path instantly cleared, allowing Everett to saunter to the stage and step up with another flourish. The man from the stage door who had offered himself followed Jewel in, along with two of the ladies, much to Joe's surprise. The ladies didn't seem to notice or care what kind of pub they'd entered.

"Lawrence, play *A Wandering Minstrel I*," Jewel commanded, thumping the top of the piano.

The admiring crowd renewed their applause at such a volume that Joe barely heard the first notes of the song. As soon as Jewel began singing, however, the crowd grew hushed and hung on every note he sang.

Joe's brow shot up. The man had talent. More than

that, there was something about his presence that held the audience in thrall, as if he radiated magic. His eyes in particular seemed to sparkle, even across a distance. Even Officer Wrexham was struck dumb as he watched the performance.

The only person in the entire pub who didn't seem impressed was Lionel, who looked sour as he cut his way back through the rapt admirers to lean against the wall beside Alistair, crossing his arms. "I'd hate him if he wasn't such a good fuck," he muttered just loud enough to be heard.

Joe burst into laughter before he could stop himself. Everything around him felt surreal—the heightened mood of the pub, its colorful patrons, and the paradoxical sense of safety that pervaded the rowdy establishment. Clearly the Metropolitan Police knew about the place, as attested by Officer Wrexham's presence, but Wrexham didn't appear particularly inclined to do anything about it. In fact, the way he watched Jewel—as if seeing his first sunrise—had Joe covering his mouth with one hand to keep from offending the man by snickering. Wrexham was currently his best hope for finding Lily.

Jewel finished the number from *The Mikado*, then launched into an upbeat, scandalously inappropriate song that involved the participation of everyone standing closest to the stage.

"This is another side to the man," Alistair told Joe, needing to lean close and speak directly into his ear to be heard. "Shakespeare it is not."

Joe laughed—barely hearing the sound he made—and nestled his back against the wall by Alistair's side. More people flooded into the pub, and within minutes, he and Alistair were wedged up against each other out of necessity. Not that Joe was complaining. He would have found an excuse to plaster himself against Alistair before too long if the crowd in the pub hadn't given one to him. The sensation was exquisite. Alistair was fit and firm, and although Joe sensed a great deal of tension radiating from him that likely had to do with the crowd, it was just as possible that that tension was Alistair's reaction to their proximity.

Jewel kept singing, his songs getting dirtier as the night progressed and his antics with his admirers, right in front of everyone, more shocking. Joe found the whole thing astoundingly entertaining, but he could sense when Alistair had had enough.

"Is there a back way out?" he asked Lionel—who watched Jewel's spectacle with crossed arms and a disapproving scowl by Joe's other side.

Lionel gestured with his thumb farther down the wall to a narrow passage just a few feet away.

Joe slapped his shoulder in thanks, then took Alistair's hand and tugged him to get his attention. He nodded to the passage, then started forward, leading Alistair through the inebriated crowd.

By the time they headed down the narrow hallway, passing more than one door from which came the unmistakable sound of men enjoying each other, through a storeroom, and out into an alley behind the pub, Joe's ears were ringing from the noise.

"Thanks for that," Alistair said, overly loud.

"For what?" Joe asked, equally loud.

"For getting me out of there. Jewel is fascinating, but I've never been one for crowds."

"They don't bother me, but that was—"

Joe's response was cut short as Alistair stepped into him, clasped the sides of his face, and slanted his mouth over his. The kiss took him completely by surprise, which gave Alistair the leverage he needed to deepen things between them, sliding his tongue along Joe's.

Joe sucked in a breath, kissing him back with abandon. He moaned as their lips teased and tested each other and as their tongues danced. He slipped his hands under Alistair's jacket, wishing the layers of waistcoat and shirt would vanish so that he could make contact with his skin.

He wasn't sure when he'd backpedaled or how Alistair managed to press him up against the wall, but he approved of the results. Their bodies ground together, the hard bulge of Alistair's cock insistent against his hip. Undiluted desire rushed through Joe, making his head spin. The suddenness of it all had him moments away from spending in his trousers.

"We can't do this here," Alistair panted, pulling back. "We can't do this tonight."

Joe was willing to concede the first point, but the second felt as though he'd been robbed. "When?" he asked, unable to catch his breath as he gazed deep into

Alistair's eyes, then answered his own question with, "Soon."

Alistair blinked, looking suddenly vulnerable. "I don't know how."

A bolt of affection shot through Joe. The simple statement could mean so many things. "I'll find a place," he said. "I'll find a way."

Alistair nodded, hesitated, then said, "I have to go home now." Joe's disappointment must have shown on his face, because Alistair rushed on with, "I don't trust what I'll do if I stay close to you."

"You can do whatever you'd like," Joe said, meaning it more than he'd meant anything in his life.

"That's what I'm afraid of," Alistair said in a whisper. He darted a glance around. "But not here. Not like this."

Joe nodded. Alistair wanted things between them to be special, more than just a grope and a fumble in the back alley behind a garish pub. "I'll figure something out."

Alistair let out a breath, but that didn't seem to be enough. He surged back into Joe, kissing him deeply and grinding their hips together. They both sighed with longing at the connection, tasting and touching. "I want you," he confessed in a whisper. "More than I've wanted anyone in my life."

"And I want you," Joe said, heart pounding. "Soon."

Alistair peeled away slowly, his gaze lingering on Joe's eyes. There was so much need, so much desperation and affection in Alistair's bright eyes that Joe was tempted to change his mind and fling Alistair across the pile of crates beside the pub's door and have his way with him right then and there. But the look in Alistair's eyes was right. Whatever was growing between them deserved more.

aiting was agony. Alistair couldn't concentrate on a damn thing as days ticked slowly by without seeing Joe's mischievous smile, without kissing his passionate mouth, and without feeling the heat of his body. The anticipation of what Joe might figure out so that the two of them could be together was made even harder to bear by the fact that his courtship of Lady Matilda was proceeding at lightning pace.

"I'm proud of you, son," Alistair's father said, thumping his back with a shaking hand as they loitered in the front parlor, waiting for the rest of the family to be ready for the ball they were about to attend at Eccles House. "Lady Matilda Fairbanks is perfect for you."

"Thank you, Father," Alistair said, certain the embarrassed heat rising to his face would give away every lie he was telling by clinging to Lady Matilda.

"I can see it in your eyes," his father went on. "The

way you look at her, yes, and the way you have taken to staring off at nothing, that mooning look of love in your eyes."

Alistair flushed hotter and cleared his throat. "I don't have a mooning look," he muttered, stepping away from where his father stood, warming himself by the fire. He pretended to examine the clock in the corner as a way to hide his face from his father.

"You can't fool me, son," his father laughed. "I've been in love. I know what it looks like. And you, my boy, are besotted."

"Yes, well," Alistair said with a shrug and cleared his throat.

His father was far too perceptive for his own good. Alistair *was* in love. There was no way around it. He might not have seen Joe for more than a week, but the delightfully dangerous bugger had sent him letters, delivered by special courier, every day since the night at The Cock and Bull. Letters that would land both of them in prison if they were ever made public. Letters that detailed everything Joe planned to do to him once they had a chance to be together. Alistair had rubbed himself raw every night, and several times in the middle of the day, reading those letters, and, God help him, he had responded with epistles that would spell his ruin if they were ever discovered. But he couldn't help himself. Joe had become as much a part of him as the blood that pounded into his cock every time he remembered the way they'd kissed in the alley.

"Besotted," his father repeated, shaking Alistair out of his thoughts.

Alistair cleared his throat again and turned away from the clock, begging his body to settle so that he wouldn't embarrass himself any further in front of his father. "Whatever you say, Father."

His father chuckled, then coughed, the rattle of premature age sounding through his amusement, and shuffled toward Alistair. "I cannot tell you how proud I am of your choice. Matilda Fairbanks is by far the prettier of the two sisters. But more importantly, this means that you and Burbage might be brothers-in-law very soon. And with such a connection as that, we're bound to uncover every dirty secret of the Eccles slave trade before long."

Alistair's awkward emotional maelstrom instantly died away, leaving old, gnawing sorrow for everything his father had become in its wake. At the same time, a new spark of curiosity flared behind the shame and disappointment he was so used to feeling at his father's ranting, though he didn't have time to examine what that spark could mean. Darren strode into the room just as their father spoke. He sent Alistair a long-suffering look, as though their father were at it again.

"I say let the law deal with legal problems," Darren said as he crossed to check on their father, "and the rest of us should mind our own business."

Alistair nodded in approval.

"But it is our business," their father insisted, allowing

Darren to help him into the chair nearest the fire. "The entire Eccles clan has hidden their nefarious activity so well. Only we can bring their villainy into the light."

Alistair winced as he crossed to stand on the other side of the chair from Darren. "We'll do the best we can, Father," he said, sharing a flat look with his brother. Then again, if there was a kernel of truth behind his father's ridiculous fancies, it might explain how a good girl like Lily could disappear from Eccles House.

"You're certainly doing well," Darren said with a grin, overriding Alistair's thoughts. "Matilda Fairbanks? Where did you ever come up with an idea like that?"

Alistair swallowed. Mentioning Lionel Mercer and his web of social connections was utterly out of the question, so he settled on, "We met at some ball or another ages ago, then met again and had a lovely conversation at the theater last week."

"Yes, I noticed you weren't the only one to rush off at the end of the show," Darren said with a teasing look. "She seemed to have somewhere to go in a hurry herself."

Alistair's brow inched up before he could conceal his reaction. Had Lady Matilda left the theater in a hurry as well? He hadn't noticed. He hadn't even seen her after the show. His thoughts had been for one person and one person only. All the same, he mumbled, "Yes, well," letting his brother and father think what they would of it.

"Three invitations to dine with the family in a week," Darren went on, his expression impressed. "Not bad."

"It's excellent," their father added from his seat,

looking up and between his sons. "We'll have just the alliance we need by the end of the spring, I'm certain. And it carries the added advantage of a solid connection to the Eccles family. The blackguards will be in prison by the time your first son is born."

Alistair and Darren exchanged another look as Alistair's heart sank. "Could I have a word with you?" Darren asked in a low voice.

Alistair nodded, then followed as his brother stepped away from their father's chair and out into the hall.

Once they were alone and well away from their father's ears, Darren faced Alistair and said, "We can't let him go on like this indefinitely."

"But what can we do about it?" Alistair asked, his brow knit in frustration. "We can't have him committed to Bedlam. There's nothing wrong with him but illness and senility."

"Perhaps not," Darren murmured back. "But we can't keep taking him out in public like this. It's only a matter of time before he says something that truly puts the entire family in hot water. This obsession with the fantasy of the Eccleses' slave trading will end with one or both of us challenged to pistols at dawn if he doesn't shut up about it."

"Agreed." Alistair let out a heavy breath and rubbed a hand over his face. Though he couldn't shake the idea that kidnapping and the slave trade weren't as different as they might have been. Could his father actually know something? But even if he did, how could they possibly separate the truth from his father's madness?

An awkward pause passed, and Darren's troubled expression slipped into a grin. "Matilda Fairbanks," he said, shaking his head. "I never would have thought you had it in you."

"To court a suitable lady?" Alistair asked.

"I've heard rumors Lady Matilda was holding out for a duke. Or a marquess at the very least."

Alistair scrambled for an explanation of how he had managed to interest the woman. "I suppose she decided she was willing to settle for a future earl." That seemed weak, so he quickly added, "We get along well."

In fact, they did, if getting along meant that they had been able to carry on conversations about innocuous topics without irritating each other in the time they'd spent together. Lionel had been right about her being cold, though. Still, Alistair rather suspected Lady Matilda liked him because, unlike so many other gentlemen, he hadn't taken aggressive control of their conversations. He'd spent more time listening to her express her opinions on every topic under the sun instead of telling her what to think. And she was intelligent. He had to give her that much.

"Well, I applaud you for choosing well," Darren said, slapping him on the arm.

"I'm just doing my duty," Alistair replied, feeling it keenly. His thoughts flew back to the letter he'd received from Joe that afternoon, the promises of sin it contained.

How he would be able to negotiate a dutiful marriage while also following his heart was a problem he did not look forward to solving.

"The two of you make a mother proud," their mother said, interrupting them as she came down the stairs, dressed for the ball they were all about to attend. "You are my solace in this difficult time," she continued with a dramatic sigh.

"Mother, you look lovely," Darren complimented her as she reached them.

She kissed Darren's cheek, then turned to Alistair, who bent so she could kiss his as well. "You're a good boy," she said, patting the cheek she'd just kissed. "I had my concerns about you, but it seems you're on the right path after all."

The look she gave him as he straightened sent a chill through Alistair. Mothers knew things. He'd always worried that his knew more than she let on. Which made the path he was on even more perilous than he'd imagined.

"Shall we go to the ball?" he asked with a smile all the same, offering his mother his arm. It was the first time in his life that he'd ever looked forward to going to Eccles House. He would look forward to any occasion when he might be lucky enough to see Joe.

His mother sighed and slipped her hand into the crook of his arm. "Let's get this over with."

.   .   .

"No, NOT THOSE CUFFLINKS, THE DIAMOND ONES," Burbage snapped at Joe with a distracted scowl.

Joe merely nodded and walked back to Burbage's wardrobe and the silk-lined box of cufflinks it contained. He returned the modest, rejected ones and selected a garish pair with diamonds.

Burbage was silent when Joe returned. He stretched out one arm, then the other, as Joe fixed the cufflinks in place. Sometimes the man was silent because he had nothing to say. Sometimes it was because he considered it beneath him to converse with a servant while getting dressed. But that evening, Joe was convinced it was because his employer had something else on his mind.

Which suited Joe perfectly. He had plenty of other things on his mind as well. Things that made it exceptionally difficult not to crack a saucy smile as he fetched Burbage's waistcoat for the ball and helped him into it. He stepped around to do up the buttons, fighting to keep his thoughts from the way he wanted to undo every button Alistair had fastening him into his stilted, noble life.

It was madness for him to write the letters that he'd sent Alistair in the last week. Anyone who happened to get even the briefest glimpse of them would know immediately what there was between the two of them. Or, at least, what there could be. That was why he'd been painstakingly careful to have one of the pages from The Chameleon Club deliver them, and why he was grateful that Alistair had done the same with the letters he'd sent in return.

Alistair, his dear, sweet, viscount, had a way with words. He had a way of describing the most salacious acts in terms that were endearing and almost innocent. With each new letter he received, Joe was less certain whether he wanted to bend Alistair over a barrel and fuck him until they were both exhausted or whether he wanted to lavish him with all the tender attention of a sentimental lover and swallow his cock to the hilt.

"What is that smile for?" Burbage snapped, startling Joe out of his thoughts.

"Smile, my lord?" Joe played innocent as he marched to retrieve Burbage's suit jacket from the stand where he'd brushed it earlier.

"I don't approve," Burbage said, though what exactly he didn't approve of, he didn't say.

"No, my lord." Joe schooled his expression and straightened his back, attempting to become part of the furniture again as he brought the jacket to Burbage.

Burbage slipped his arms into the sleeves with an irritated breath. "You don't have a sweetheart, do you?" he asked in a sour voice.

"No, my lord," Joe answered immediately.

"Good. Because I've had enough of my staff run off with their sweethearts to last a lifetime. It's disgusting."

Joe's heart caught in his chest, and all the things he'd recently let slip to the wayside leapt back into his thoughts. "You've had staff run off with their sweethearts?" he asked, then added, "My lord," when Burbage glared at him in the mirror.

"Maids are forever dashing off with milkmen," Burbage grumbled.

It was all Joe could do to keep a straight face as he brushed Burbage's shoulders and stepped back as his employer studied his appearance in the mirror. Lily. In the past week, in spite of Officer Wrexham's information at the pub, Joe had only had time for Alistair in his thoughts. And as delicious as those thoughts had been, Burbage's words now wracked him with guilt. Was Alistair pulling him away from what he should have been doing? Had Lily run off with the milkman after all, or was she another victim of the man, Adler, that Wrexham had mentioned?

"Balls are such a nuisance," Burbage sighed as he turned away from the mirror and crossed to the door. "They were a necessity when I was finding a wife, but I've got one now. I'd rather go to my club, or any of a dozen, far more interesting parties."

Joe remained silent, stepping toward the wall and attempting to blend in with the wallpaper. Burbage wasn't talking to him in any case.

Rather than leave to attend the ball, Burbage turned back to Joe as he reached the door. "When you're finished cleaning all this up, pack a bag for me."

"My lord?" Joe blinked. He was usually informed days or weeks in advance when Burbage traveled.

"I'm going on a short trip," his employer confirmed.

"For how long?" Joe asked. "Should I bring formal or informal clothes?" His heart sank at the idea of being dragged away from London and Alistair for any length of time.

But Burbage surprised him with, "Not you. I won't need a valet on this trip. I'm going alone, and it will be for a week. Possibly more."

"Yes, my lord." Joe nodded, unable to think of anything else to say.

"Plain clothes will do," Burbage said before striding out of the room.

Joe stood where he was for a moment, the sudden jumble of his thoughts working to resolve themselves. Burbage never traveled without notice, and never without a valet. The man was useless on his own. But Joe wasn't about to look a gift horse in the mouth. If Burbage traveled alone for a week, that meant a week with far lighter than average duties. And if he didn't have to shower attendance on Burbage every second of the day and night—especially the night—it meant he could finally spend the time with Alistair that he'd been longing to.

That thought sent his pulse racing as he went about his work, tidying up Burbage's dressing room and putting away all the bits and bobs he'd needed to get his employer ready for the ball. A week without waiting on the tosser would be like heaven, especially if it meant he ended up in Alistair's bed at last. He would have to find out what sort of emergency errand would call Burbage away without a valet and make certain whatever it was happened frequently.

There was a spring in his step by the time he headed downstairs, taking Burbage's day clothes with him to the laundry. The jacket Burbage had worn that afternoon had a loose seam that needed repairing, but rather than getting right to it, he draped the jacket over a chair in the servants' hall, then headed back to the main staircase as discreetly as he could. Guests for the ball were already arriving, and Alistair was meant to be there that evening. It would take him all of three minutes to let Alistair know their time was coming soon.

"Oy! You scold me for spying on the toffs, but here you are doing the same."

Joe jumped within seconds of slipping through the servants' door into the main corridor of Eccles House as Toby called out to him from behind one of the potted palms lining the wall.

"Toby." Joe sent the young hall boy a lopsided grin, glanced around to see if either of them had been noticed, then strode across the hall to pretend to hide behind the palm with him. "You're going to get far more than a scolding if Mr. Vine catches you."

"He won't catch me," Toby whispered. "He's too busy telling Ned and the rest where to put the nobs's coats."

Joe laughed and tousled the boy's hair. "You've got the makings of a right good spy, Toby," he said. "Where's Emma tonight?"

"Not sure," Toby went on. "She had stuff to scrub in the scullery, but I ain't seen her for hours."

Joe nodded, continuing to glance down the hall. Guests had been arriving for at least half an hour, so for all he knew, Alistair was already in the ballroom, or one of the side parlors.

He stood a little straighter as the unmistakably glamorous figure of Lady Matilda Fairbanks swept through the foyer and into the front hall. Joe's gut tightened with irrational jealousy at the sight of her. Irrational, because no matter how beautiful, well-placed, or sought-after Lady Matilda was, and no matter how likely it was that she would end up as Alistair's wife, she would never have Alistair's heart. That was all his, bold as it was of him to make that assumption. Still, the woman was competition, of a sort. And if she was there, Alistair couldn't be far behind.

Joe straightened and stepped out from behind the palm to walk casually down the hall. Maybe he would be seen and called out for being where he shouldn't be, but maybe he wouldn't. Either way, he had to find Alistair and share the good news of their upcoming torrid affair with him.

CHAPTER 10

*A*listair arrived at Eccles House already on edge, but walking up the steps and into the grand home, knowing that he would be under the same roof with Joe for the entire evening, had his heart dancing a jig in his chest and his stomach flipping. That, coupled with the sure and certain knowledge that he wouldn't be able to recognize or acknowledge Joe in any way, that he probably wouldn't actually see him—but perhaps, if he were lucky, he would—had his emotions in a complete muddle.

"Careful on the step, Father," he said distractedly, practically lifting his father the last few steps into the house.

"Be on your guard, my boy," his father said in return, glancing around the front hall like a terrier in search of a rat as they entered. "There are enemies around every corner."

Alistair shared a look with Darren, though he fully

intended to follow his father's advice to be on his guard. The ball was a bad idea. He would have begged the whole family not to attend if the ball hadn't been a chance to see Joe.

They deposited their coats with the footmen, then made their way into the ballroom. Already, the ball was in full swing. Lord Chisolm had hired one of the most sought-after orchestras to play waltzes for his guests, and they were already earning their keep. Alistair and Darren steered their parents to a suitably free spot between a potted palm and a bust of Pericles, where they could watch the proceedings in relative peace, but within minutes, Darren graciously offered to dance with their mother. Alistair grinned as the two headed to the dance floor, a dozen or more envious mothers watching them and likely wishing their handsome, young sons were so dutiful. If Darren was attempting to win the place of most favored son, he was doing a good job.

At least, on the surface. If the contest were about which son made the greater sacrifice for the family, Alistair would win that hands down, a point that was punctuated by the arrival of Lady Matilda. She spotted him quickly, burst into a smile, and strode over to him in a way that drew attention to her approach.

"Lord Farnham." She greeted him with the widest of smiles, extending her hand in a clear command for Alistair to make a show of taking it and lavishing affection on her.

"Lady Matilda," Alistair said, playing his part

expertly, as he knew he had to. He grasped her hand and bent to kiss it lingeringly, then straightened and stood closer to her than was strictly proper, closer to her than he truly wanted to. "You look stunning this evening."

Lady Matilda laughed modestly, though the sly look she sent him said she knew exactly how she looked. Her striking, blue gown was the height of fashion, with a cinched waist, full, short sleeves, and a swooping neckline that any other man would find exceptionally intriguing. Her hair was styled with a pin that matched her glittering necklace, making her appear as valuable as she was beautiful.

"Lord Farnham, you are too kind," she said, tapping his arm playfully with her fan. "But no ball gown is complete without the ultimate accessory."

"Which is?" he asked, knowing she expected him to.

"Why, a handsome beau, of course." She grinned wolfishly at him, shifting to his side and slipping her arm through his. "Would you care to take a turn about the room?" she asked, already searching the guests, likely for people she knew or who she wanted to see her on Alistair's arm.

"Alas, I cannot leave my father unattended," Alistair murmured, leaning close to her ear to do so. That much might satisfy her, even if she were disappointed by his refusal to show her off.

Her expression soured for a moment as she glanced over her shoulder to Alistair's father, whom she hadn't greeted yet. She hesitated, peeking at Alistair for a moment, before plastering on a false smile and turning. "Lord Winslow. How lovely to see you this evening," she said, as if it were an afterthought.

"What?" Alistair's father snapped, looking as though someone had fired a shot near him. "Have the slave ships set sail already?"

Heat flooded Alistair's face, and he glanced sideways at Lady Matilda, anxious of what she thought. "Lady Matilda is saying hello to you, Father," he said, repositioning Lady Matilda so that his father couldn't help but look right at her.

"My lord." Lady Matilda curtsied, shooting Alistair a worried look as she straightened. "I cannot tell you how gratified I am to see that you are well enough to attend tonight's ball."

"Yes, yes," Alistair's father answered. "Our work isn't done here yet. We must defend those who are weaker than us whenever we can."

Alistair's face grew hotter. "Are you certain you wouldn't like to sit down, Father?" he asked.

"No, no, boy. Go about your business," his father answered, squaring his shoulders and returning to his observation of the room.

There was nothing Alistair could do but leave his father be and turn with Lady Matilda to face the swirling crowd in the room instead. "As soon as my brother returns from dancing with my mother, I'll take you out for a waltz," he said.

"Thank you, Lord Farnham. You are too kind." Lady

Matilda inched closer to him, resting against his arm. "I'm certain that by the end of the evening, half of London will be buzzing with rumors of our impending union."

Alistair glanced down at her, one eyebrow raised. He should have been happy about her assumptions, but they only filled him with dread.

"Just think," Lady Matilda went on. "In a short time, I'll have more than fashion and fortune to lord over them all, I'll have position too. Won't my sister be green with envy when she sees me making a splash in society as a countess."

Alistair tried to smile, but his gut churned. Anyone who glibly assumed the man standing not more than ten feet behind her would be dead soon, and in a way that would work to her advantage, was not someone he would have wanted to associate with. Under normal circumstances. But he needed Lady Matilda. He was trapped by that fact.

The feeling of being squeezed by a vise of duty and propriety intensified acutely as Alistair spotted Joe stepping unobtrusively into the ballroom through the door the footmen were using to carry refreshments in and out of the room. Alistair's heart immediately knocked against his ribs, and the heat of embarrassment over his father flashed to the flames of desire. He knew full well he should do everything in his power not to look at Joe, but his gaze was fixed and immovable within seconds.

Better—or perhaps worse—still, Joe found him staring

a few moments later, locked eyes with him, and smiled far more boldly than was good for either of them. Alistair's heart thumped harder. Joe's smile dropped slightly as he gestured toward the door with an appealing look. He wanted to meet. Alistair had no earthly idea how that would be possible. He inclined his head toward Lady Matilda and his father, then nodded. Joe nodded back, as if he understood the complications involved in Alistair getting away, then slipped back out of the room once more.

Alistair let out a breath, and his shoulders dropped. Whatever else happened, whatever mischief Lady Matilda wanted to get up to and however troublesome his father's behavior was, he had to find a way to break away from them and find Joe.

It was no easy task. The second Darren returned with their mother, Lady Matilda all but demanded Alistair lead her out to the dance floor for not one, but two dances. Two dances in succession was more than enough to set every society gossip in London talking about the connection between the two. As much as Alistair loathed the idea of being whispered about that way, there was no getting around the fact that the gossip would work to his advantage. His and Joe's advantage.

Once the string of dances was over, Alistair found himself dragged around the room by Lady Matilda, showering attention on her as she gloated to her friends about how lucky she was to have a future earl as a beau. She made no secret of her satisfaction at snagging a man who would have a respectable title someday soon. So much so that Alistair wondered if he could have handed her a marionette made to look like him to carry around and show off instead of accompanying her himself.

After the turn around the room was finished, he began to look for an excuse, any excuse, to leave the ballroom and seek out Joe. But instead of finding an excuse, he ended up mired down in a conversation with Burbage.

"Of course, I detest balls like this," Burbage said, eyeing Alistair as though he were expected to agree wholeheartedly. "It's such a bore to have so many people invading one's home."

"It's my home as well, dearest," Lady Burbage said with a tight smile.

"One would think you would be happy to have so many people come to see how plump and adorable your wife has become, Lord Burbage," Lady Matilda said with a smile, sending her sister a sneer.

Lady Burbage blanched. "Plump and productive," she snapped in return.

"I'm sure I'll sail my way through such a condition with elegance and grace," Lady Matilda replied, resting a hand on Alistair's arm.

It was Alistair's turn to blanch. His collar felt too tight and misery infused every cell of his body. He glanced around the ballroom for a way out.

"Such delightful conversation makes me almost sad I'll be going away tomorrow," Burbage said sarcastically.

Alistair focused on him with a frown. "You're going

away?" Would he take Joe away with him? Was that what Joe wanted to talk to him about?

"Just a short errand," Burbage said. "There is a bit of delicate family business I need to take care of."

"Ha! I knew it!" Alistair's father bounded into the conversation before Alistair realized that he was close enough to hear what was being said at all. "I can just imagine what your family business is. Opium, no doubt."

Alistair winced. At the same time, he wanted to shout in triumph. At last, he had an excuse to leave the ballroom. "Father, are you certain you're feeling quite well?" He shook Lady Matilda's arm out of his and moved to rest a hand on his father's back.

"Where are you hiding your sins, Burbage?" Alistair's father demanded. "Your family's shame will be brought into the light, I swear it."

"That's quite enough of that, Albert." Alistair's mother swept up to join them. Darren wasn't far behind.

"Please excuse us," Alistair said, certain his face was bright red. "Excuse us," he repeated to Lady Matilda.

It was an embarrassment and a blessing to usher his father out of the crowded room and away from the stares of the ball's attendees. Having his mother and brother there to deflect some of the attention helped, but it wasn't until they were across the hall, working to convince his father to settle quietly into a parlor in a quiet corner, that Alistair began to feel relief.

That small bit of relief blossomed into an entirely different sort of nervousness when Joe unexpectedly walked into the parlor as they were trying to convince Alistair's father to sit and asked, "Is there anything I can do to help?"

The undeniable sense that everything would be all right filled Alistair. He stood a bit straighter and said, "Father, you remember Mr. Logan from last month, don't you?"

His father instantly stopped fussing and narrowed his eyes at Joe as if trying to remember him. "Oh, yes. The valet."

Darren and Alistair's mother turned to study Joe curiously. Joe nodded to each of them with the deference that was reasonable for his position and stepped cautiously closer.

"What seems to be the problem this evening, my lord?" he asked Alistair's father, crouching beside the sofa where he sat and speaking to him from a lower level.

Alistair's heart caught in his throat at the bold tactic Joe was using to address his father. He stole a glance at his brother and mother to see what they thought of it. The two of them stared on with interest and surprise.

"It's these blackguard Eccleses," his father growled. "They preen and pose, but all the while, we know they are as black-hearted as the devil."

"Father, you cannot say such things," Darren sighed, rubbing a hand over his face.

But Joe said, "Yes, it truly is unjust, isn't it?" He reached for Alistair's father's hand, and surprisingly, his father let him take it.

"There is too much injustice in this world," his father said. "We must work harder to fight it."

"And we will, my lord," Joe said with a nod, clasping both of his hands around the frail one he held. "We will fight whomever we must to make this world a safer place for those who are persecuted."

"Yes, yes."

Alistair's pulse raced as his father's shoulders dropped and the tension he'd been carrying all evening left him. Joe had such a remarkable manner and such a strong effect that Alistair's affection grew to the point where he was suddenly terrified he wouldn't be able to hide it. He turned away, searching the room for any sort of excuse not to look at Joe.

"Now, my lord," Joe went on. "Would you really like to stay here, dancing the night away with London's finest, or would you rather rest, safe and secure, in the comfort of your own home?"

"We don't have to stay here," Darren quickly backed up Joe's question.

"I've had my dance," his mother said with a sigh. "I've no deep desire to stay."

"Then let's go home," Darren concluded, appealing to their father.

Alistair's nerves tightened again, and he turned from where he'd gone to study the clock on the mantel back to Joe. Joe sent him only the briefest of looks before focusing on his father again.

"What do you say, my lord? Bed, and perhaps a hot chocolate, or dancing until dawn?" he asked.

Alistair's father huffed out a breath. "I've never been one to stay up 'til dawn. And I do like hot chocolate."

"It's settled, then." Joe smiled his endearing smile that made Alistair want to run to the ends of the earth for him, patted his father's hand one last time, then stood. "If you'd like, I can ask Mr. Vine to have your carriage brought around."

"That would be lovely, young man," Alistair's mother answered with a genuinely grateful smile. When Joe started forward, she stopped him with a hand to his arm. "And thank you ever so much."

Joe smiled and nodded to her, then left the room. Alistair followed him with his eyes, his gaze lingering on the empty doorway when he turned the corner. Lady Matilda be damned. He knew whom he wanted to face the slings and arrows of life with.

"What a charming young man," his mother said, smiling for the first time that evening.

"A capital fellow," his father agreed, attempting to stand.

Alistair rushed over to his side to help him as Darren did the same.

"He's the valet who helped Father last month?" Darren asked.

"He is," Alistair answered, too afraid that his emotions were written in bold on his face to meet his brother's eyes.

They escorted their father to the hall, then waited while their coats were fetched.

"I think I'll stay behind," Alistair said, near panicking at the thought of missing out on an opportunity to spend more time with Joe. When his brother glanced questioningly at him, Alistair went on with, "Lady Matilda would have my head if I abandoned her to face the ball on her own."

Understanding and mischief dawned on both Darren and his mother's faces.

"Of course, son," his mother said, stepping over to kiss his cheek. "You go court your beauty, and the rest of us will wait eagerly for happy news."

It was all Alistair could do to keep his smile from giving away his true excitement as he watched his family prepare to leave. That was made even harder when Joe was the one to bring them their coats. He didn't bring Alistair's coat, and considering he hadn't been there for the discussion about staying for Lady Matilda's sake, Alistair dreaded the moment someone would put the pieces together and figure everything out.

"Thank you once again, Mr. Logan," Darren nodded to Joe as he prepared to escort his father down the stairs. "If you ever find yourself in need of employment...." He left the offer hanging.

Prickles raced down Alistair's back at the thought. Employment. As a valet. A man with constant, intimate access to his employer. His pulse raced so fast it made him dizzy.

As soon as his family exited into the night, Alistair felt the brush of Joe's hand against his.

"Come with me," Joe whispered. "I know where we won't be disturbed."

Those words turned Alistair's dizziness into fervent expectation. Without a word, he turned and marched down the hall with Joe. There was no possible excuse that he could think of for a viscount like him to be following a valet deeper into another family's house, but he walked with bold steps, his head held high, as though he were on a mission of great importance. Blessedly, after turning a few corners, they were in a part of the house unoccupied by guests, or anyone else, for that matter. The entire wing where Joe led him was silent, as everyone in the household was needed or expected elsewhere.

"I'm not sure who knows about this room," Joe said, slightly louder and much faster, as he turned the handle on a small, unremarkable door at the end of a long hall-way. "I'm not even sure they use it."

He took Alistair's hand and pulled him through the doorway into what appeared to be a small, cramped study. The curtains on the two windows at one end of the room were open enough to let in just enough moonlight for Alistair to see Joe, but not many details of the room. It had a desk, bookshelves, and a small, leather sofa, like any other study. The embers in the fireplace were banked, proving that the room was used, but that was all Alistair could see and all he had time for before Joe surged into him.

Alistair's back thumped against the closed door as Joe pressed his body against him, slanting his mouth over his. Alistair groaned with sheer joy at kissing Joe at last, deepening their kiss and sliding his tongue along Joe's. He'd wanted to entwine with Joe that way so badly for so long that finally getting what he wanted had him trembling with need in no time.

"Burbage is going away," Joe panted between kisses, working open the buttons of Alistair's jacket and waistcoat as he did.

"Then we should make the most of this moment," Alistair said, fumbling with Joe's buttons as well. He was far clumsier than Joe was and ended up abandoning the complicated task to slide his hand down. He cupped Joe's erection through his trousers, going hard himself.

Joe let out a rough sound of approval and ground against Alistair's hand, then managed to say, "You don't understand. He's not taking me with him. I'll have a week off."

Alistair sucked in a breath as though Joe's words were a caress and sought out his lips again. Every shred of caution he'd been clinging to vanished as he kissed Joe, exploring him fully and passionately. Joe finished with his buttons and pushed and tugged at Alistair's jacket. Alistair pivoted away from the wall, shrugging out of his jacket while also making another attempt at Joe's buttons. There were too damn many buttons in the world.

They stumbled a few steps across the room toward the sofa, pulling at each other's clothes and doing an awkward job of exposing each other's skin. Somehow, Alistair ended up stripped from the waist up while managing to unfasten Joe's trousers to free his prick. Sliding his hands around Joe's thick, hard cock, feeling its heat, had him dangerously close to coming. But he adored every second of it. His body throbbed with need that he'd denied himself for too long.

When they reached the sofa, breathless, kissing and groping without any art or focus, Joe suddenly took charge. He twisted Alistair in his arms, tipping him off his feet so that he landed splayed on his back across the sofa. Alistair drank in the sight of Joe tugging off his shirt in the moonlight, the strong, firm lines of his bare torso with his prick standing up over the sagging waist of his trousers, before he rushed forward. Joe made quick work unfastening Alistair's trousers, tugging them down to his thighs in a gesture that was so demanding and possessive that Alistair had to grip whatever parts of the sofa he could to keep himself from bucking off.

He barely had time to think before Joe grasped his cock, stroking it a few times before bending down to close his mouth around it. Alistair let out a long, low moan of pleasure, instinctively flexing his hips to drive himself deeper into the hot wetness of Joe's mouth. His split-second of worry that he'd gone too far melted as Joe let out the most sensual sound of enjoyment Alistair had ever heard. He threw his head back and added pleasured sounds of his own to the song.

Joe knew exactly what he was doing. He bore down on Alistair, sucking and stroking with his tongue, before moving in a hard, steady rhythm that had Alistair breaking out in a sweat. The pleasure was so acute that Alistair shot straight to the edge in no time, spending himself in Joe's mouth with a sharp curse of surprise. For a moment, he was suspended in the all-encompassing pleasure of an orgasm that shook his whole body.

All too quickly, that pleasure turned to guilt.

"Sorry," he panted. "I'm sorry."

"For what?" Joe asked, still panting and aroused, as he slid his way up Alistair's overheated body, kissing as many spots as he could as he went. When he reached Alistair's shoulder, neck, and jaw, he ground his still iron-hard cock against Alistair's softening one.

"I should have held out longer," Alistair said, turning his head so he could kiss Joe. The heady musk of his taste sent shivers of renewed arousal through him.

"I'm certain I can make you come again before the night is through," Joe hummed in a saucy voice.

A thrill of lust and affection shot through Alistair, and he put his full energy into kissing Joe, already certain Joe would be able to make good on his promise. That certainty doubled as Joe's sensual grinding turned into deliberate thrusts against him. The heat of Joe's cock throbbing against his belly as he sought his own orgasm had Alistair panting with arousal. He wished to God his trousers weren't around his thighs so that he could spread his legs and offer Joe a far more enticing part of him to fuck. He settled for gripping Joe's backside and teasing the pucker of his ass with his fingers.

It was enough to send Joe into a powerful orgasm. Alistair sucked in a breath as warm wetness spilled across his stomach. He'd done that. He'd caused the gorgeous, kind, wonderful man in his arms to come, and the sensation of the evidence of that across his skin was glorious. As glorious as the way Joe collapsed above him, letting out a sound of satisfaction as the urgency of the moment turned into a tender embrace. The world may have been a mess around him, but he'd brought satisfaction to the man he loved. Nothing else mattered.

CHAPTER 11

Joe had no idea of how the mechanics of the situation could possibly work out, but as the potent rush of lovemaking began to fade into the afterglow, he and Alistair managed to entwine in each other's arms on the impossibly small sofa. Their position was awkward and cramped, but at least he still had his arms around the man he'd just shared a life-changing experience with. Their damp bodies were plastered together, and their faces were mere inches apart as they struggled to catch their breaths.

"That was everything I hoped it would be and more," he finally managed to say, threading his fingers through Alistair's hair. "And I want more."

"As do I," Alistair said, still breathing heavily. His hands brushed Joe's sides and back before caressing his backside. The simple touch was magical. "So much more."

"When?" Joe asked, propping himself above Alistair so he could study his handsome, sated expression in the dim moonlight. "Just tell me when and where and I'll be there."

"I would say tonight, if I thought we could get away with it." Alistair reached up to caress the side of Joe's face. "But we both know that's impractical."

"Everything about us is impractical," Joe laughed. He couldn't have wiped the grin off his face if he'd tried.

"Impractical, but so perfect," Alistair said with a tender sigh. "I need you in my life, Joe. All of my life. The rest of my life. I can't imagine going on through this mad existence without you."

His words felt like stardust poured into Joe's heart, radiating heat and perfection through his entire body. "I don't want to go on without you either," he said, sentiment thick in his voice.

He lowered himself to kiss Alistair tenderly, with all the passion that coursed through him. But it was different from the passion of lust, from every other encounter, no matter how satisfying, he'd ever had in his life. He wanted to be with Alistair, to share his life, his troubles and his joys. Yes, he wanted to make love with him in every conceivable way, until they were both silly with satisfaction, but it was more than just that. He wanted to be able to call Alistair his and for Alistair to do the same with him.

Their kiss quickly heated as their tongues danced together and their lips explored one another. Alistair's prick began to stiffen again between the two of them, which caused a matching reaction in Joe. He wanted nothing more than to grind against Alistair, to join with him in earnest and come inside of him, but they weren't prepared for any of that. And a dusty office in the house of his employer was not the right scene for fucking all night long.

"A hotel," Alistair panted, caressing Joe's face with both hands and gazing deep into his eyes. "What we need is to check into a hotel."

"Yes," Joe agreed, victory surging through him. "Just tell me where and when."

"This week," Alistair went on, surging up to steal light kisses from Joe's lips as he spoke. "I'll book us a room at a discreet hotel somewhere here in London, where no one will question us. As soon as I've made the reservation, I'll send you what you need to know. I'll make it for tomorrow."

"That's hardly soon enough," Joe teased, jerking his hips against Alistair's. "Would that it could be tonight."

"Would that it could be every night." Alistair responded with fervent movements of his own, increasing the heat between them as they both hardened further.

Joe groaned in agreement and captured Alistair's mouth in a searing kiss. There might be time yet. They could get each other off once more before he had to return to his duties and Alistair needed to go home.

"I had a thought," Alistair said, his breathing growing shallow as his hands roved Joe's body once more. "There is a way we could be together without anyone questioning it."

"God, that would be wonderful." Joe shifted to kiss his jaw and nibble on his neck. How dangerous would it be for him to leave a mark there?

"My brother gave me the idea, actually," Alistair went on, squeezing Joe's backside. "I could hire—"

Alistair stopped dead and both of them froze as a thump sounded in the hall outside the office. Joe's heart pounded against his ribs, but no longer from lust. If they were caught, it would be a catastrophe.

The thump was followed by footsteps, then a voice. Joe and Alistair held perfectly still, not even breathing. The voice said something else which, to Joe's ears, sounded like a complaint, before the footsteps moved on. Slowly, cautiously, Joe relaxed. If he had to guess, he'd say one of the maids had passed by the office, possibly dropped something, and cursed herself as she picked it up and moved on. Chances were, she didn't have a clue what was going on behind the door she passed. All the same, he and Alistair remained utterly still for several more seconds.

"So much for another go-around," Joe whispered at last, peeling himself away from Alistair with the greatest reluctance.

"Cooler heads prevail," Alistair joked, sitting up as soon as Joe rolled to the side to stand.

"Do you need any help straightening yourself up?"

Joe asked, tugging up his trousers and fastening them. He was a mess, and likely Alistair was as well.

"I don't think anything short of a bath will truly straighten me up," Alistair chuckled, standing with a wince that Joe could just make out in the dark. "I should probably slip out the back way so that no one sees me in this condition."

No sooner were the words out of his mouth then the sound of footsteps returned in the hallway. Both Joe and Alistair quickened their pace, scrambling for their clothes and throwing them on as fast as possible. They'd been far more careless in undressing than Joe had thought and had to search for shirts, waistcoats, and jackets in the near-dark room, throwing them on and tucking and tugging without any guidance to make themselves look even partly presentable.

When at last they were together enough to leave the office, they crept out into the deserted hall, but didn't get farther than the unused library.

"Wait here," Joe whispered. "I'll fetch your coat. Then I'll get you out one of the side entrances."

Alistair nodded, then pretended to be perusing the shelves while Joe darted out into the main hall and the room where the footmen were keeping coats. He was fairly certain anyone who took a close look at him would guess that he'd been doing something other than standing sedately in a corner, waiting to be called on to serve, but the advantage of being a servant was that few people noticed him. He caught sight of his pink-cheeked reflection in a mirror in the hallway and worked to tidy his tousled hair as he reached the room where coats were being kept.

It was a stroke of luck that retrieving Alistair's coat, taking it to him, and stealing through the halls with him until they reached the conservatory, where a set of French doors let out into a courtyard with access to the street, passed without trouble. It was foolish to risk kissing Alistair goodbye, but he stole a peck anyhow.

"I'll send you notice of arrangements tomorrow," Alistair whispered before slipping off into the night.

Joe stood where he was in the cold courtyard for a moment, smiling up at the patch of stars above him. His heart had never felt so full, and he loved the sensation. He loved everything about the madness that swirled around him, because he knew without a doubt, beyond reason, that he loved Alistair.

The ball was far from over, which gave him ample time to dash back into the house and up to his garret room in the servant's quarters to wash up and change clothes before heading back to Burbage's dressing room. The later it got, the more likely Burbage was to return, and he would need help undressing. Joe also had to pack his bag for whatever trip his employer was about to take. He didn't care where Burbage was off to. The man could travel to Peru, for all he cared, and stay there indefinitely.

Those thoughts were still fresh in his mind when Burbage marched into the dressing room just after midnight.

"Is my bag packed?" he asked without preamble, loosening his tie as he crossed to the wardrobe.

"Yes, my lord," Joe said, grateful he'd finished the job less than five minutes earlier.

"Good," Burbage snapped. "Help me to change. I need to be at Victoria Station by one-thirty."

Joe fought to hide his surprise. He said nothing as he helped Burbage change out of his ball suit and into one more suitable for traveling. A thousand questions flooded him, but he was in no position to ask any of them. For a change, it irritated him that Burbage was in no mood to talk either. He didn't give so much as a hint of where he was going or why he needed to leave in the middle of the night. He didn't criticize the job Joe was doing or acknowledge him at all.

"See to it that the stain is cleaned off the cuff of that jacket." They were the only words Burbage spoke before gesturing for Joe to take up his suitcase and follow him out of the dressing room.

The ball was still ongoing as they made their way down to the ground floor. Not unlike Alistair, Burbage chose to leave the house through one of the side doors that let out into the courtyard. Joe followed him to the front of the house, handing the bag over as Burbage climbed into a waiting carriage. Without a word, Burbage slammed the carriage door. Moments later, he was gone.

Something wasn't right, but Joe couldn't put his finger on it. There were very few reasons a man would dash away from home in the middle of the night, leaving without saying goodbye to anyone. Then again, Burbage could very well have made his goodbyes to his family before coming up to his dressing room. Or not. The uneasy feeling that Burbage's swift departure had something to do with Lily's disappearance struck him, but he rejected the idea. He'd already searched for clues that might connect his employer with Lily's disappearance and had found nothing. It was far more likely the man was rushing off to a clandestine affair. Joe grinned as he headed back into the house. He certainly knew what that was like, or at least, he was about to.

By the time he returned to the dressing room to fetch Burbage's jacket and carried it down to the servants' hall to see about the stain, exhaustion was well on its way to taking over from curiosity. He deposited the jacket on the pile of other clothes Burbage needed repaired before heading out for what he considered a well-deserved sleep.

"Oh, Mr. Logan, do you have a moment?" Lucy, one of the maids, stopped him before he got to the stairs.

"Certainly," Joe replied with a smile.

Lucy chewed her lip and frowned before asking, "Have you seen Toby?"

"Toby?"

"Or Emma," Lucy went on.

"Emma isn't in the scullery?" Joe asked.

Lucy shook her head. "Cook's in a right temper about it. Says Emma's been shirking her duty."

"That's not like Emma at all," Joe said with a frown.

That frown softened. "Although it might be like her, considering the ball. Toby was upstairs earlier, spying on the toffs."

Lucy made a frustrated sound. A sound exactly like the one Joe and Alistair had heard in the hall that interrupted their tryst. If that had been Lucy in search of Toby and Emma, they'd been damned lucky she hadn't checked in the study after all.

"Keep looking around upstairs," Joe advised her. "I would be willing to bet the two of them fell asleep in a corner of the ballroom while watching the guests dancing."

"You're probably right," Lucy said, shaking her head. "Goodnight, Mr. Logan."

"Goodnight, Lucy."

Joe continued on, mounting the stairs to his tiny room two at a time. In spite of the strangeness of Burbage, his heart was light. He was eager to get to bed, though he wasn't sure how well he'd be able to sleep. He was already anticipating the letter he would get from Alistair and the nights they were about to have together.

ALISTAIR TRIED TO FIGHT THE GIDDY FEELING IN HIS gut as he strode swiftly through the streets of Mayfair on his way home. He walked with his hands thrust in his pockets and the collar of his coat turned up, not only against the cold, but because he knew he looked a mess and probably smelled of sweat and sex. Which was why he couldn't keep the foolish grin off his face.

It didn't matter that it had been little more than an impromptu fumble in the dark, finally being so intimate with Joe, tasting his skin and feeling his mouth around his cock, had been the single most gratifying experience of his life. He replayed every detail of the sounds Joe made, the way Joe's body had felt under his hands, and the friction of Joe's hard cock against his belly until the memories alone made walking extraordinarily uncomfortable. The sooner he made a reservation at a discreet hotel and met Joe there, the better. He made a note to himself to purchase lubrication, because he had every intention of sinking himself deep inside of Joe and begging for the same once they were finally alone, without danger of discovery.

When he reached home, he had the feeling that at least someone was still up, perhaps waiting for him, but he rushed up to his room before anyone could intercept him, going so far as to take his coat with him instead of handing it off to the footman on night duty. The last thing he wanted was for anyone in his family to see him in his current state.

Duty got the best of him, though, and he decided that after washing up and changing into his night clothes, he would head out to make certain his father and mother had made it home in one piece.

The reflection that he saw of himself in his bedroom mirror made him grunt with amusement as he removed his coat. His clothes were rumpled, and he hadn't buttoned his waistcoat correctly. He couldn't help but laugh as he removed the layers of soiled clothes and set them aside to be washed. His shirt was skewed and didn't seem to fit right, though as he removed it, he saw why.

Somehow, a piece of paper had plastered itself to his torso as he'd dressed. His shirt had ended up on the desk in the small office, and he supposed he must have picked up the paper when he retrieved it. He set it aside as he finished undressing, then scrubbed himself in the sink of the bathroom attached to his bedroom. He'd take a full bath in the morning, when he had more energy. Once cleaned up, he wandered back into his bedroom, put on his pajamas, then went back to the paper to see what it was.

His tired, cozy mood vanished as he read the signature at the bottom of the letter—J. Adler. Instantly, his gut clenched, and he dragged his eyes to the top of the page to tear through the contents of the letter. It wasn't addressed to anyone in particular, but Alistair wasn't certain it mattered. It simply read, "In receipt of cargo. Buyer waiting in Brighton. Shipment to proceed next Tuesday."

Alistair's scowl deepened as he scanned the letter for any sort of date or any indication what the cargo in question was. There was no date, but something about the letter seemed recent. The letter held no other information, but it set Alistair's nerves on edge all the same.

His mounting anxiety was interrupted by a knock on

his door. He quickly put the letter face down on the dressing table beside his wardrobe, then crossed to answer the door.

"I thought that was you I heard coming in," Darren greeted him from the hall.

"I should have come to tell you or Father and Mother that I'd made it home," Alistair said, unaccountably flustered by his brother's presence.

Darren laughed and let himself into the room, thumping Alistair's arm as he did. "How old are you, Alistair? Nearly thirty? You're well past the age when you have to tell Father and Mother you're home. Well past the age when anyone should hold you accountable for staying out a little late to court your sweetheart."

Alistair's face flamed at the statement. If only Darren knew. "Yes, well, old habits die hard," he said, not quite able to meet his brother's eyes.

Judging by the teasing in his expression, Darren knew exactly what Alistair had been up to, just not with whom. "So should we expect a spring wedding?" he asked with a rakish grin.

"Probably," Alistair said with what he hoped was a casual shrug. "I don't think there's any point in delaying things." Delaying the inevitable marriage to Lady Matilda would only give him the chance to get cold feet about the entire thing.

"You should have heard the way Father went on and on about you once we got home," Darren continued. "I don't know how I'm ever going to be able to measure up to you, the favorite son, once you finish marrying the perfect bride and producing the ideal heir."

"I'm sure you'll figure out a way to outshine me and gain their favor a thousand times more than I have," Alistair mumbled, crossing to the clothes he'd left out. The urge to hide them in case Darren could smell them the way he could was acute. "How is Father now?" he asked, changing the subject to something that would wipe the sly grin from his brother's face.

Darren sighed and rubbed a hand over his face. "All right, I suppose. If you consider a long and inevitable decline all right. Mother convinced him to go straight to bed. I hate the way she suffers over this whole thing."

"We all hate it," Alistair agreed. "We have to stop letting him go out like he has been. It only upsets him."

"If only we had someone like that Mr. Logan to keep him calm," Darren said.

Alistair tensed, certain his brother would be able to hear the pounding of his heart. "Yes, Mr. Logan is one in a million," he said quietly, glancing away.

When he looked back, Darren was studying him with a frown that chilled Alistair's blood. Darren wasn't a fool, and he'd known Alistair his entire life. It wouldn't take much for him to see the truth.

"I'm going away for a short trip tomorrow," Alistair blurted in an attempt to stop whatever thoughts his brother was having.

"Oh, yes?" Darren's sly grin returned. "This doesn't have anything to do with Lady Matilda, does it? Only, I heard her tell her sister that she was off for a quick jaunt to the countryside."

Alistair blinked. Had she said that? He'd barely listened to a word Lady Matilda had said through the entire ball, but if she was leaving London, it was a blessing.

"Yes," he answered Darren, turning away and forcing himself to grin as though Darren had caught him in a naughty plan. His actual naughty plan certainly wouldn't make his brother grin the way he did at that answer.

"You sly dog," Darren said, stepping forward to slap Alistair's back. "I honestly didn't think you had it in you. I'll make a suitable excuse to Mother and Father for you, and to Beth, if she deigns to spend her time here at home instead of out with her friends."

"Thank you," Alistair said, sending his brother a sheepish look. "And if you ever want to sneak off on a similar errand, I'll support you too."

"Of course, you will." Darren gave his back one more pat before heading for the door. "A June wedding is just the thing," he said before winking and stepping out into the hall, shutting Alistair's door behind him.

Alistair huffed out a breath and shook his head, not sure whether he'd convinced Darren everything was above board or not. All he knew was that the life he wanted to live and the path he seemed doomed to follow were two very different things, and it would be his job to reconcile them.

CHAPTER 12

The note Joe was waiting for came just after midday, as most of the Eccles House staff was busy cleaning up after the ball.

"This just came for you," Lucy said, handing Joe a tiny slip of paper as their paths crossed in the downstairs hallway.

Joe's heart bounced from his stomach to his throat as he opened the note to read, *"The Savoy under the name Mercer"*. His elation lasted for only a second, though.

"Is something the matter?" he asked a distracted Lucy.

Lucy could hardly stand still. Her brow was furrowed, and she had chewed her lip so much that it looked as though she was wearing cosmetics. "Did you ever find Toby or Emma last night?" she asked, worry lining her face.

Joe's already heightened emotions turned anxious

and squeezed his chest. "They weren't upstairs, spying on the guests?"

Lucy shook her head. "I thought you were right, that they would be found sleeping in some corner after the guests all left, but they weren't. No one has seen hide nor hair of them."

Alarm quickly swallowed everything else Joe felt. "We'll search downstairs," he said, launching into motion. "They have to be here somewhere."

"I've already searched three times over," Lucy said, following him. "And up in our quarters too, though neither Toby nor Emma would have any reason to be up there."

She was right. The hall boy and scullery maid generally slept downstairs, wherever they could find a spare corner. They were the ones who were expected to wake up first and go to bed last every day and to work harder than anyone else in the house. A few minutes of searching brought to light things Joe should have noticed earlier but hadn't—the way Mr. Vine was grumbling about downstairs fires not being lit on time, Cook's complaint about dishes piling up in the scullery with no one cleaning them, the irritation of the maids who had been set to do Emma's jobs. The life of a scullery maid was hard and thankless, but Emma had always been diligent and cheerful.

"You're right," Joe was forced to admit at last, after he and Lucy had been all through the servants' hall and garret bedrooms. "They're gone."

Admitting as much was painful. It brought to mind how the staff must have felt when Lily went missing months before. The anger bubbling under the surface of every maid and footman he came across, the resentment that the lowliest servants in the house had shirked their duty, only added to his biting frustration at the situation. He couldn't shake the feeling that Toby and Emma—and Lily—were in horrible danger, and the people who spent their days around them, who should care the most, were angry instead of anxious.

He paused in the crossway of two downstairs hallways, shoving a hand through his hair. The note from Alistair was still in his pocket, and he took it out to look at it again. His aristocratic lover wanted to meet him in a posh hotel for sex—something he'd wanted from the moment the two of them had met—right as two vulnerable young people whom he cared about had vanished. Just as his sister had vanished. The timing couldn't have been worse.

"I'm going out to look for them," he told Lucy, who had lingered in the hall, watching him as though he would burst forth with the answers at any moment. "I'm not certain when I'll be back."

He strode forward, heading for the stairs that would take him up to his room, where he could pack a bag for a night in the hotel. But his thoughts were as far from The Savoy as could be. Foul play had to be involved. Toby and Emma wouldn't just wander off. He couldn't just stand by and let their disappearance stand, like the staff had done with Lily. He had to do whatever he could to find them.

He began with stopping in at the kitchen doors of all the neighboring houses to ask if anyone had seen the children run off the night before, or if they had seen anything suspicious at all. No one had. The search continued with him walking to the nearest parks and checking to see if Toby or Emma had skipped off to play there. He found nothing. He even backtracked to Eccles House to speak to Mrs. Harris, the housekeeper, to ask if anyone had been at the house before, during, or after the ball that had seemed suspicious or unusual.

"It was a ball," Mrs. Harris laughed at his question. "Half the tradesmen in London were in and out of the mews yesterday, delivering food, flowers, and wine. There were the musicians, the extra help, and the guests themselves. The house was swarming with people yesterday."

It wasn't the answer Joe wanted, and Mrs. Harris balked when he asked for a list of names of all the tradesmen whom she'd had dealings with. Her lack of willingness to help his search, the lack of willingness of everyone he spoke with, had him boiling with frustration by the time he gave up and continued on his way to The Savoy. Somewhere, there had to be an answer. Someone had to have seen Toby and Emma—and Lily—leave the house, in company or alone. He even considered that Burbage could have taken the two children with him, that his trip had something to do with missing children after all. But he'd seen Burbage's train ticket on his dressing table, confirming that he'd departed from Victoria Station in the middle of the night. He wasn't sure that fit with the timeline of when Toby and Emma had gone missing.

The scowl Joe wore as his thoughts tumbled over each other must have radiated a warning around him as he stepped through the grand doorway into the lobby of The Savoy. The hotel was new and reported to be one of the most modern, fashionable hotels ever created. Every bit of marble, metal, and mirror shone, screaming prosperity and progress. Ladies and gentlemen in the latest fashions, jewels shining, seemed to be showing off, like glamorous statues in a museum, as they waited around the lobby's vast and beautiful space for whatever engagements they had. The hotel's staff, their liveries crisp and attractive, lingered at key points around the room or rushed to and fro, assisting the hotel guests.

Joe barely noticed a few of them glancing his way with turned-up noses and lips curled in distaste as he strode toward the hotel's front desk. He was too lost in the riddle of missing children. It wasn't until he reached the desk and told the concierge, "Reservation for Mercer," that he realized anything was out of the ordinary.

Rather than bowing or nodding and hurrying to fetch a room key, the concierge narrowed his eyes and stared at Joe down the length of his long nose. "Are you saying you have a reservation, sir?" he asked.

Joe clenched his jaw and met the man's imperious gaze with stubbornness. "Yes."

The concierge broke into a condescending laugh. "I think you must be mistaken."

"I'm not mistaken," Joe growled. "Reservation for Mercer."

The concierge's lips twitched as though he were eating a lemon, and he glanced down at the reservation ledger in front of him. The desk was low enough that Joe could see the names listed as clearly as the concierge could, and the name John Mercer was written in a clear hand near the top of the page.

"I'm afraid I don't see anything under that name," the concierge said all the same, sweeping Joe with a look.

Joe had enough fury inside of him from the events of the morning already. The last thing he needed was for some snobbish concierge, whose background was probably no better than his own, to question his right to be where he was. "We both see the reservation," he said, his tone threatening.

The concierge laughed nervously. "I'm certain it's a mistake. The Savoy caters to a very specific clientele. We do not take in just anyone off the street." He glanced down his nose at Joe's less than stylish clothes once again.

"And I am telling you," Joe went on in a low growl, "I have a reservation under the name John Mercer, and it's right there." He jabbed the ledger over the name to prove his point.

The concierge rocked back in alarm at the aggressive

gesture and glanced quickly from side to side. Two large bellmen left their positions of readiness on either side of the desk and closed in on Joe from both sides.

Joe stepped back, ready for a fight. Fighting was exactly what he needed to defuse the anxious energy that had been surging through him all morning. He was hungry for it. But he didn't get his chance.

"Is there a problem here?"

Alistair's cool voice instantly calmed Joe's defensiveness. Joe turned to see him striding across the lobby, his suit impeccably tailored, a gold watch fob shining against the grey of his waistcoat, not a hair out of place. His blue eyes were bright with expectation as he glanced to Joe, but otherwise, he was the picture of aristocracy.

Joe found himself drawn to and repelled by the image at the same time, which unsettled him. Particularly when the concierge instantly snapped to attention and leaned forward, as if ready to fawn all over Alistair.

"It's nothing, sir," the concierge told Alistair, dripping with deference. "My assistants were just in the process of removing this riff-raff."

Joe's back went up, and he glared at the concierge.

Alistair, on the other hand, laughed casually and shook his head as though it were all some childish misunderstanding. "This man is not riff-raff," he told the concierge. "He's my valet. I've been waiting for him."

By the look he sent Joe, Alistair clearly expected claiming Joe as his valet would make everything better. In fact, Joe felt as though he'd been slapped.

"Very good, sir." The concierge bowed and smiled obsequiously at Alistair. "So sorry for the misunderstanding."

"Mind you don't judge books by their covers in the future," Alistair told the man with a brittle smile, then turned to Joe. "Shall we go up?"

The excitement in Alistair's eyes was unmistakable. It was almost enough to melt Joe's heart. He loved Alistair, but even he had to admit that no one was perfect. He nodded and followed as Alistair headed toward a row of shiny, brass elevator doors.

They couldn't speak in the elevator, what with the attendant on duty to run the contraption. Alistair's silence as they swooped up to what appeared to be a high floor, brimmed with giddiness. Joe found it endearing, but not quite enough to make everything better. As they reached their floor and stepped out into an empty hallway, Alistair's grin began to fade.

"You don't look happy to see me," he said at last, once they were alone behind the closed and locked door of the fanciest hotel room Joe had ever been in.

The furnishings were of the highest quality. A gilded mirror hung above a polished bureau against one wall. A fire crackled merrily in a small grate as a clock ticked on the mantel above. An open door led to one of the modern bathrooms that the hotel was famous for. The bed was an enticing, large presence in the heart of the room, but even the sight of the small jar already set out on the bedside table couldn't quite cut through Joe's sour mood.

"Of course, I'm happy to see you," he grumbled, shrugging out of the strap of the satchel that held his change of clothes and tossing it on the bed. "But it's been a trying morning, and that bastard of a concierge didn't make it any better."

Alistair's affectionate smile faltered. "Sorry about that. I suppose the man was just doing his job."

"By calling me riff-raff and attempting to have me thrown out?" Joe demanded. He knew he needed to calm down and let it go, but he wasn't ready to yet. "And what is this nonsense of you telling him I'm your valet?"

A brief look of uncertainty flashed across Alistair's face, followed by a wince as his shoulders dropped. "What other excuse do you have for the two of us entering a hotel room together?"

Joe stepped to the bed and sat on the edge, rubbing his hands over his face. "You're right," he muttered. "Though I hate it."

Alistair moved cautiously to the side of the bed. He flinched as though he would sit, but changed his mind. "Would it be so bad if you were my valet?" he asked.

Joe glanced up at him, finding the sort of endearing innocence that only Alistair could pull off while still looking masculine and alluring. "It means we aren't equals," he said honestly. "It means you're above me."

A sensual spark lit Alistair's eyes. "I don't mind being below you," he said, his expression warming.

Joe couldn't help but grin in reply to that. He patted the bed beside him, and Alistair sat. "I'm sure we can come up with a thousand variations of above and below between the two of us that way." He curled his hand around Alistair's thigh, brushing his fingers against the already increasing bulge in Alistair's trousers, before irritation got the better of him once more. "But the way I was treated down there, the way I will always be treated in public when I'm with you...." He rolled his shoulders and frowned. "It stings."

"It's class," Alistair answered with more seriousness than Joe would have expected. "It's ingrained in the system. Nothing you or I do can change it. At least, not in the short term."

Joe stared at him incredulously. "And you can live with that? You can live with that sort of inequality between us?"

"What other choice do I have?" Alistair asked, suddenly serious. "If I want you—and I do—I must accept you as you are, and you must do the same with me. At least as we present ourselves to the world. But behind closed doors, we can be whomever we want to be."

It was a hard truth, but Joe saw it clearly for what it was—the conditions of love for men like them. It was their lot in life to love in secret, whether they were a valet and a viscount or two farm hands living out in the country. He had to take what he could get.

"I do want you," he said with a sigh.

"Good," Alistair answered, pivoting to face him more fully and taking Joe's face in his hands.

He kissed him with enough passion to push the frustration to the back of Joe's mind, though that frustration and anger tried to hold on in spite of the joy of being kissed so hard. It took a few good seconds of their lips pressing against each other and their tongues entwining for his tension to begin to subside.

"That's more like it," Alistair murmured as he began to relax. "Forget everything in the outside world and just be with me. Kiss me, embrace me, fuck me."

Joe sucked in a breath at the demanding invitation. Blood surged through him, pushing everything bad even further into the back of his thoughts. He worked open the buttons of his jacket and waistcoat, shrugging out of them and tossing them to the floor as Alistair did the same.

It was far more efficient for the two of them to undress themselves, and within minutes their clothes had been thrown about the room and the bedclothes pulled back so that they could slide between the sheets. Joe couldn't remember the last time he'd been in a bed that was so soft or so luxurious, but that was nothing to the hard planes of Alistair's naked body. It was a sight to behold in the sunlight that streamed through the tall windows. Every line and curve of him was magnificent— his broad shoulders, his powerful chest with enough hair to tempt him, his narrow waist, and his sizeable cock standing proud between his hips. Joe remembered the taste of that cock and how much it had filled his mouth. He wanted to taste it again, but Alistair had other plans.

"I don't care who we are out there," Alistair whispered as he kissed and nibbled Joe's shoulder and brushed his fingernails down Joe's sides in a move that had him catching his breath. "Alone, we are equals."

"We are," Joe said, his words turning into a gasp as Alistair cupped a hand around his balls.

"But this afternoon, as soon as I finish priming the pump, I want you to use me like a French whore," Alistair went on. He kissed his way down Joe's chest, flickering his tongue over one nipple as he went until Joe writhed beneath him. "I want you to fuck me without mercy, show me that you own me in every way."

Joe could barely breathe, let alone answer the demand. He threaded his fingers through Alistair's hair, and tugged tightly as Alistair's mouth made its way across his stomach. Alistair groaned in approval, then closed a hand around Joe's throbbing prick, lifting it so that he could kiss and lick the tip.

It was exquisite. Everything about the intimate act had Joe's heart pounding. He shifted his hips wider and arched his back as Alistair bore down on him, sucking hard. Almost too hard. If they weren't careful, Joe would come long before either of them were ready. But in the meantime, the hot wetness of Alistair's mouth encompassing him was so good that he answered each movement with moans of pleasure.

"Enough," he panted at last, pulling Alistair's hair hard to get him to let go. The passion-hazed expression on Alistair's face, coupled with his open mouth, was so erotic that Joe had to fight the urge to orgasm then and there. Alistair had asked for something, though, and Joe wanted to give him everything he'd ever asked for and more. "On your knees," he said as commandingly as possible.

A small, deep moan of victory sounded from Alistair as he shifted positions. Joe rolled to the side, reaching for the jar on the bedside table. The thrill of the moment he'd been dreaming about for weeks finally arriving made his hands shake as he unscrewed the top and dipped his fingers into the cool lubricant.

He set the jar aside and returned to Alistair, who was bent forward, poised and waiting, in a position so suggestive that it made Joe dizzy. "You look like a green lad begging for his first fuck," he said, not sure whether to laugh or growl with lust.

"I feel like it," Alistair panted, inching his legs farther apart and lifting his backside.

Joe wanted to capture the image of Alistair, submissive and eager, in his imagination forever. He planted his knees between Alistair's spread calves and stroked his salve-covered fingers over the pucker of Alistair's arse. Alistair gasped in response, which only made Joe want him more. He took his time, though, teasing and stroking, inserting one finger to test him, then two as Alistair rocked back, asking for more. He spread the remaining salve over his own cock, close to trembling with need, before guiding himself to Alistair.

It was almost too good to be true. Alistair accepted him with an impassioned moan, his thighs shaking with pleasure as Joe slowly drove deep inside of him. The tightness and pleasure of it had Joe hungry for more, but he moved slowly, not sure how long it had been for Alistair or how ready to accept he was.

"More," Alistair panted after a few strokes, answering the question. "Give it all to me. Don't hold back."

Joe moved deeper and faster, not sure he could have held himself back if he wanted to. He curled around Alistair's back, clasping his hand over Alistair's as it gripped the sheets and threading their fingers together. He moved his other hand around Alistair's hip to close around his iron-hard cock. There wasn't much he could do, as his focus was narrowed on jerking his hips against Alistair's backside as a delicious urgency built within him, but by the ecstatic sounds ripping from Alistair's throat, it was enough.

"You're mine," Joe growled as his thrusts peaked in intensity, the pleasure of it almost unbearable. "Mine."

He was so close that his body felt as though it were on fire. Tension poured off of Alistair as well. Joe hid the desperate sounds coming from him by biting Alistair's shoulder, and when he did, Alistair let out a fierce cry. Warm wetness spilled into Joe's hand. That was all it took for Joe to let go himself and fire into Alistair with an orgasm so powerful the edges of his vision went dark for a moment.

For a few, delicious heartbeats, they were no longer two entities. They were one—one heart, one body, one soul. The sweetness of the moment wrapped around Joe like angel's wings as his spent body loosened. Alistair collapsed, face down, into the sheets, and Joe relaxed with him, covering him.

"I love you so much," he panted as any will to move or exist apart from Alistair vanished.

"And I love you too," Alistair said, pure happiness in his voice.

CHAPTER 13

The afternoon passed in a haze of pleasure. Alistair couldn't remember the last time he'd been so happy. Within the walls of the hotel room, he didn't have to pretend to be someone he wasn't. Duty didn't press down on him, and the scrutiny of his family didn't hang above him like the Sword of Damocles. Even when he and Joe cleaned up enough to leave the hotel to seek out supper and entertainment at The Cock and Bull pub, the world seemed just as it should have been.

The night passed with as much fire and tenderness as the afternoon. Something was bothering Joe, something more than the vagaries of class and position, but Alistair chose to put his efforts into distracting Joe rather than talking about it.

By morning, he was beginning to wonder if that had been a mistake.

"You're still moody," he said as the two of them lay

naked and entwined in each other's arms in bed. Early morning light filtered through the sheer curtains over the tall windows, giving the room a fairy tale feeling.

Joe didn't answer, though his body tensed. Alistair had come to know Joe's body so well in the last day and stroked a hand up to Joe's shoulder to rub his muscles loose again as they lay face to face. Joe let out a breath and softened a bit, but the underlying tension was still with him.

"The only way to change the world is to find a way to get around its rules," Alistair said, then stole a light kiss from Joe's lips.

Joe didn't flinch away, but he didn't respond with the ardor Alistair hoped for either. "So many things are wrong about this world," he muttered.

"I agree. The world is wrong, but we aren't." Alistair's brow inched up hopefully. All he wanted to do was to find the words that would set Joe at ease and make him smile again.

Instead, Joe's frown deepened and he said, "Toby and Emma have gone missing."

It was Alistair's turn to frown. "Toby and Emma?"

"The hall boy and scullery maid at Eccles House."

Alistair shook his head slightly and adjusted the way he held Joe, hoping to give him more comfort. "Do they disappear often?"

"No," Joe answered immediately. "It's unlike them. Just as it was unlike Lily."

An uncomfortable feeling crawled through Alistair.

He'd entirely forgotten about the letter he'd accidentally taken home from the ball until that moment. He'd been so wrapped up in meeting Joe at the hotel that everything else had fallen by the wayside.

But before he could mention it, Joe wriggled away from him and said, "I've let too many things get in the way of what I should be doing, looking for Lily. And now Toby and Emma."

He rolled to the side, throwing back the bedcovers and swinging his legs around to stand. Alistair would have enjoyed the sight of Joe's bare back and backside as he rose and crossed the room to the bathroom, but all the lust, love, and tenderness they'd explored in the past day had been thoroughly replaced by frustration. It radiated from Joe like heat.

Alistair slipped out from under the sheets and sat on the edge of the bed, watching the open bathroom doorway until Joe came out.

"The situation might not be as hopeless as it seems," he said, rising and walking to meet Joe. He couldn't help but lose his train of thought for a moment at the sight of Joe's naked body. It didn't help solidify his thoughts when Joe raked him with an appraising glance as well. As much as they'd enjoyed each other in the last several hours, Alistair was ready for more. He would be ready for more for a long time to come.

Rather than reach for Joe, though, he shook his head to clear his thoughts and changed direction, crossing to the bureau where he'd stored his clothes the day before when he'd arrived. He took the letter from Eccles House out of the top drawer and turned to show it to Joe.

"I accidentally took this with me from the office the other night," he explained. "It's cryptic. It might be nothing. But the name Adler caught my attention."

Joe's reaction was far stronger than Alistair anticipated. "Adler?" His voice rose as he snatched the letter from Alistair and read it. His eyes grew wide with anger. "Why didn't you show this to me yesterday?" he demanded.

The reaction was so far beyond what Alistair had expected that it unnerved him. "I intended to tell you right away, but we got distracted." He took a slight step back.

Joe hissed and crumpled the letter in his fist. "Everything is a distraction. We've been distracted far too much for far too long."

"We've waited weeks to be together," Alistair reminded him, feeling his temper rise at the harshness of Joe's response to what he thought was a step in the right direction in so many ways.

"Maybe we should have waited longer," Joe grumbled, marching across the room to the chair where his satchel sat, still unpacked. He yanked it open and began pulling clean clothes out.

As much as Alistair tried to fight the sentimental feeling, he was hurt. "Are you saying we shouldn't have met here? That we shouldn't have fucked the way we did?"

Joe winced, as though he recognized the offense he'd

caused. "No," he said, a wealth of emotions packed into the single word. He huffed out a breath and threw the drawers he'd just taken from his satchel onto the table before turning to Alistair. "I don't mean that at all. You're right. We've waited a long time to be together, and I don't regret a second of it."

Alistair wasn't convinced Joe believed his own words. He crossed his arms. "But being together isn't as important as finding your sister."

Joe didn't contradict him right away. The hurt pounding in Alistair's chest grew. Joe was right, of course. Family meant everything. His sister was and should be the most important thing in the world to Joe. But knowing that did nothing for Alistair's pride or his heart.

"You are important to me, Alistair," Joe said, defeat and frustration in his voice as he walked slowly closer to Alistair. "God knows how important you are, now more than ever." He came close enough to rest a hand on the side of Alistair's face. "But is fucking, no matter how great it is, more important than the lives of three young people?"

"No. I'm not saying it is," Alistair answered immediately, though part of his heart felt like he was lying. Joe was important to him. Joe was everything he'd ever wanted, and everything he knew he would have to fight to be able to have. But he hadn't anticipated he'd have to fight Joe as well.

"I don't mean to hurt you," Joe said, letting his hand slide down to Alistair's chest for a moment before turning and walking back to the chair with his satchel. "I mean that. I really don't. But my conscience won't let me rest until I know I've done everything possible to find my sister, and now Toby and Emma too. And it feels like you withheld information from me that could be the lynchpin in the whole thing."

"I didn't withhold anything from you deliberately," Alistair insisted, following him to the chair. "I was just caught up."

"I know," Joe said, anger creeping back into his voice again. "But we can't afford it."

"So we're just supposed to...to put us aside while we attempt to locate missing children based off of a cryptic note that might not mean anything at all?" Alistair demanded, growing angry as well.

"No," Joe answered, exasperated, then turned to Alistair, meeting his eyes, and said, "Maybe yes."

Alistair flinched. He couldn't stop himself. "No," he said, crossing his arms and staring hard at Joe. "I refuse to believe that's the answer. We stand a far better chance of finding your sister, and finding the hall boy and scullery maid, if we approach this together."

"You're right," Joe said with a sigh, beginning to dress. As he straightened after putting on his drawers, he said, "But the children have to be a priority."

Alistair's gut disagreed. The two of them, what they had together, had to be the priority. If they didn't nurture what they had and put it above all else, they wouldn't be as effective. Instead, he said, "Staying in Burbage's employ isn't going to help things. Leave him and come work for me."

Joe froze halfway through reaching for his shirt. "Work for you? As what?"

"My valet," Alistair said with less patience than he should have used. "What else?"

Joe made a sound of disgust and continued dressing. "I bet you would love that," he said, sending Alistair a sour look.

"As a matter of fact, I would," Alistair said, fast approaching the point where he wasn't sure whether he wanted to kiss Joe or punch his perfect jaw. "I would love having you near me all the time, having a perfectly reasonable excuse for you to have intimate access to me at all times."

"And like any toff, you'd love to keep the country boy servant in his place," Joe sneered.

"When have I ever said that class matters to me? When have I ever given a fuck where you came from or what your job is?"

"When you told that cunt of a concierge that it was all right to let me into this goddamn place because I was beholden to you," Joe snapped.

"We talked about this," Alistair fired back, fighting to keep his voice at a volume that wouldn't carry through the walls and give them away. "What you and I need and what the rest of the world demands are two different things, and all the wishing in the world isn't going to change that."

"I refuse to be relegated to second class in the eyes of the man I love." Joe had no such qualms about being loud.

"Do you love me?" Alistair demanded, struggling to keep his emotions in check and failing. "Because last I checked, love was about making sacrifices."

"Then why do I feel like the only one sacrificing here?" Joe turned away to throw on his shirt, then the rest of his clothes.

"I am risking everything to be with you," Alistair hissed. "My family assumes I've dashed off to the country for an illicit rendezvous with a woman I can barely tolerate, but whom I will have to marry and, God help me, bed to produce an heir."

"And how is that you sacrificing something for me?" Joe asked, fastening his trousers and tucking in his shirt. "You'd end up doing the same, whether I was in the picture or not."

He had a point, and it stung. "It wouldn't feel like such a curse if I hadn't fallen in love with you."

"Then maybe you shouldn't have." Joe finished dressing and darted around the room, retrieving his clothes from where they'd ended up the day before and stuffing them into his satchel.

Alarm made Alistair's hands and heart go numb. "I could no more have stopped myself from falling in love with you than I could have stopped the blood from pumping through my veins," he said in a hoarse voice.

"And I'm not going to stop now because you're offended at the bitter truths of life."

"I'm offended," Joe began, whipping to face Alistair, "that someone out there thinks that snatching children is acceptable. I'm offended that my beautiful, funny, intelligent sister disappeared and that no one thought to question it or look for her. I'm offended that the man who should support me more than anyone is more concerned with who will suck his cock and put him to bed each night than he is about injustice."

"That is not what I'm concerned with," Alistair raised his voice again. "I want to find your sister and the others, but even you have to admit that we have a better chance at pursuing this case if we are able to be together and work together as much and as closely as possible."

He could tell he'd made his point by the way Joe's face pinched in frustration. He could also tell they were at an impasse. Joe had a stubborn streak a mile long and enough will to stick doggedly to what he believed in against all odds. That was one of the things Alistair admired the most about him, one of the things that attracted him. But at the moment, it made him want to throttle the bastard.

Joe let out a heavy breath and slung his satchel over his shoulder. He stared down at the floor for several, aching seconds before dragging his gaze up to meet Alistair's eyes. For a moment, he merely stood there, looking at him. Joe was fully dressed while Alistair was still naked and exposed. It seemed only right, somehow.

"I can't stay here and go around in circles with you. I have to go look for them," Joe said at last in a defeated voice. "I won't be able to live with myself if I don't at least try to find them. I'll go to Brighton to follow that lead on Adler if I have to, but I can't just stay here, whittling away my time in bed with you—as much as I might want to—when those children are in danger."

He glanced away from Alistair as he headed to the door.

"So you're just going to leave?" Alistair followed him, panic growing in his gut. It felt too much as though everything he'd ever wanted and had finally gotten was slipping through his fingers. "Just like that?"

"Yes." Joe reached for the handle on the door, but paused, letting out a long breath. "No." He glanced at Alistair over his shoulder. "I'm leaving you, but not that way," he said, the tenderness in his voice running riot with Alistair's emotions. "I love you. I want you. But not now, and not like this."

Alistair's lips pressed together as if to form the word "But—" to begin a protest, but the words wouldn't come out. He wanted to beg Joe to stay. He also wanted to kick him through the door with a "good riddance". In the end, he stood by, unable to do anything but watch, as Joe opened the door and slipped out into the hallway as discreetly as possible.

As the door clicked behind him, the panic Alistair had managed to hold at bay overwhelmed him. He stumbled back until he sat on the edge of the rumpled bed, breathing heavily. In spite of what Joe said, it felt as though things were over, as if his world were ending. He didn't understand how things could have fallen apart so soon after being heaven itself. It was as if he were starring in some romantic play, but the script had been switched with that of a tragedy after the first act.

He sat where he was for so long his backside started to go numb before getting up and heading into the bathroom to wash up. As he splashed cold water over his face and body, he forced himself to summon up the will to continue on. He hadn't lost Joe yet. And he refused to believe that the children were truly lost either. Joe was right that finding them was the most important thing in that moment. Alistair wracked his brains, seeking out all the ways that a man of his position might be able to do more than the average man to find out who Adler was and what he was up to. And with that, he searched his thoughts and his heart for a way he could win Joe back and convince him that they were fighting on the same side after all.

CHAPTER 14

Walking out on Alistair was the stupidest thing Joe had done in years. He knew it within hours of leaving the hotel, as he stormed fruitlessly through the streets, no idea where to even begin his search for Toby and Emma. He had no clues to go on other than the note Alistair had shown him, which he'd barely glanced at before flying off the handle. The only thing he could think to do was to travel to Brighton, but by the time he reached the seaside town that evening, he didn't have any more of an idea where to search or even what he was looking for than when he'd started. Beyond that, he didn't have enough money to spare for a hotel for the night and ended up sleeping under one of the piers with a dozen other, shadowy, down-on-their-luck men and women.

It wasn't until he was huddled against one of the pier's damp, stinking support columns, shivering to block out the icy wind blowing from the Channel, that the full impact of his foolishness hit him. He'd walked out on Alistair, a man who loved him beyond reason and whom he, strange as it was to admit it, loved to a ridiculous degree. They'd spent a night together that he wouldn't soon forget, giving and taking pleasure like he'd never known. Joe truly had never experienced anything half as sensual or satisfying as bedding Alistair. He had to face the fact that the reason it had felt so good was because their hearts were connected as intimately as their bodies.

And he'd run from that. Run like the dickens, because the idea that he could give himself over so completely to someone who was born into a different world and a different class than him, someone who would always have just a slight advantage over him, no matter what promises Alistair made, unnerved him. His pride rebelled at the idea of submission to another man. And yet, hadn't he laid himself bare, submitting fully to Alistair's lusts at least once during their long night together? Taking a turn in that role had been a pleasure and then some. And wasn't his position with Burbage, the position he depended on for his salary and for clues about where to find Lily, a lower one? Hadn't his apprenticeship at the tailor's in Leeds been inferior to his master as well? Why, then, did it sting so much more to think that his only chance to be with Alistair was in a role where society would disregard him as just a servant?

Because he loved Alistair. The answer came to him as the lap of the waves against the end of the pier finally lulled him into a restless sleep. He loved Alistair beyond reason, and love demanded partnership, equality. Love demanded something almost impossible for him and Alistair. But could he be willing to reach for something just short of ideal if it meant the two of them could be together?

His fitful slumber was awakened suddenly at the first hint of light as police officers combed the beach around the pier, chasing away the vagrants who had made it their home for the night. Joe leapt up and scattered along with the others before he could be found out and possibly arrested. He couldn't think of anything to do other than to search up and down the Brighton waterfront for any sign of illicit activity.

Unsurprisingly, he found more of it than he bargained for—prostitutes selling themselves, smugglers looking to unload illegal cargo, and even an attempted kidnapping. He watched in horror as a man in a colorful but ragged coat tempted a young boy away from his family with a stick of candy. Only at the last minute, when Joe spotted a shadowy accomplice waiting behind the pier with a burlap sack did he launch into action.

"You shouldn't talk to strangers, son," he said, stepping out from his concealment and walking boldly up to the boy.

The man in the ragged coat lost the cheery smile he'd put on for the boy and glared at Joe with narrowed eyes, but Joe ignored him. He walked up to the boy and took his hand, heading on as though he truly were the boy's father. The ragged coat man and his accomplice rushed off as Joe marched the boy back to his family, who had only just noticed he'd gone missing.

"Billy, where did you wander off to?" the boy's true father asked, approaching Joe with a dark, suspicious look.

"He nearly got himself into trouble," Joe informed the man. "Have a care for him."

He returned the boy to his family, but the eeriness of the encounter stuck with him as he doubled back to look for the ragged coat man. Had Lily been snatched from Eccles House as easily? Had Toby and Emma been lured away in a similar fashion, when no one was paying attention? And if it was so easy to steal a child, what could possibly be done to keep other children safe?

The next few days passed in a similar fashion, but without as much excitement. Tuesday came and went, but Joe witnessed nothing that matched the letter from Adler that Alistair had found. Again, he cursed himself for not staying by Alistair's side or getting a better look at the letter to work out what it meant. His whole journey had ended up being pointless. By the time he returned to London, almost a week had passed. He'd had no contact with Alistair, and it was beginning to wear on his nerves.

"And just where have you been this week?" Mrs. Harris asked him with a scowl when he finally joined the rest of the Eccles House servants in the downstairs hall after unpacking his things and dressing in his work clothes the day of his return.

"I went to the seaside," Joe answered truthfully. They didn't need to know where he was or whom he'd been with before going there. When Mrs. Harris continued to frown at him, he went on with, "Burbage is gone, and I haven't had a holiday since I came on here."

Mrs. Harris hummed, then moved to the end of the table, where servants' tea was set, to fix herself a cup. "There are duties a valet could fulfill, even without his master being home."

Joe ignored the comment as he moved to help himself to a much-needed cup of tea. If he were truly in trouble, it would be Mr. Vine who took him to task, not the house-keeper. All the same, he'd always been on good terms with the rest of the staff at Eccles House, but now it felt as though things had changed. Perhaps he shouldn't have vanished for a few days after all.

"I'm certain it will be the wedding of the decade," Lucy said to one of the other maids, Martha, as the two of them walked into the hall and made their way to the table. "A match like that is sure to end up in all the newspapers."

"According to Lady Burbage, her sister won't settle for anything less than a full-page announcement in the Times," Martha laughed.

Every nerve in Joe's body snapped tight. It felt as though his heart stopped beating. He did his best to casu-ally sip his tea, but it suddenly seemed difficult to breathe, let alone swallow.

"Lady B is beside herself with envy," Lucy went on

in a quiet voice, peeking at Mrs. Harris, who clearly didn't approve of the maids gossiping about their mistress, but who also seemed interested in what they had to say. "Word is that old Lord Winslow doesn't have much longer, which means her sister will be a countess before she is."

Joe's chest squeezed tighter. Any hope he had that the maids were gossiping about someone other than Alistair was gone. He moved slowly to the bench on one side of the table and sat heavily before his legs and his hope gave out.

"I wouldn't count old Lord Winslow out yet," Martha said. "Certainly, he's mad as a hatter, but he didn't seem as frail as all that when he was here for the ball."

"He left the ball early," Lucy reminded him. "Poor Lord Farnham and his brother practically had to drag him out to keep him from making a scene."

Joe arched one eyebrow subtly. That wasn't what had happened, but it was interesting to see how the story had grown in the past week.

"Either way," Lucy went on with a wave of her hand as she and Martha sat, several feet down the table from Joe, "the old bat will be pleased that his son is marrying into such a prominent family."

Misery flooded through Joe. He shouldn't have run off. He should have stayed with Alistair and battled things out between them.

"Any man who is destined to inherit an earldom will marry into a prominent family," Mrs. Harris told the maids, a light in her eyes as if she, too, found the whole topic fascinating.

"Do you suppose this means we'll be seeing more of Lord Farnham?" Martha asked as she sipped her tea. "You could say he's marrying into the family, in a way. I do hope he comes to Eccles House more often. He is a treat to look at."

Martha grinned and Lucy giggled. Joe's heart sank to his feet. Alistair was a treat to look at. The silly maids had no idea. The sight of Alistair, naked and aroused and spread across the bed, jumped to Joe's mind, bruising his heart further. He would have given anything to see Alistair like that again, to run his hands over Alistair's chiseled body and to bring him to orgasm with his hands, his mouth. What kind of a damned fool was he to let his pride get in the way of all that?

The kind of fool who knew that searching for vanished children was just as important as sex.

That thought sprang into his mind as a small boy he didn't know dashed into the room with a bucket of shoe polishing supplies and took a seat meekly in the corner, where several pairs of servants' shoes were piled.

"Toby never returned?" he asked no one in particular as he stared at the boy, his heart sinking so far it felt like it would dissolve into dust.

"No," Mrs. Harris replied unkindly. "Neither did that Emma. If the two were older, I'd bet my best brooch they eloped."

"They were only six or seven," Joe reminded her.

"Doesn't mean they aren't old enough to get fool ideas in their heads and to run off," Martha commented with a sneer.

Joe felt sick. He should have done more to look for Toby and Emma rather than going home to Leeds. He should have stayed in London to work things out with Alistair. Guilt assailed him from all sides. He couldn't have made the right move if he'd had an angel standing on his shoulder, telling him what he should do every step of the way.

He stood suddenly, leaving his half-empty teacup on the table. He had to do something. Anything. Any action at all to figure out what had happened to Toby and Emma, and to Lily. Anything that might help him heal the rift he'd caused between him and Alistair, and hopefully before Alistair went through with a marriage that was, apparently, already in the works.

Without a word to the others, he left the servants' hall, taking the stairs to the ground floor two at a time, then striding through the halls of Eccles House until he reached the out of the way office where he and Alistair had experienced their first moments of passion together. If Alistair had managed to find the cryptic letter mentioning Adler and Brighton there, perhaps he could find more information.

To his surprise, the door was locked. He tried the handle twice, but it was definitely locked. Joe's heart raced. A locked door was proof that something sinister was going on, as far as he was concerned. Especially if someone had discovered the office had been infiltrated the night of the ball. He only hoped that whoever had discovered the state of the office—which, admittedly, he and Alistair hadn't had the time to tidy up—didn't know what had happened there. Either way, he wasn't about to let a locked door stop him.

It only took minutes for him to head back downstairs to Mrs. Harris's office. The housekeeper had keys to every room in the house tucked away in her desk. Fortunately for Joe, she was still in the servants' hall, listening to Lucy and Martha speculate about Alistair's upcoming wedding to Lady Matilda. There were advantages to working in a household where the servants were far laxer than they should have been. He was back upstairs, unlocking the office door, before anyone noticed.

The office seemed vastly different in the light of day than it had in the black of night when he and Alistair had been there. The small room was crowded with papers, books, and newspapers, none of which were arranged in any sort of order. Dust covered a few of the shelves, telling Joe that the maids didn't clean the office regularly, if at all. That explained the slightly musty smell he had noticed the night of the ball. The room didn't have an abandoned feeling, however. Quite the contrary. It felt like a room that was used often.

He strode around the desk, pushing a large chair aside so that he could study the documents on the desktop. At first glance, they looked like any business records. There was a ledger that held information about sales and transactions, profits and losses. More telegrams, similar to the one Alistair had showed him referencing Brighton and Adler, were stacked in a corner. Nothing held specific information, though. There wasn't a trace of what merchandise was being delivered or sold, which sent a chill down Joe's back. He had a horrible feeling he knew just what commodities Burbage—or whoever used the office, it might have been Lord Chisolm—was selling.

An odd, sick feeling filled Joe's gut. He'd spent months assuming there was no way Burbage could be involved in something as trivial as one of his maids disappearing. He'd figured Burbage wouldn't see Lily as a person and that she would, therefore, be beneath his notice. But Burbage—and his father—guarded their assets zealously. The more Joe looked at things from the point of view of Burbage seeing Lily—and possibly the others—as an asset, the more likely it seemed that he could very well be involved. And he'd been serving the man for months.

Nothing on the desktop stood out to Joe, until he noticed a crisp slip of paper, a telegram, with that day's date on the top. It simply read, "Thursday. Dock. 11:30."

Joe held his breath. It was the most specific information he'd seen about whatever business dealings the owner of the office was up to. And with Toby and Emma missing, with Lily gone for months, he had a terrible feeling he knew what might take place at some London dock on Thursday. But which dock? London had hundreds.

That thought had just begun to slither down his back, giving him a chill, when Burbage stepped suddenly into the doorway. "What are you doing here?" he demanded.

Panic made Joe clumsy, and he knocked the ledger he'd been looking at to the floor. He met Burbage's eyes, but there was no point in even attempting to explain his presence or his activity.

Burbage's initial shock shifted into a wry grin, as though Joe were an insect specimen he was about to pin to a board. "You're the one who was in here the other night, no doubt," he said, stalking menacingly closer to Joe. "Thought you could catch me out at something? Servants are never satisfied with what they have," he went on without Joe's prompting. "Always trying to get more out of their betters."

"You aren't my better," Joe said, standing straighter and squaring his shoulders.

Burbage laughed. "Of course, I am. You're a pitiful country slob and a sodomite at that."

Joe's chest squeezed so hard the edges of his vision went black. How could Burbage possibly know about him?

"Don't look so surprised," Burbage went on with a sneer. "It's obvious, if one knows how to look for the signs. The way you linger a little too long while undressing me, the way you study me out of the corner of your eye. And I've heard whispers from downstairs that you aren't even remotely interested in the maids, no matter how blatantly they flirt."

Acid filled Joe's stomach at the idea of Burbage thinking he had even a shred of attraction for him. "You are mistaken," he growled, hoping Burbage would take the statement as a whole and not just as it pertained to him.

"I am not," Burbage said with absolute certainty. "I had a valet before you who was just as perverted and thought he could act on it." A vicious, lopsided grin tugged at his mouth. "I believe the only employment he could find afterwards was servicing peculiar sailors down on the docks."

Joe didn't try to hide his disgust, though it was all for Burbage and not the unfortunate soul he'd driven to ruin.

But before he could say more, Burbage continued with, "Don't think I didn't see the way you and Farnham were ogling each other the night either. Farnham is a notorious pouf, in spite of this supposed liaison with my wife's sister. I've known that much since university."

Whatever confidence had been building in Joe flattened. Damn him, but Burbage was more observant than he seemed. "You're wrong," he said, knowing there wasn't enough conviction in his words.

"I'm not," Burbage said with too much confidence. "I despise men like you and Farnham. Sick bastards. The lot of you should be exterminated."

"And crooked businessmen, like yourself, shouldn't?" Joe asked, scrambling for a way to keep from being humiliated and also hoping to provoke Burbage into a confession of some sort.

Burbage merely laughed and shook his head. "So that's what you're after, is it? Some kind of proof that I'm engaged in untoward business? Well, you won't find it. My business dealings are none of your concern."

There was something sinister, something far less confident, in the way Burbage spoke than before. His eyes flashed with defensiveness, giving Joe the distinct impression that the man was hiding something. Something that would take place on Thursday at eleven thirty at an unspecified London dock.

But before Joe could think of how to approach the subject, Burbage took a breath, shifted his stance, and said, "I'll give you twenty minutes to get out of my house. If you are not gone by then, never to darken this doorstep again, I will inform the police that you are an unrepentant sodomite." Joe opened his mouth to protest, but Burbage went on with, "Furthermore, I understand that a hall boy went missing from this house a week or so ago. I will also inform the police that the poor lad ran away because you were buggering him at every chance you got."

"It's a lie," Joe hissed, repulsed by the thought.

Burbage shrugged. "Whom do you think the police will believe? A gentleman or a queer valet?"

The truth was so bitter that it turned Joe's stomach. He knew as well as Burbage whom they would believe. He had no choice at all but to take Burbage at his word. With nothing more than a look of seething hatred for the man, Joe turned and marched out of the room. He'd never known hate so potent, and he vowed he would bring an end to Burbage, if it was the last thing he ever did. But there was no point in firing those words at the bastard and no time.

He sprinted up to his garret room and packed his things as fast as he could. He wouldn't put it past Burbage to call the police immediately instead of waiting twenty minutes. If he wanted to have any chance of putting Eccles House behind him, he had to get out.

The trouble was, he had nowhere to go once he was out. He fled Mayfair only to wander aimlessly through Westminster, for how long he wasn't sure. The only friend he had in London was Alistair, and under the current circumstances, he wasn't certain if he could turn to Alistair.

It wasn't until he spotted the dome of St. Paul's Cathedral in his wandering and headed toward The City that he realized there was somewhere else he could go. He could go where men like him went when they were in a tight spot.

With a seed of his confidence renewed, he marched on toward the heart of London and the offices of Dandie & Wirth.

CHAPTER 15

The moment Joe stepped through the door into the offices of Dandie & Wirth, Lionel Mercer raised his head from the paperwork on the desk in front of him, smiled broadly, and said, "The prodigal son returns."

Joe blinked, freezing with his hand on the door as he shut it. "How did you know I was gone?" he asked, letting go and taking a few more steps into the heart of the room.

Lionel sent him a flat look, as if to ask, "Have you learned nothing about me?" as he stood and stepped out from behind the desk. His suit was expertly tailored as usual, with a lavender waistcoat that made the blue of his eyes stand out like beacons. The vaguely supernatural feelings Joe had had the first time he and Alistair had met Lionel returned.

"Is that Joe Logan?" David Wirth's voice sounded

from the adjacent office, moments before he strode into the front room.

"It is," Lionel answered, approaching Joe and taking his satchel from his shoulder. "Right on schedule."

Wirth nodded and moved in to shake Joe's hand as Lionel stepped away with his satchel, crossing to rest it on one of the sofas, then moving on to the stove to make tea, as if Joe had entered a home instead of a place of business.

"I thought you would show up here eventually," Wirth said with a sympathetic smile.

"And why is that?" Joe asked, the hair on the back of his neck standing up. He hadn't known he would turn to Dandie & Wirth until half an hour ago.

Wirth shrugged, then stepped back to sit on the edge of Lionel's desk. "Alistair told me everything."

A chill passed down Joe's spine, one that was sharp with jealousy. He fought to hide his emotions, but feared it was impossible to hide anything from Wirth and Lionel. "You saw him?" he asked, shoving his hands into the pockets of his trousers, since he didn't know what else to do with them.

"At The Chameleon Club." Wirth nodded again. "Last week. He said he was there because he'd told his family he would be out of town for a few days. It only took one glass of port to get the real story out of him, though."

Wirth grinned sympathetically. The man was as dark as Lionel was luminescent, but just as perceptive. Where

Lionel had the effect of an avenging angel who could force confessions from a stone, Wirth radiated brotherly compassion and confidence. His soothing smile put Joe at ease. So much so that he stepped to the closest sofa and slumped to sit against its back.

"I was an ass to leave the way I did," he said, rubbing a hand over his tired face and feeling as though he was putting down a burden he'd carried for a week. "I know he was just trying to be helpful."

"But he could have done it in a less aristocratic way," Wirth finished the thought for him, arching one of his dark brows.

Joe eyed him with consideration. "You're not a nob, are you? I mean, you have a certain poshness about you, but you don't act like one of them."

Wirth let out a self-deprecating laugh. "I'm as middle-class as they come. My father was a solicitor, and his father before him. My mother was a school teacher." He nodded to Lionel. "Lionel there's the nob in this operation."

"Leave my nob out of this," Lionel said with a charmingly lopsided grin as he brought a cup of tea to Joe. "It's on sabbatical at the moment anyhow." He handed Joe the tea—which was prepared exactly the way Joe liked it—then went on with, "And I'm not aristocracy, just gentry, and a younger son at that."

"So really, you're nothing," Wirth teased him with a grin that was wry enough to make Joe wonder if there was something between the two men.

"Honey, I am everything," Lionel replied with an equally flirty flicker of one perfect eyebrow, then moved to sit on the arm of the sofa beside Joe.

Joe smiled at the exchange, in spite of his own, roiling emotions. "I should be more sympathetic to Alistair. He can't change who he is, and I'm not sure I would want him to."

"Of course not," Wirth agreed, focusing on Joe once more. "But I understand how irritating gentlemen can be sometimes." He shot another, teasing glance to Lionel, then said, "Do you want to send for him?"

"I suppose we'd better." Lionel stood and crossed in front of Joe, heading to the office door, then out into the hall.

Once he was gone, Wirth grew serious. "Alistair also told me that you were upset with him because he failed to inform you of some key information he received before your night together."

Heat raced up Joe's neck to his face. What else had Alistair revealed? "We should be following every lead we get when it comes to finding the missing children."

"Agreed," Wirth said, standing. "Which is why I passed the information along to Patrick Wrexham as soon as Alistair gave it to me."

Joe's spirits lifted, and he sat straighter. "Has Wrexham discovered anything?"

"Not specifically," Wirth said, pacing in front of Joe. "Though the information does match what he already has. Confirmation is as good as new information sometimes."

With renewed excitement, Joe jumped to his feet. "I have new information," he said. "At least, I think I do." Wirth paused and turned to face him. "I found a note in Burbage's office that said a transaction would take place at some unknown London dock at eleven-thirty on Thursday."

Wirth's eyes went wide. "Which dock?"

Joe let out a breath. "I have no idea. The note wasn't specific."

Wirth's face fell into a frown, and he continued his pacing. "It's still the most specific information we've had to date." He glanced to Joe as he crossed in front of him. "And you say you found this in Burbage's office?"

"I did."

Wirth rubbed a hand over his tense face. "That all but proves Burbage is involved. Or someone in the Eccles family. Perhaps the entire family."

The statement hit Joe hard. It was one thing to drag himself to the conclusion that he had while rifling through Burbage's papers, but it was another to have someone on the outside point out the truth as though it were obvious. He felt like a fool for not figuring it all out from the start. Had he not looked hard enough, possibly because Burbage was an aristocrat, not to mention the man paying him a wage? If that was so, he was as guilty of buying into the lie of class distinction as much as Alistair was.

He let out a breath and shoved his hands through his hair. "I have been in a position to discover the truth all these months, and I squandered it."

"You found out when a transaction is going to take place," Wirth assured him. "And you were instrumental in Alistair finding that paper connecting Adler to the transaction. I think it's likely that transaction is transporting the missing children."

"But I could have done more," Joe sighed. "And now I've been sacked and banished from the one place where I could have been of use." He bristled with frustration, hating himself for being stupid and acting without thinking.

"Don't castigate yourself yet," Wirth said, leaning against the desk once more. "The investigation is far from over. In fact, I have a feeling it's just heating up."

He didn't have a chance to go on. The office door opened, and Lionel returned, leading Alistair behind him. Alistair wore a puzzled frown. He froze the moment he spotted Joe, his brow shooting up and his face flushing pink.

Joe's heart shot to his throat as he stared at Alistair. How he had managed to forget how devilishly handsome Alistair was in the scant space of a week was beyond him. At the same time, Alistair had a decided tension around him that seemed to make the lines of his face harder and his shoulders tighter. The overall effect made Joe want to run to him and fold Alistair in his arms, both to apologize and to tell him that everything would be all right. In actuality, he stood where he was, unable to move.

"You're back," Alistair said, removing his coat at Lionel's prompting and stepping slowly forward.

"I went to Brighton," Joe blurted, taking two fast steps toward Alistair, then stopping. "I found nothing. It was a fruitless trip."

"You went all the way to Brighton on your own?" Alistair asked, his expression softening.

Joe nodded. He wanted to say so many things, to apologize and to confess how much he loved and missed Alistair. He wanted to say that it didn't matter what people thought of them or their stations in life, he just wanted to be with him. But the words refused to push past his lips.

"I told David about that note," Alistair said haltingly.

Joe swallowed the pinch of jealousy at hearing Alistair refer to Wirth by his given name. He nodded. "He told me. And I told him about another note I saw, just this morning." He stepped closer to Alistair, taking in a cleansing breath and forcing his mind to things that were more important than his bruised heart. "Something is going to happen on Thursday at eleven-thirty at a dock on the London waterfront."

Alistair looked surprised, but it was Lionel who stepped forward and said, "You have a day and a time?"

"But not a location," Wirth said. "All the same, we need to inform Patrick so that something can be done. A sweep of the dockyards, perhaps."

"The dockyards are extensive," Lionel answered, as if Joe and Alistair weren't even there. "And as much as it pains me to say it, they're out of the purview of my sphere of information."

"Someone might know something." Wirth shrugged. "Even gentlemen have business interests at the docks."

"You know more about the underworld than I do," Lionel said, crossing his arms and frowning.

"I do, but I generally need more than four days to follow up on information this vague."

Joe only gave half of his attention to the conversation between Lionel and Wirth. He stared at Alistair, desperate for a way to communicate his regret without having to swallow his pride. It didn't help the brittle state of his nerves that Alistair stared right back at him, like some sort of confession was hovering just behind his pursed lips.

"I was sacked," Joe said at last.

"You were?" Of all things, a flash of hope filled Alistair's expression.

"Burbage caught me in his office and sacked me on the spot. He suspects something between us as well," Joe added.

Lionel and Wirth stopped their conversation, turning to them.

"Burbage caught you snooping in his office and he suspects the two of you are involved?" Lionel asked, color splashing across his pale face. He cursed under his breath and shook his head in disgust as he marched behind his desk and began rifling through papers. The only part of his mutterings that Joe could make out were, "careless" and "amateur".

Alistair seemed to notice Joe's satchel on the sofa for the first time. "Where are you staying?" he asked, more hope in his eyes.

"I don't know," Joe sighed.

"I can arrange for accommodation," Wirth said, glancing cautiously between Joe and Alistair.

"Nonsense," Alistair said. "You'll come home with me."

"I can't do that," Joe said, though the pull to do just that was powerful.

"I need a valet," Alistair went on with a shrug. "It's what I told you last week. No one would question your presence in my house."

Joe had a feeling everyone would question it, starting with Burbage, as soon as the bastard found out. How long could things go on once that cat got out of the bag?

He opened his mouth to reply, but Alistair spoke over him with, "I won't hear of anything else. You're coming home with me."

Joe glanced to Wirth, surprised to find he wanted the man's guidance in the matter.

Wirth shrugged. "It will be easier to keep you both informed of the investigation if you're in the same place."

There was more to Wirth's answer than met the eye, Joe was certain. He glanced to Lionel, whose sharp stare seemed to tell him he would be a fool for not jumping at the chance to quietly slip into his lover's house in a manner no one would question or find untoward. Joe damned the two men for being so perceptive and meddling, even though neither said a word.

"All right," he sighed, turning back to Alistair.

Alistair cracked a relieved smile that shot straight to Joe's heart. Twin feelings of disgust with himself for feeling so maudlin and relief that Alistair didn't seem to be irreparably hurt by his actions left Joe feeling utterly off-balance. He smiled in return before he could stop himself, which only widened Alistair's grin. The two of them would be blubbering in each other's arms in no time if he didn't put his foot down.

"What do you plan to do about the information I gave you?" he asked Wirth, clearing his throat when his words came out in a croak.

"Like I said, I'll inform Patrick and get him working on things immediately," Wirth answered.

"And I'll send out my feelers in all the appropriate directions," Lionel added, walking back around the desk to take the cold cup of tea that Joe hadn't touched from his hands. Joe was startled that he still held it. "Why don't the two of you go on and see if there's anything you can do to infiltrate Burbage's cabal again."

Alistair blinked. "Burbage's cabal?"

Joe blew out a breath, his thoughts flying back to where they had started this interaction with Wirth and Lionel. "Burbage is clearly involved in the disappearance of all these children," Joe said. "Something I should have figured out far sooner than I did. Particularly since he left for his trip the night Toby and Emma disappeared."

His back snapped straight as the thought struck him. Why had he not made the connection before?

Because he'd assumed Toby and Emma were concealed somewhere in the house, spying on guests, not missing, on the night of the ball. And because his thoughts had been so consumed with lust for Alistair that he hadn't had room to think of anything else.

"I'll find out where exactly Burbage went on his little trip up north," Lionel said, returning from the stove, where he'd deposited Joe's teacup.

"He traveled north?" Joe asked.

"He left from St. Pancras on a train destined for Edinburgh," Lionel said. "Though that particular train made a dozen stops before it got there. I didn't realize it would be important to know more, otherwise I would have had someone follow him."

Joe couldn't imagine who Lionel might have had working for him, but it hardly mattered. As difficult as it was to step away from the investigation, he knew the whole thing was in good hands.

Wirth nodded to him as if acknowledging the thought. "You're not in this alone," he said. "We'll find those children, and we'll find your sister."

ALISTAIR'S HEART HADN'T STOPPED RACING SINCE the moment he stepped into the offices of Dandie &

Wirth and saw Joe standing there, teacup in hand, looking utterly lost. He'd barely known what to say through the business at the office, and he knew even less what to say when he ushered Joe outside to the carriage waiting for him.

"You look well," he said, opening the carriage door and waiting for Joe to get in.

"No, I don't," Joe said. He stared at Alistair for a long moment before frowning and climbing into the carriage. "Shouldn't you get in first?" he asked as he settled.

Alistair jumped in, shut the door, and called for the driver to take them home. "I don't know, and at the moment, I don't care."

Joe hummed and adjusted his satchel on his lap like a shield.

"I'm sorry," Alistair blurted before he could lose his nerve.

"What about?" Joe asked, sounding tired.

"About all of this. About fighting with you. I know you don't want to be my valet, but—"

"I want to be your valet," Joe sighed. Alistair wasn't convinced, which must have shown on his face as Joe went on with, "It was never about the job to begin with."

"Only the position," Alistair finished for him.

"It won't work if we don't feel equal," Joe said.

"I know, I know." Alistair slumped back against the seat. Joe's frown shouldn't have been encouraging, but the very fact that they were there together, in a carriage heading home, fanned the ember that had never gone out in Alistair's soul. "Let's take one thing at a time," he went on. "You'll settle in my house as my valet, and we'll work out what to do next."

"Honestly, nothing is going to settle until we've found Toby and Emma and Lily and brought the people who took them to justice," Joe said, his shoulders loosening as he rubbed his hands over his face. "I can't believe I didn't see how involved Burbage was from the start."

"Things always look clearer when you look at them after the fact," Alistair said, his heart brimming with compassion for the man he loved beyond reason. "If I had a farthing for every time something stared me in the face without me seeing it for what it was, I'd be richer than Rothschild."

"Yes, but that's because you're so good and sweet that you only see the goodness and sweetness in others," Joe said.

The compliment settled over Alistair like a warm, summer breeze. He smiled before he could stop himself. "God, I would throw myself on you and kiss you within an inch of your life if I didn't think the driver would hear my sighs of ecstasy and know all," he hissed.

"Like this?" Joe breathed, then surged forward.

Joe braced his hands on the back of the seat behind Alistair, closing his mouth over Alistair's and kissing him with a week's worth of denied passion. The carriage was too cramped for their bodies to meld together, but that didn't stop Alistair from reaching under Joe's jacket to dig his fingertips into his sides. The warmth and solidity he felt there was like heaven after hell, and he gave himself over fully to their kiss, in spite of the sounds he couldn't help but make.

"This is madness," he panted at last. "We're not going to be able to do this without being caught."

"We will," Joe promised, following his long, deep kiss with half a dozen shorter, teasing ones. "We'll just have to be careful." He ended with one final, searing kiss, their tongues brushing, before leaning back. "But we have to put the investigation first."

"Yes, of course," Alistair said. His lips tingled with the force of Joe's kiss, his body was hot with need, and his prick strained against his trousers. "I don't know how, though."

Joe fell back into his seat, struggling to catch his breath. "Are you really engaged to Lady Matilda?" he asked.

Alistair blinked. That was the last thing he expected Joe to ask. "No," he answered, then shifted awkwardly in his seat, sitting straighter. "Not yet. But it's expected and inevitable."

"I see," Joe said, his jaw tight.

A flush of satisfaction raced through Alistair. Joe was jealous. "I'm supposed to see her tonight," he said, toying with the idea of making Joe even more jealous to see what he would do about it. "We're to dine at—" He stopped, his eyes snapping wide.

"What?" Joe asked, leaning slightly forward.

"We're to dine at Eccles House tonight," Alistair said.

The feeling of triumph at what he saw as a chance to discover more about Burbage's involvement with the missing children crashed when Joe looked grimmer than ever.

"Burbage suspects something between us," Joe reminded him.

Alistair's confidence shattered. "Damn. How am I supposed to sit across the table and make polite conversation with the man, let alone pry for information?"

The silence between them bristled. Joe's expression soured. "By showering attention on Lady Matilda," he answered.

The inevitability of his marriage gnawed at Alistair's gut as sharply as ever. "Damn," he said, sinking back against his seat.

Neither of them said another word as the carriage completed the journey to Mayfair. Both of them knew what fate had in store for men like them. Within the span of minutes, Alistair went from feelings of giddy gratitude that Joe had accepted the position of his valet to resentment that they were doomed to be trapped in that relationship forever.

"We need to focus on one thing at a time," Joe said as the carriage stopped and he let himself out first. Alistair followed him out to the street, waved to the driver, then gestured for Joe to walk with him up the steps to the front door as Joe went on with, "We have to find the children first."

"Agreed," Alistair said, knocking, then walking

through the door as the footman on duty opened it for him. He didn't think about the propriety of Joe entering the house through the front door with him until they were already in the hallway. "My greatest hope is that we have enough information for—"

He nearly ran headlong into Darren, who stood in the hall, looking incredulously at Joe.

"What is the meaning of this?" Darren asked, glancing down his nose at Joe as though Alistair had let a stray dog into the house.

As smoothly as he could, Alistair said, "You remember Mr. Logan. I've just hired him as my valet."

"Sir." Joe nodded crisply to Darren. The practiced subservience of his bow sent a chill through Alistair.

Darren continued to study Joe suspiciously. "You didn't tell me anything about looking for a valet."

"Unnecessary," Alistair said, alarmed at how hot his face felt. "Besides, you saw how good Mr. Logan was with Father the other night. You were the one who said if he ever needed a job he should turn to us. Perhaps he can be of use with Father as well tending to me."

Darren made a considering noise, but it didn't change his apprehensive stare. For a few seconds, the hall crackled with tension as none of the three of them moved a muscle. Darren broke the tension by sucking in a breath and saying, "You'd better hurry up and change. We're expected at Eccles House in less than an hour."

"Yes," Alistair said, certain his brother would be able to hear his furiously pounding heart. "That's just where we were heading. Mr. Logan can help me change, then I'll have Jennings take him downstairs and introduce him to the rest of the staff as my valet." He glanced past Darren to the family's butler, who had entered the hall in time to witness the exchange.

"Very good, my lord," Jennings said with a bow, acknowledging Joe with a nod.

Joe nodded back, making Alistair wonder if there were an entire language among servants that he knew nothing about. There wasn't anything more to say or do in the situation, so he started upstairs, gesturing for Joe to come with him.

"We can make this work," he whispered as they neared the top of the stairs.

"If you say so," Joe said doubtfully.

Alistair swallowed, reaching subtly to brush Joe's hand as they turned the corner and headed down the hall toward his room. If he were honest with himself, he wasn't certain they could pull it off either.

CHAPTER 16

*A*listair's heart and mind were a mess as he rode through the darkened streets of Mayfair to Eccles House. It didn't help matters that he'd agreed to pick Lady Matilda up along the way. Though the distance between her family's home and Eccles House was crossed in a matter of minutes, Lady Matilda spent the entire trip complaining about her sister.

"It's as if she wants everyone to comment on her increasing shape," she said with a long-suffering sigh as the carriage slowed. "All it would take is a few, minor alterations to her existing wardrobe and the right under-garments, and her condition would hardly be noticeable at all."

Alistair nodded, but he barely heard her. His gut roiled with the thought that Burbage was suspicious of his connection to Joe and that he was about to walk into the lion's den because of it. Darren had seemed to find

Joe's presence at home suspicious as well, though God only knew why. As far as he knew, Alistair had never given his brother any reason to doubt his tastes. Although it was a blessing Beth was in the country with her friends again. His sister would pick up on the undercurrents between him and Joe much more quickly.

"She shouldn't be in public at this point at all," Lady Matilda went on as the carriage stopped in front of Eccles House. "She should be off in the country somewhere, enjoying her confinement, and leaving London to me."

Alistair hummed, trying to drag himself out of his thoughts as he stepped down from the carriage and offered Lady Matilda a hand. There were more things on his mind than his relationship with Joe being discovered. Thursday was only a handful of days away. He couldn't stomach the idea that the children who had gone missing might find themselves enduring a fate worse than death in such a short time. If Officer Wrexham wasn't able to figure out the exact location of whatever exchange was about to happen, Alistair felt it was his duty to jump into action.

He offered his arm to Lady Matilda, who took it silently, thank God. It was only when they walked up the stairs and through the front door, held open by a smartly-dressed footman, that Alistair realized her silence was sharp disapproval.

"Aren't you going to say anything?" she asked once they were safely in the front hall and the footman took their coats.

"I'm not certain what to say," he admitted.

Lady Matilda pursed her lips in irritation. "You could comment on my gown or the trouble I went through to style my hair this evening."

Alistair blinked and looked at her, trying to notice the details she would want to have noticed. "You do look lovely," he said. He could admit that objectively, though her diamonds would never be a match to the sparkle in Joe's eyes when he smiled.

Lady Matilda tilted her head up and studied him with narrowed eyes. "Thank you," she said, still not pleased. "You're too quiet this evening."

Alistair sent her what he hoped was an apologetic smile. "I have a great many things on my mind." When she arched an eyebrow at him, he went on with, "That I wouldn't want to trouble you with."

She let out an impatient sigh as they started toward the parlor, where most of the other guests, including Darren, were already assembled. "If we are to continue forward in this partnership, you must learn to trust me with your concerns."

Alistair glanced sideways at her. That wasn't going to happen.

He was saved from having to say anything as Lord Chisolm came forward to greet them.

"Ah, there's the shining couple of the moment," he said, fawning over Lady Matilda in a way that made her cheeks pink with pleasure. "My dear, you look delightful this evening."

"Thank you, Lord Chisolm," Lady Matilda laughed playfully. "You're such a flirt." When Lord Chisolm turned to acknowledge a glance from his butler, who had just stepped into the doorway to announce supper, she muttered to Alistair, "You would do well to take lessons in flattery from Lord Chisolm."

"Yes, of course," Alistair mumbled back. "I'm terribly sorry."

His feeble apology seemed to be enough for her. She tightened her grip on his arm, her expression softening, and said, "It's all right. You can be trained."

Alistair bristled inwardly at her condescending tone. Clearly, the woman thought she was miles above him, though God only knew why. It struck him that he must be feeling something akin to what Joe felt every time someone of Alistair's class addressed him. No wonder Joe had flown off the handle with him at the hotel.

Alistair only had moments to greet the other guests before the lot of them headed into the dining room. He was grateful to be separated from Lady Matilda, though it meant he was seated next to a dowager countess who was infamous for her affairs and a timid ingénue who had only just come out and seemed overwhelmed by everything. Burbage was seated across the table from him. Alistair had a hard time deciding if that was a good or a bad thing.

"You seem awfully out of sorts this evening, my lord," the dowager on Alistair's right said to Burbage. "That is very out of character for you."

"I had a bit of unpleasantness with staff this morning," Burbage answered with a smile that didn't touch his eyes. "I had to sack my valet." His cold gaze snapped to Alistair. "Turns out he was a bloody sodomite."

Several of the ladies sitting within earshot of Burbage gasped. The ingénue to Alistair's left coughed so hard she had to reach for her serviette, then down a few large gulps of wine.

"Paul, there are ladies present," Lord Chisolm grumbled from the head of the table.

"My sincerest apologies, Father." Burbage nodded to his father, then met Alistair's eyes again. "It's just that I detest such perversion."

The hair on the back of Alistair's neck stood up. Burbage seemed to be daring him to agree or to contradict him. There was nothing Alistair could do but clear his throat, reach for his wine, and mutter, "Quite," before taking a long swig.

When he set his wine glass down, Burbage was still staring at him, calculation in his eyes. Alistair stared back, feigning confusion over the look. Playing innocent was a defense mechanism, but at the moment, it was necessary. There were far bigger things at stake than revelations about his personal life, and he owed it to Joe to fight for those things.

"I understand you have just returned from a trip," he began, still holding Burbage's gaze. "Was your trip a success?"

Burbage's mouth curved into a wry grin. "My business ventures are always a success, my lord," he said.

"Congratulations." Alistair nodded, fighting to keep his expression neutral as his mind scrambled for something to say that would trip Burbage into admitting his involvement with the missing children. The best he could come up with was, "What precisely are your business ventures?" It was feeble and far too obvious, so he rushed to add, "I am still not used to men of our situation engaging in business."

"Yes, it is a modern development that I heartily disapprove of," the dowager added. "Gentlemen of our class should confine themselves to government and leisure and leave business to the other classes." She tilted her nose up and sniffed.

"I believe that not everyone's financial situation allows for the same life of leisure it once did, my lady," Alistair said.

Burbage laughed. "I have no problem with that. My financial situation is beyond sound." He reached for his wine. "No, my business speculations are purely for entertainment. One might call it a little pet project that has been in the family for generations."

Alistair's breath caught in his throat. Something about the statement struck him, struck a memory he couldn't quite put his finger on. Burbage was a little too sly, a little too smarmy about the whole thing. But Alistair didn't have a chance to press the man further. The next course was served, Burbage was pulled into conversation by the woman seated next to him, and the dowager on Alistair's right launched into a discussion about the merits of a good marriage, all the while trying to wheedle a confession about his status with Lady Matilda out of him.

It was almost a relief when supper ended and the gentlemen retired to the billiard room for cigars and brandy.

"That Lady Carmichael is a bore," Darren commented to Alistair as they walked over to fetch brandies, referring to the dowager. "I felt terribly sorry for you when I saw who you were seated with."

"On the contrary," Alistair answered with a shrug. "It meant I had very little work to do to maintain the conversation."

Darren laughed and slapped his back.

"He'll have even less work to do if he goes through with this mad plan to marry my sister-in-law," Burbage said, striding over to join them, his usual haughty grin in place. "That is the plan, is it not?"

Alistair's nerves bristled. There had to be a way to get Burbage to confess to his involvement with the missing children, even if obtusely. "That does seem to be the way things are headed," he answered, standing taller as he faced Burbage.

"More's the pity," Burbage laughed, stepping past Alistair and Darren to help himself to brandy. "As your future brother-in-law, allow me to give you a piece of advice. The best way to navigate marriage to a Fairbanks woman is to keep your mouth shut and their legs spread."

Alistair nearly choked on the brandy he was in the process of swallowing. "I beg your pardon?" he croaked.

Burbage took a drink, flickering one eyebrow rakishly as he did, then said, "Let Matilda do all the talking she wants, but when it's just the two of you alone, fuck her hard and fuck her often, whether she wants it or not, to show her who's lord of the manor. It also has the advantage of getting a shrew with child so they have something else to keep them quiet."

Disgust poured through Alistair, leaving him speechless and, unfortunately, too shocked to formulate a way to get the information he needed from the man. It was enough to make him wonder if Burbage had deliberately shocked him to throw him off-balance.

"I say, that's a bit extreme, isn't it?" Darren asked with a nervous laugh.

"Not at all," Burbage said with a shrug. "What is a woman for if not to please her husband and give him children?"

"Women are capable of a great deal more than that," Alistair managed to say.

Burbage laughed. "Of course, *you* would say that," he sneered.

A thread of panic joined the outrage pulsing through Alistair, but it was Darren who asked, "What is that supposed to mean?"

Burbage's brow flew up and he grinned as though

attending some sort of comedic entertainment. "You mean you don't know about your dear brother?"

Sweat broke out on Alistair's back. He was certain his face had flushed, but he prayed anyone looking at him, particularly Darren, would think it was anger.

"He's as meek as a lamb," Burbage went on with a laugh. "Everyone knows that he's destined to be brow-beaten by whatever lady is unfortunate enough to marry him. Which appears to be my sister-in-law."

Alistair couldn't tell if Burbage was toying with him or if he truly didn't know what he was. "Just because I treat women with respect and admiration doesn't make me a lamb," he said, assuming the best, but staying on his guard.

"We were raised to be better men than that," Darren added, shifting to stand shoulder to shoulder with Alistair in solidarity.

Burbage huffed a laugh. "Raised by a lunatic."

"You leave our father out of this," Darren hissed.

Alistair rested a hand on his arm to stop him from attacking Burbage.

"Your father will be out of it permanently before too long," Burbage sniffed, then took a long drink of brandy. When he finished, he set his tumbler carelessly on the table. "But enough of this feud. Our families are to be intimately joined soon. We should be friends."

Alistair would rather have died than befriend Burbage, but he held his tongue.

Once again, Darren was the outspoken one. "A

connection through marriage is hardly an intimate bond," he said. "I see no need for our families to have anything to do with each other."

"I suspect you see very little." Burbage smirked.

"I've seen quite a bit," Alistair said, narrowing his eyes at Burbage. If he was going to take a chance and call the man out, he had to get it over with. "Where have you been this past week?"

"My whereabouts are none of your concern," Burbage snapped, tensing.

"Brighton, perhaps?" Alistair asked.

Dark wariness filled Burbage's expression, but it was replaced within seconds by a snide grin that chilled Alistair's blood. "Nowhere near the place," Burbage answered, then rushed on with, "You wouldn't happen to know of a competent valet looking for a position, would you? I've been caught in the lurch after being forced to dismiss that filthy sodomite this morning." He crossed his arms and stared challengingly at Alistair.

"I wouldn't know," Alistair said, fighting to stay cool in spite of the sweat trickling down his back. He caught Darren staring at him out of the corner of his eye, a puzzled frown creasing his brow.

"Where did you find your valet?" Burbage asked on, an infernal light in his eyes as he glanced between Alistair and Darren before settling a vicious look on Alistair.

"I don't have a valet," Alistair answered.

Darren flinched but, blessedly, remained silent.

"I wager you will have soon," Burbage laughed.

Alistair hated everything about the conversation. He hated the insinuations Burbage was making, the suspicion that clouded Darren's expression, and worst of all, the fact that he was no closer to discovering where Burbage had been or what he had been up to than when he'd arrived. He was utterly on the back foot, and there didn't seem to be anything he could do about it.

Before he could scramble for a way to salvage the situation, the Eccles's butler strode discreetly into the room and up to Burbage's side. He whispered something in Burbage's ear. For a split second, Burbage's expression betrayed surprise and possibly annoyance.

"Dammit," Burbage hissed as the butler leaned away from him. "Tell them I'll be there as soon as I can."

"Very good, my lord." The butler bowed, backed up a few steps, then turned to leave the room.

"Gentlemen," Burbage said, thumping Alistair's arm, "it has been a pleasure crossing swords with you this evening, but if you will excuse me, a rather pressing engagement I had planned for later in the week seems to have been moved to this evening." He nodded to Darren, sent Alistair a teasing smirk, then marched swiftly out of the room.

Alistair's heart thundered against his ribs. He had no doubt at all that the engagement Burbage was referring to, the one that would take place that night instead of later in the week, was whatever exchange had been supposed to happen on Thursday night at the docks. Burbage's contacts must have been alerted to the fact that someone was onto their game. Alistair had to reach Joe and tell him as soon as possible. He had to let David and Lionel know, and Officer Wrexham.

"Excuse me," he hissed, attempting to step past Darren.

Darren caught his arm, holding him to the spot. "What in the devil is going on?" he asked in a tight, hushed voice.

Alistair hesitated, studying his brother's frustrated expression. There simply wasn't any way he could reveal so much as a shred of what was really going on. "Burbage is up to no good," he said. "I have reason to believe his business endeavors are criminal in nature. I've been working with some people to discover—"

"That's not what I'm talking about," Darren growled, staring so hard at Alistair that it felt as though knives were piercing him. "What is going on with that valet?"

It took everything Alistair had to continue to meet his brother's eyes. "I can explain," he said, bristling with anxious energy. "But not now."

He tried again to leave, but Darren wouldn't let go of his arm. "Alistair," he said, his tone warning. "Are you—" The question was plain as day in his eyes, but he couldn't bring himself to ask it.

Alistair let out a breath, feeling as though the foundations of his life were crumbling. "There isn't time to discuss it now. I have to act against Burbage and his plans while I still can."

The two brothers stared at each other for a long,

tense moment before Darren let out a breath and let go of Alistair's arm. As soon as he did, Alistair shot forward, ignoring the attempts of the other men in the room to engage him in conversation as he marched through the room and into the hall. He had to find Joe and let him know what was going on. For more reasons than Burbage. The storm they had been hoping to avoid was about to break.

CHAPTER 17

The Bevan house was oddly quiet after the turmoil and rush of the offices of Dandie & Wirth and the manner in which Alistair had brought Joe home and left him there. Joe had helped Alistair dress for dinner as best he could, but once Alistair was gone, he couldn't help but feel abandoned in a place where he knew no one and hadn't been introduced. The footman had informed the butler and housekeeper of his hiring, but that didn't stop the startled looks Joe got when he found his way downstairs to introduce himself to his new fellow staff members.

It was surreal and unsettling. There wasn't a spare bedroom for him among the servants' rooms at the top of the house. Joe insisted he would be fine sleeping in Alistair's dressing room until other arrangements could be made, knowing that wasn't where he would end up sleeping at all. Everyone from Joe to the butler to the hall boy found the arrangement and Joe's sudden presence in the house awkward and vaguely wrong.

After a meal eaten in painful silence with the rest of the staff, Joe made the excuse of familiarizing himself with Alistair's wardrobe and ventured back upstairs. But hiding away in Alistair's room, waiting for his lover to come home, felt just as strange as loitering below stairs with a dozen people he didn't know.

In the end, his restlessness propelled him to walk through the house, familiarizing himself with the layout, and his wandering brought him into a cozy family parlor where Lord Winslow sat, reading a book by the fire. As soon as Joe stepped into the room, Lord Winslow glanced up, then blinked.

"Good heavens. What are you doing here?" he asked, removing his reading glasses and closing his book.

"Your son, Lord Farnham, hired me as valet, my lord," Joe explained. "It was all rather sudden, and I still haven't quite gotten my bearings. I was investigating the house. I didn't realize anyone was in this room. I can leave, if you'd prefer."

"Not at all, not at all." Lord Winslow gestured to the ottoman beside his chair. Joe winced internally at being invited to sit like a child, but he crossed the room and took a seat all the same, if only because he knew Alistair's father was ill and fragile. "You were a great help to me at Lord Chisolm's ball," he said. "I didn't thank you properly."

"No thanks are necessary, my lord," Joe said. "It was my pleasure to be of assistance."

"Thanks are always necessary," Lord Winslow corrected him. "Kindness is a rare gift, as I well know. And I'm glad my son hired you away from that villain, Burbage."

Joe smiled, lowering his head slightly. "To tell you the truth, my lord, I am as well." Oddly enough, he had to fight the urge to confess more to Lord Winslow. Something about the man touched his heart and made him want to be as honest as possible. Perhaps it was because he saw so much of Alistair in the man.

"Good men should stick together," Lord Winslow went on. "It pained me to think of you mired in the filth that Chisolm and Burbage wallow in."

Joe's compassionate smile tightened at the statement. He felt as though someone had lit a match in his thoughts. "What do you know of Lord Chisolm and Lord Burbage's dealings, my lord? If you don't mind my asking."

"I don't mind at all," Lord Winslow said. He set his book on the table beside him and adjusted the blanket that was draped over his legs. "The entire Eccles family is as black as coal. Always have been. They're slave-traders, every one."

Joe was familiar with Lord Winslow's delusion, but at that moment, he didn't seem deluded at all. "Do you mean they built their family's wealth on the slave trade in the eighteenth century?" Joe asked, scooting closer to the man and resting his elbows on his knees as he waited for an answer.

"Yes, they did that," Lord Winslow said. "But the trade never stopped."

"The slave trade was made illegal generations ago, my lord," Joe reminded him.

Lord Winslow snorted. "Legal, illegal, it doesn't matter to those Eccleses. And it doesn't matter to the devils who see innocent souls as theirs to use in whatever black-hearted way they see fit."

Joe's pulse quickened. "My sister was a maid at Eccles House. She went missing last year. That's why I came to London from Leeds, to find out what happened to her."

Lord Winslow let out a sad sigh. "If that is the case, then we can only hope God is watching out for the poor girl."

"Do you have any idea where she might be?" Joe leaned closer to the man, placing a hand on his knee.

"I wish I did, my boy." Lord Winslow patted Joe's hand. "I've been trying to discover exactly what sort of evil that family is involved in and to bring an end to it, but they are clever, as devils often are."

"Anything you can tell me would be of help," Joe said.

"If only my mind were what it once was." Lord Winslow sank back into his chair looking as feeble as ever. "As Hamlet said, I am but mad north-northwest. When the wind is southerly, I know a hawk from a hand saw. Unfortunately for me, the wind is north-northwest more and more these days."

He lapsed into a contemplative silence that Joe didn't feel right breaking, no matter how important the information trapped in the man's head might be. It was a strange sort of comfort to him to know that Alistair's father wasn't as mad as everyone seemed to think he was. Or, if he was indeed mad, that the spark of the man Lord Winslow had once been hadn't gone out entirely.

"Would you like me to read to you, my lord?" Joe asked at length.

Lord Winslow roused himself from his contemplation and smiled. "That would be lovely," he said.

He handed Joe his book and pointed out where he'd stopped reading. Joe scanned the page quickly, then read in as soothing a voice as he could manage. He'd read to his younger siblings before leaving home, and entertaining an increasingly drowsy Lord Winslow the same way stirred every sort of nostalgia that Joe could imagine.

Time passed, and just as Joe was about to check whether Lord Winslow had fallen asleep or whether he was merely listening with his eyes closed, a door opened and closed somewhere toward the front of the house and hurried footsteps rushed down the hall. Alistair sailed right past the parlor doorway before skidding to a stop and rushing into the room.

For a moment, his expression was all surprise. When it settled into an anxious frown, he said, "Burbage

received word that an important meeting he had sched-
uled for later in the week has been moved to tonight."

Joe jerked around to stare up at Alistair in alarm.
Lord Winslow opened his eyes, proving that he was
awake after all. Alistair glanced between the two of them,
looking as though he didn't know what to do.

"Wirth needs to know about this as soon as possible,"
Joe said, standing and setting the book aside.

Alistair nodded in agreement, shoving a hand
through his hair. "I think we both know what is about to
transpire."

"We do." Joe stepped away from Lord Winslow and
went to meet Alistair. The panic in Alistair's eyes felt like
a knife in his gut. His instinct to comfort Alistair in every
way was almost overwhelming. Alistair might have been
educated and capable, but his heart was too tender for the
evil they were facing.

"Perhaps you could summon one of the footmen to
help me up to bed?" Lord Winslow asked, attempting to
push himself out of his chair and stand. The fruitlessness
of his efforts was difficult for Joe to watch.

"Certainly, my lord." Joe smiled at Lord Winslow,
sent Alistair a brief look, then marched out into the hallway. A footman was waiting nearby. Alistair was already
helping his father out of the chair when they returned.

"Your father knows more than you've given him
credit for," Joe whispered to Alistair as they watched the
footman lead Lord Winslow out of the room.

"He does?" Alistair's reply was slow and heavy as he

watched his father leave. He then turned to Joe. The pain of watching a man he'd likely spent his whole life looking up to was vivid on his face.

Joe rested a hand on Alistair's arm. "His mind might be slipping, but it's not gone entirely. He's known all along what Burbage and Chisolm are up to."

"I should have listened to him," Alistair said in a haunted voice, shaking his head. "I've had my suspicions about the things he's been saying for weeks now. But it's been such a long, slow decline that I've grown used to writing off the things Father says as symptoms of his illness. I shouldn't have dismissed the things he's said as the ravings of a madman."

"You weren't to know." Joe gripped both of Alistair's arms, forcing him to meet his eyes. "From everything you've told me, his claims have sounded outrageous. You are not to blame for assuming they were baseless."

"But I should have—"

"And besides," Joe cut him off. "He doesn't know any more than we know about who else is involved in this modern slave trade or how to stop them. Listening to him sooner wouldn't have changed things."

"I'm a terrible son," Alistair hissed, his miserable heart on his sleeve, as he lowered his head in shame. "All I ever wanted to do was my duty to him, to make him proud of me. I wanted to be the ideal son and heir, but I've failed him at every step. I haven't been man enough. I haven't married well and given him an heir. I haven't even listened to him when he was trying to tell me something desperately important."

"You are who you are, Alistair," Joe told him, resting a hand on the side of his hot face. "And I would venture that you've been the most amazing son to him that a man could ask for. You've cared for him. You've loved him and sheltered him from the cruelty of the world. You've stood by him when so many other sons would have abandoned him as a lost cause. Everything else, the duty and the marriage and heirs and all that, it's inconsequential compared to the way you've loved him. Even I, though I haven't been part of your life for that long, can see that."

"I don't know what I would do without you," Alistair whispered.

"You won't have to find out," Joe reassured him.

He hesitated for only a second before leaning into him and kissing him with all the bottomless depth of emotion in his heart. Alistair was a good man, the best Joe had ever known. It didn't matter what sacrifices he had to make. They wouldn't be sacrifices at all if the two of them could fight their way through life together. He sank every bit of that determination and that love into his kiss as Alistair parted his lips to allow him in. Joe slipped his tongue alongside Alistair's, blending passion with devotion to show Alistair, beyond a shadow of a doubt, just how much he loved him.

"Good God. What is the meaning of this?"

A deep shout from the parlor doorway ripped Joe and Alistair apart. They turned to see Alistair's brother and

Lady Matilda standing in the doorway, their faces masks of shock.

"Darren," Alistair said, pivoting to face his brother but not stepping away from Joe.

His brother marched fully into the room, eyes wide with outrage as he glanced between Alistair and Joe. "Is this what Burbage was attempting to hint at this evening?" he demanded.

Lady Matilda followed him into the room, though her steps were much more cautious and she looked as though she might be sick.

Joe was caught between wanting to stand up for Alistair and the deference that had been ingrained in him.

Alistair wasn't as stuck. He grabbed Joe's hand. "I see no point in denying things now," he said. "Joe is my lover."

Joe's brow shot straight to his hairline at the speed and surety of Alistair's confession.

"Your what?" Alistair's brother boomed.

"You heard me." Alistair squared his shoulders and faced his brother bravely. "He's my lover and has been for some time now."

"And you dared to bring him into our house?" his brother shouted.

"Keep your voice down," Alistair hissed. "And yes, I did. I love Joe and I want him near me."

"Disgusting," Lady Matilda hissed, sinking into the chair closest to her. "I refuse to marry a man who is mired in such wickedness."

"I never asked you to, my lady," Alistair told her with kindness in his voice that Joe never could have managed, given the circumstances.

Lady Matilda stared up at Alistair with an oddly heartbroken expression.

"This is outrageous," Alistair's brother continued to rage. "I never would have thought you were capable of this sordid kind of perversion." He flung a hand toward Alistair and Joe and made a sour face.

"Love is not a perversion," Alistair insisted. "You may not understand it, but my feelings toward Joe are most certainly love."

"As are my feelings for Alistair," Joe added, though he didn't think his input would help the situation at all.

Indeed, Alistair's brother sneered at him as though he were something dirty and soiled. "Get out of this house at once," he spat.

"No," Alistair answered, gripping Joe's hand harder. "Joe will stay right where he is."

"I'll tell Father and Mother," his brother threatened. "They'll be so disgusted they'll disown you."

"Then they disown me," Alistair said with surprising calm. "And you'll become the heir." He paused, glancing to Lady Matilda, who continued to watch the scene as though witnessing something horrific. "You're more or less the heir already," Alistair went on, letting out a breath as he turned back to his brother. "I tried being a dutiful son and marrying as I should, but it's no use. Not

241

when I've found the man I wish to spend the rest of my life with."

An odd blossom of emotion erupted in Joe's chest at the ill-timed confession of love and fidelity. It felt wrong for him to so much as blush at that moment.

"You're sick," Alistair's brother grumbled, pacing a few steps across the room and back. "Perhaps there is a cure."

"There is no cure," Alistair assured him. "And there is no time to debate inconsequential things when children's lives are at stake."

"This is not inconsequential," Alistair's brother shouted as he turned to storm back to Alistair.

"What children?" Lady Matilda asked, pressing a hand to her chest.

Alistair didn't back down from his brother's charge, but it was clear to Joe that the force of his brother's anger intimidated him.

"Several children have gone missing," Joe said, taking control of what truly mattered. He let go of Alistair's hand and moved closer to Lady Matilda. "The hall boy and scullery maid from Eccles House, for one, and my sister, Lily. She disappeared from Eccles House several months ago."

"She probably ran off," Lady Matilda said, still visibly unsettled. "Staff runs off all the time."

Joe shook his head. "Not these children. And there are more, all across London. There's an investigation ongoing, spearheaded by the solicitors of Dandie &

Wirth. We believe we have enough information at this point to determine that there is a...a ring of kidnappers and those who traffic in human cargo."

"Trafficking in children?" The color drained from Lady Matilda's face.

"And your lot is involved, no doubt," Alistair's brother hissed, breaking away from his staring battle with Alistair. "You're all a bunch of filthy pedophiles."

"No, we are not," Joe insisted, sickened at the idea, but knowing how common the notion was. "Alistair and I have been doing everything in our power to catch the perpetrators and bring them to justice, and to retrieve the children."

"For your own ends, no doubt," Alistair's brother said with a grimace.

"How dare you speak such filth in our home," Alistair growled, glaring at his brother. "Do you really think me capable of harming a child?"

"I didn't think you were capable of buggering a valet, until I saw it with my own eyes," his brother snapped.

"It was a kiss," Alistair said, raising his voice. "A much-needed kiss at that. The world is not divided into angelic and sordid. Or do you expect me to laugh off the way you dallied with that maid, Rosie, last year until she was forced to quit?"

Joe's brow shot up. Alistair's brother glanced quickly away, his face going red. Lady Matilda's mouth dropped open before snapping shut as the full impact of what must have happened hit her.

"None of us is perfect, Darren," Alistair went on. "You can rail away at me for being who I am later. For now, the lives of children are at stake. Burbage is deeply involved in the disappearance of these children and—"

"Burbage?" Lady Matilda squeaked, clutching a hand to her chest. "No. No, no, no. It can't be. We were just at his house."

"He and his father are deeply involved," Joe informed her, trying to soften the blow, even though it was impossible. "We found evidence in his study proving as much."

"And the exchange that we thought would happen on Thursday is, in fact, happening tonight," Alistair went on. "We need to cease this pointless madness and go tell David Wirth and Officer Wrexham what is happening immediately."

Alistair nodded to Joe, then started across the room to the doorway. Joe began to follow, but when Alistair was stopped by his brother, he stopped too.

"You're not going anywhere," Alistair's brother said. "I'm not letting you out of my sight."

"Unhand me." Alistair shook out of his brother's grip.

"I want that man gone from my house immediately." His brother pointed at Joe.

"Joe stays with me," Alistair insisted.

"I will not have your sort of perversion under my roof," his brother argued.

"This is my house as much as it is yours," Alistair insisted. "We don't have time for this. It's already late. Burbage left his house before I did. And we still need to determine the location of whatever exchange is about to take place."

"I won't let you go anywhere until that man is out in the street where he belongs." His brother held firm.

Lady Matilda burst into tears where she sat, shaking her head and burying her face in her hands. Joe would have done something to comfort her if he thought any sort of gesture would be welcome.

"Would you throw me out in the street as well?" Alistair asked his brother.

"If I have to," his brother answered.

"I'll go," Joe said, holding up a hand to end the argument. "I'll go of my own accord."

"No." Alistair stepped closer to him, determination mingling with desperation in his expression. "You don't have to go."

"I'm causing more trouble here than I am doing good," Joe told him in a frustrated voice. "We have to focus on what is important first."

"You are important," Alistair insisted, resting a hand on the side of Joe's face. His brother let out a disgusted hiss, but Alistair ignored it. "Nothing is more important to me than you."

"I understand." Joe rested his hand over Alistair's for a moment before moving it away from his face. "And you are everything to me." He darted a glance to the side. "But we've bungled this a bit."

"To say the least," Alistair agreed through clenched teeth.

"I'll go to Wirth and Lionel, tell them what's happened," Joe said in a fast whisper. "They offered to find me a place to stay before, and I'm certain that offer still stands."

"Let me know where it is as soon as you can," Alistair said.

"You will do no such thing," his brother roared. "The two of you will never see each other again. Alistair will marry Lady Matilda as planned and—"

"He will do no such thing," Lady Matilda snapped, standing. "I couldn't bear it. No decent woman could bear it."

"Then he'll marry someone else," Alistair's brother said. "And soon. Before rumors begin to circulate."

Alistair let out a breath and rubbed a hand over his face. "If you're going, you'd better go," he told Joe. "Our only chance of helping those children is if one of us reaches them before it's too late."

Joe nodded, lowering his hand to squeeze Alistair's arms. He leaned close to Alistair's ear and said, "I'm leaving my things in your room so I have to come back for them."

The barest hint of a smile touched Alistair's lips before his expression turned grave again. "Understood."

Joe stepped away from him, glaring with undisguised venom at Alistair's brother. It didn't matter how high above him the man was, his actions that evening were unforgivable. "If you truly cared about your brother," Joe said, "you'd understand when he's found happiness, and you'd let him have that instead of forcing him to be miserable." He took a few steps toward the doorway before turning back and adding, "You're going to win everything in this situation anyhow. The least you could let Alistair have is me."

He didn't wait to see what Alistair's brother's reaction was. With his heart aching with frustration and uncertainty, Joe marched out of the room and away from the man he loved.

CHAPTER 18

*D*eep, roiling anger, like magma beneath the surface of a volcano, was not a feeling Alistair was accustomed to. But from the moment Darren had forced Joe out of his house, through an interminable night of waiting to hear if Joe had been able to contact David and Lionel to intercept whatever mission Burbage was on, and for the next few days when word came that nothing had been discovered or thwarted that night, all Alistair felt was anger.

"Why are you so sour when we're at a children's concert," his sister, Beth, whispered to him as they mingled among the guests at Bardess Mansion.

Alistair sent Beth a wary look. She had returned from the country only that morning, which meant she'd missed the family melodrama that had unfolded the night Darren and Lady Matilda discovered him with Joe. "I'm not sour," he lied.

Beth pursed her lips and hugged his arm as they strolled around the ballroom, which had been set up as a concert hall. Two separate choirs of barely-presentable children were clustered near a tiny stage at one end of the room. One choir was overseen by a group of nuns in threadbare habits. The other was being kept in order by an attractive young man with spectacles and, if Alistair wasn't mistaken, Maxwell Hillsboro was hovering nearby as though eager to help. Alistair took a second look at the man with spectacles. Hillsboro had good taste.

"This is because Lady Matilda broke with you, isn't it," Beth whispered, leaning closer to Alistair with a sympathetic smile.

"Certainly not," Alistair snapped, his mood sinking. "There was never an understanding between me and Lady Matilda."

"I don't believe that for a moment," Beth said, nodding to an acquaintance as more people entered the room. "When last I heard, Mama was certain you'd be making an announcement any day now." She paused, turning to face him fully with a frown, and said, "That's the only reason I can think of that Mama would be so angry with you now. She was looking forward to a wedding."

Alistair couldn't think of an answer to Beth's implied question. All he could do was arch one eyebrow. Darren had deemed the truth about Alistair's affections too outrageous to tell their father, but that hadn't stopped him from blurting the whole thing to their mother when she had come downstairs to ask what all the shouting was about and to tell them to stop so their father could sleep. The most awkward part of the whole, messy revelation was that their mother didn't seem surprised at all to learn of Alistair's true nature. That hadn't stopped her from upbraiding him for failing to keep his personal business to himself and to do his duty to his family.

"You're never going to be happy until you tell me why our family is suddenly at sixes and sevens," Beth said as they continued on their stroll around the room. Many of the guests were already claiming seats, even though the benefit concert wasn't due to begin for several more minutes. "You've never kept anything from me in the past."

"Perhaps I should have," Alistair sighed. "Or perhaps I never had any secrets worth keeping in the past."

"So you are keeping a secret." Beth's eyes lit up and she grinned at him as though he were about to hand her a bag of sweets.

"I'm not telling you anything, Beth," Alistair said. "How old are you again? Barely twenty?"

"Twenty is old enough to be let in on shocking family secrets," Beth informed him in a whisper as she leaned closer.

The mischief in her eyes sent an itch down Alistair's back. She knew. She had to. She wouldn't be staring at him as though he'd stolen biscuits from the kitchen and she were about to tell Father on him if she didn't.

"Isn't that Lord Norton over there?" He nodded

across the room to one of the ridiculous young men Beth always seemed to moon over at balls.

"You know that servants talk, don't you, dear brother?" Beth said, ignoring his attempt at a diversion.

Alistair stopped near one of the ballroom's French doors and hissed out a breath. He glanced around to make certain no one was near enough to overhear them, then faced her. "You obviously have something to say, so please say it."

"I want to meet this valet of yours," she said, eyes bright. "I wasn't there either of the times Mama, Father, and Darren met him."

"It's out of the question," Alistair hissed.

"So you intend to keep him locked away in some sort of den of love, do you?" Her mouth twitched into a saucy grin.

"Mind your tongue," Alistair scolded her.

"Is he handsome?"

"It's none of your concern."

"I bet he's handsome."

"You shouldn't even know about these things, let alone speak of them."

"But I do."

"How?" He narrowed his eyes, wondering if they'd kept a close enough watch on who Beth's friends were.

Beth shrugged. "I'm a modern woman." When Alistair stared disapprovingly at her, she went on with, "Don't give me that look. You're the one bedding another man."

"I'm not—" Alistair started, but huffed out a breath. In fact, he was. "You shouldn't know about these things," he repeated.

"It's too late for that," she said, leaning closer to him, her eyes glittering with mirth. "I want to meet him."

"No, you can't."

"I can and I will. Particularly if you intend to keep him."

She had a point there. He couldn't very well hide Joe from her if he expected to spend the rest of his life with him. "There are other things going on at the moment that require my and Joe's attention."

"His name is Joe? How sweet," Beth said, the light of romance in her eyes.

"Why are you not condemning me like Darren has?" Alistair asked, surprising himself with the question.

Beth shrugged again. "Darren is a stick in the mud traditionalist. I told you, I'm a modern woman."

Alistair shook his head.

"And Rebecca's brother is a homosexual as well," she went on in the quietest of whispers, referring to her closest friend. Her smile brightened. "I feel as though I have joined some sort of prized, secret organization now."

Alistair rolled his eyes. "I'm glad my peculiarities have enhanced your social life."

Beth had the nerve to laugh. "I love you, Alistair. You're my brother. I will always love you, no matter what Darren says or how old-fashioned Mama is."

Her outpouring of support touched Alistair so deeply

and so suddenly that he was in real danger of showing too much emotion in public. He covered the potential embarrassment by clearing his throat and squaring his shoulders, then offering Beth his arm to continue escorting her around the room. "I love you too, Beth. And it means the world to me to hear you say you won't abandon me."

"Never," she said. "No matter what Father and Mama or Darren say."

Alistair's throat squeezed with sentiment. If Joe's little sister was half as spectacular as Beth was, it was no wonder the man was willing to turn over every stone in Christendom to find her.

His burst of warm emotion was quelled all too suddenly as he spotted Lady Matilda marching toward him from the ballroom's entrance. Alistair stopped, his stomach tying in knots.

"Should I prepare for battle?" Beth asked, leaning closer to him.

"I don't know," Alistair answered truthfully.

Lady Matilda's expression was a mask of determination as she ignored everyone who tried to speak to her as she approached Alistair. Alistair could practically see the whispers of curiosity turning into gossip as more people glanced over to see what would happen.

"I need to speak with you," Lady Matilda said, marching right past Alistair and Beth and gesturing for them to follow.

Alistair exchanged a look with Beth before following. Lady Matilda charged on to one of the French doors, unlocking it and stepping out into a cold, dormant garden. One of the footmen attending the ballroom hurried after them, pausing in the doorway as though he didn't know whether to tell them off for going somewhere out of bounds or to guard against anyone else joining them. Blessedly, he appeared to choose the latter.

"I still think you're an abomination," Lady Matilda began, whipping to face him when the three of them were alone.

"I beg your pardon." Beth defended him, looking like a wildcat about to attack.

Alistair rested a hand on her arm to still her. "I'm sorry if I have hurt or disappointed you in any way, Lady Matilda," Alistair said.

"I have half a mind to spread word of what you are to everyone I know," Lady Matilda went on, tilting her chin up and staring down her nose at Alistair.

"You wouldn't dare," Beth hissed. "If you do, I'll tell everyone you're nothing but a fortune-hunting—"

"Beth, hush," Alistair stopped her. He saw more than simple disgust in Lady Matilda's face. She was anxious, upset about something other than his habits. His gut told him she'd taken him aside for more than just a dressing down. "If there is anything I can do to make this situation less painful for you, my lady, I will."

Lady Matilda's expression tightened, but more with regret than fury. "It would be easier if you weren't such a gentleman," she said, so quietly Alistair almost didn't hear.

"The others are always so—" She paused. "But you have always been—" Again, she stopped, shaking her head and letting her shoulders drop. "It seems unfair somehow."

"Good men are out there. Men who will appreciate you for all that you are," Alistair said, praying it was the right thing.

Lady Matilda nodded once, lifted her head to meet his eyes, and swallowed. "Burbage is a monster," she rushed on. "My sister has told me things." She turned suddenly to the side, pressing her gloved fingers to her mouth and looking as though she might burst into tears.

A moment later, she recovered, took a breath, and went on. "There is a property on Batcliff Cross Docks."

Every nerve in Alistair's body jolted to life as she spoke.

"I don't know what happens there, only that Burbage is involved," Lady Matilda went on. "Katherine, my sister, has heard him and his father speak of it frequently. She's seen things she's had to pretend she didn't see. When you mentioned the children—" Her face crumpled into grief and pain. She clapped a hand to her mouth, unable to go on.

"Understood," Alistair said in the gentlest voice he could muster, stepping forward and resting a hand on Lady Matilda's arm. "I'll leave at once to tell the men working on this case where to look. In the meantime, Beth will see to you."

"I will?" Beth asked uncertainly.

Alistair sent her the most serious look the two of them had ever exchanged. "You will," he said.

Beth nodded, clearly confused, and slipped to Lady Matilda's side.

"I'll send word if anything happens," Alistair said, turning and marching toward the door to the ballroom.

The footman opened it for him with a puzzled look, but Alistair didn't have time to explain. "See to Lady Matilda," he said before hurrying on.

"THERE HAS TO BE SOMETHING MORE WE CAN DO," Joe grumbled as he paced through the heart of David and Lionel's office. "Something better than sitting here."

"If criminals were transparent and easy to catch, there wouldn't be any," Lionel told him from his seat behind the desk. He shot Joe an impatient look as he worked, as if Joe were in danger of wearing a hole in his carefully-selected carpet.

"We're doing everything we can," David assured him, entering the room from his office and depositing a file on Lionel's desk. "Patrick has an entire taskforce within the Metropolitan Police helping him with this investigation. He has the ear of Assistant Commissioner Jack Craig, Lord Clerkenwell."

"If anyone can get anything done in the Met Police, it's Clerkenwell," Lionel said, reaching for the folder.

Joe knew they were right, but he hated every moment that he sat idle all the same. Nothing seemed to be going right. He hadn't seen Alistair for days. He'd managed to send one note, informing Alistair that Lionel had found a temporary flat for him in Earl's Court, but the second note he'd sent was returned. Alistair's brother had to have something to do with that. The man was an annoyance more than anything else, but at the moment, Joe didn't need any more annoyances.

"Has anyone been able to uncover anything about Adler?" he asked, pacing his way back to Lionel's desk.

"No," Lionel answered, looking as though his luminous blue eyes might actually shoot daggers at Joe if he didn't stop his incessant questioning.

"No," David repeated, much more patient. "We really are doing everything we can."

They were, but it wasn't enough. Toby and Emma were out there somewhere. Lily was out there somewhere. He believed that with all his heart. They needed him. They needed action, not endless waiting.

He was on the verge of trying Lionel's patience and risking his wrath with more questions when the office door banged open and Alistair flew in. The sudden burst of joy at the sight of him made Joe dizzy.

"Thank God," he said, charging across the room to greet him.

Alistair opened his arms for a brief embrace, but was too tense for more. "Batcliff Cross Docks," he said, as breathless as if he'd ran the whole way there. Which he might have, given the state he was in.

"What?" David asked, rushing to join them in the center of the room.

Lionel left his desk work to meet them as well. "It's a smaller dock. Not a lot of important trade."

"Lady Matilda tells me her sister, Burbage's wife, has heard the location discussed before," Alistair went on.

Joe's pulse pounded. He had to fight the urge to run there immediately. "We need to go at once."

"I'll inform Wrexham," Lionel said, striding to the coat stand near the door and throwing on a fine, wool overcoat. He was out the door before Joe could think to go with him.

"We should all go," Joe said. "Time is of the essence."

"We don't know what we'll find there," David cautioned him. "Even if it's not one of the larger dock-yards, Batcliff Cross is more than one building. And we can't be sure we'll find anything. It's not Thursday yet on the one hand, and even if it was, we don't know whether Burbage was able to complete his business the other night or not."

"It's the best lead we've had in the case so far," Alistair argued.

"He's right," Joe agreed. "We're bound to find something if we search hard enough."

"It's better than standing around doing nothing," Alistair finished his thought.

Joe glanced to him, glowing with happiness just to be standing next to Alistair again, no matter how dire the circumstances. Together, they might actually be able to thwart whatever Burbage was up to.

"I'll get my coat," David said before disappearing into his office.

Joe turned to Alistair, grateful for a few seconds alone with him. "I've missed you," he said, surging into Alistair for a quick kiss.

Alistair kissed him in return, gripping Joe's arms as he did. There wasn't time for a more serious kiss, but the heartfelt buss was enough. "I feel like victory is within our reach," he said. "We'll find those children, find your sister, bring Burbage and his father to justice, and then we'll figure out how to build a life together."

"Every bit of that sounds amazing," Joe said, then stole another kiss. "And I'm not going to stop until we've ticked everything off that list."

"Neither am I," Alistair said.

Joe let go of him and crossed to the coat stand, retrieving his own coat as David came out of his office. The three of them darted out of the office, through the hall, and into the street. For the first time in days, Joe was filled with palpable confidence that justice would be served and he and Alistair would have a happy ending.

The feeling lasted all the way until they made it to the street and nearly ran headlong into Alistair's brother on the sidewalk in front of the office.

CHAPTER 19

*A*listair nearly tripped down the last stair from the building housing Dandie & Wirth to the pavement at the sight of Darren. Deep self-consciousness rushed through him, particularly as he could still feel Joe's kiss on his lips, but he pushed it away. He'd done nothing wrong.

Darren flinched at the sight of Alistair and Joe. "I didn't want to believe it was true, but now I see it with my own eyes," he said, resting his glare on Joe.

"What do you see?" Alistair crossed to stand in front of his brother, standing tall and defiant.

"A sick man and his disgusting lover," Darren spat. "Having some sort of rendezvous after being explicitly told that if he so much as thought of that man again—" he nodded to Joe, "he'd be disowned."

"That's not what this is," Alistair informed him.

"You deny that you sought out that man after I told you what would happen if you did?" Darren demanded.

"We don't have time for this." Joe strode forward to stand by Alistair's side. "We need to reach Batcliff Cross as soon as possible."

"And what is that?" Darren asked, looking as though he would strike Joe at any moment. "Some sort of sordid meeting spot for men like you?"

"It's a dock where we believe criminal activity has been taking place," Joe said.

"The only criminal activity I care about is what I see in front of me," Darren snapped at him.

"We truly don't have time for this," David cut in, coming down the stairs and walking past them. He gestured for Alistair and Joe to follow.

Alistair couldn't just ignore his brother, though, particularly when Darren asked, "And who is that? Is this whole repugnant affair between three of you or more?"

David stopped, turning back to Alistair and Joe impatiently, but for all the determination in his expression, it was as if he hadn't heard Darren's comment at all. It made Alistair wonder how often David had been the butt of those same sort of cruel comments.

"As I told you days ago, we have been tracking children who have gone missing," Alistair said. "We have only just received information—from Lady Matilda, no less—about where they might be."

"Lady Matilda deigned to speak to you?" Darren balked. The disbelief in his eyes went beyond disgust, giving Alistair reason to hope all was not lost between them.

"She cares about these children too, apparently," Alistair said. "But there isn't time to stand here chatting about the whole thing. Lives are at stake."

He marched past Darren, intending to follow Joe, who had joined David, but Darren grabbed his arm.

"How can I believe a word you say after you've lied to me all these years?" Darren asked.

"I never lied to you," Alistair said.

"Lies of omission are still lies," Darren said.

Alistair blew out an impatient breath. "What would you have done if I'd told you years ago? If I'd said something when I first realized who I was?"

Darren said nothing. He merely pressed his lips shut.

"Precisely," Alistair said as though he'd answered. "We need to find these children."

He turned to rush on, but was met with the sight of Lionel, Officer Wrexham, and another police officer alighting from a carriage that had pulled up several yards down the street.

"Another team is on their way to Batcliff Cross," Lionel said, stepping onto the sidewalk and approaching David and Joe, looking like an angel of vengeance.

"Who is that?" Darren asked, clearly arrested by Lionel's appearance.

"Your worst nightmare," Lionel answered, then turned back to David. "I took the liberty of discovering Burbage is not at home at the moment."

"How on earth did you have time to find that out?" Alistair asked, abandoning Darren for infinitely more important problems.

"Magic," Lionel answered in a deadpan, then backed toward the waiting carriage. "There should be enough room for all of us if we squeeze."

"We were lucky," Wrexham told David, glancing to Alistair and Joe as he started toward the carriage. "By chance, we spotted Burbage getting into a cab near Trafalgar Square as we drove through."

"Magic, eh?" Joe grinned.

"You don't think he could be heading to Batcliff Cross too, do you?" Alistair asked as Joe stepped up into the carriage.

"Not if he's smart," Wrexham answered.

"I'm going with you," Darren said, surprising them all as he marched up behind them.

Alistair whipped to face him with an incredulous look. "You're doing no such thing."

"Either you're lying and something sinister is going on between you all or you're not and lives are at stake," Darren said. "Either way, I want to see it with my own eyes."

"Why? So you can manufacture some new reason to have me disowned?" Alistair snapped. "I've already more or less given you everything. Do you want more?"

"I—" Darren pursed his lips and exhaled through his nose. "I want to help."

Alistair couldn't believe what he was hearing. He'd

never taken Darren for the meddling type. A little too aggressive sometimes, maybe. But not one to elbow his way in where he wasn't wanted. All the same, if it came down to some sort of confrontation at the dock, they might need his help.

"How did you get here?" Alistair asked with a frown.

"I drove." Darren nodded to what Alistair now recognized as one of their family carriages at the end of the street.

"Then make sure your driver keeps up."

"I'll go with him," Lionel offered, stepping down from the carriage he'd just gotten into, a look of pure mischief on his face. "That'll keep him on the straight and narrow." He swayed over to Darren's side, fixing him with a flirtatious look that was bound to rile Darren into a state of shock.

"You brought this on yourself," Alistair told his brother with a smirk, then lunged into the carriage where Joe, David, and the other police officer were waiting.

"I'd better ride with them," Wrexham told David with a knowing look, stepping back to join Lionel and Darren. Lionel looked ready to eat Darren, though which definition of that phrase Alistair couldn't tell. Wrexham would probably prevent some sort of murder from happening on the way to the docks.

They set off. Alistair's feeling of confidence, like they might actually be able to do something based on Lady Matilda's information, had been flattened by his brother's continued bull-headedness. It wasn't the feeling he wanted on his way to what could be one of the most important moments of his life.

"It will be all right," Joe told him from the seat across from him.

Alistair shot a sideways look to the officer seated next to him. There was no way to tell if the man was like them or if he had any understanding of the situation he found himself in, so he opted to stay quiet.

They all remained nearly silent as the carriage wound its way through London traffic to the dockyards east of the city. Alistair had few reasons to travel so far east and was amazed by the sheer volume of trade and shipping he could see out the dirty carriage window. Steel ships rose up above row after row of brick and stone warehouses. It was a far cry from the more patrician buildings of Mayfair, Westminster, and Kensington. The closer they got to the waterfront, the drabber the people around the carriage appeared. And yet, there was a steady resilience to them that made Alistair certain they were the backbone of everything he held dear.

He glanced across to Joe, who also studied the world outside of the carriage window, but without a hint of surprise or fascination in his eyes. The people around them were Joe's people. Or, at least, Joe had come from the same, hearty stock. There was something comforting in knowing that. The world was filled with men and women of strength and heart, people Alistair had never bothered to consider until then. There was so much more to existence than rigid social structures and fulfilling family duties. He could be a part of it. He and Joe could forge a whole new kind of life together in a place between class and birth. They could make a difference in the world.

By the time the carriage rocked to a stop, Alistair's confidence had returned.

"Lady Matilda didn't know anything more than that whatever Burbage is up to, he does it at Batcliff Cross," he said as he stepped down from the carriage after David.

"There are more buildings here than I thought there'd be," Joe said with a frown as he stepped down and looked around.

Alistair watched Darren's carriage pull up behind theirs and waited for his brother and the others to get out. The door opened almost immediately and Darren jumped down as though the devil himself were on his tail. And by the devil, he meant Lionel. Lionel climbed carefully out of the carriage, a smile as bright and impish as a sprite on his pale face.

"That was fun," he said, beaming even wider as he crossed the grubby street to join David.

"You behaved, I trust." David arched one eyebrow.

"Of course not." Lionel grinned. "Did you think I was going to behave myself when trapped in a carriage with a man like that?"

David rolled his eyes. Alistair caught the same, wary expression on Wrexham's face as he got out of the carriage and came to join them.

"This had better not be some sort of sick joke,"

Darren growled as he marched up to Alistair's side. He leaned in close enough to whisper, "That man should be hung for what he is."

"For your information, darling, I'm well hung," Lionel said, flickering an eyebrow at Darren.

Darren shot Lionel a look of murder, which Lionel returned with three times the threat. On any other day, Alistair would have enjoyed the spectacle. But not then. Especially not when a small team of policemen approached them from the far end of the street.

"Those are my men," Wrexham informed them before walking to meet the policemen.

Alistair fell in behind him, Joe rushing to match his steps. Whatever game Lionel was playing with Darren was forgotten as the two groups met halfway down the street.

"We found their lair," one of the new officers said.

Joe reached to grab Alistair's arm. He wore a look of desperate anticipation. Alistair's own heart pounded in expectation. "Did you find Toby and Emma?" he asked. "Or Lily?"

"We didn't find anyone," the officer said, his expression stern. "We were too late. According to one of the dock workers, there was a lot of activity there last night, but that was hours ago."

Joe swore under his breath, then whipped around to glare at Darren. "This is your fault. If you hadn't been so caught up in things that don't matter, we could have found them last night. We could have caught them."

Darren took a step back, his eyes wide with indignation.

"We didn't know where to look until Lady Matilda told me this morning," Alistair reminded Joe, holding him back from charging at Darren.

"If he hadn't been such an ass, she might have said something last night," Joe said.

Alistair couldn't argue with that. Neither could Darren, apparently. Darren's face fell.

"Never mind about that now," David said, taking charge. "What's done is done."

"We need to scour the area," Wrexham stepped up beside him. "Speak to anyone who might have seen or heard anything."

"Already done, sir," the officer said. He turned and gestured to one of his men. That man gestured into one of the buildings. A moment later, a third officer came out, leading a bedraggled woman who looked as though life had been cruel to her.

"This is Maude," the first officer explained. "She works on the docks."

Alistair had a sick feeling in his stomach at the sight of her, a feeling he didn't want to know what kind of work she did on the docks.

"Tell them what you know," the officer ordered her.

Poor Maude glanced at the collection of well-dressed men in front of her with fear in her eyes. She shook visibly and swayed on her spot, cowering back. Whatever the miserable woman's experience with men was, Alistair could tell it wasn't good.

It was Lionel who stepped forward, approaching her with a gentle smile and soft manners that were in direct contrast to the way he'd teased Darren. "Tell me, sweetheart. I won't let any of these big, bad men hurt you."

To Alistair's shock, Lionel's tactic worked. Maude took one look at him, his impossibly fine clothes, his suddenly effeminate movements, and his compassion-filled face, and burst into tears. "I won't never forget their crying," she said, flopping into Lionel's open arms as he reached to embrace her. "Those poor babies. They kept them locked up there for weeks on end. And then they took them all away last night. Poor things was begging for their mamas."

An acidic knot formed in Alistair's gut, but it was nothing to the look of horror that made Joe's face go pale. Alistair didn't care who was watching or what they would think, he looped his arm around Joe's back and held him close.

"Do you know where they went, sweeting?" Lionel asked Maude, his voice higher and softer than hers, as he stroked her greasy hair.

"They didn't know I was listening," Maude told him. "I hid in the shadows."

Alistair's back itched with impatience for her to tell them what they needed to know.

"That was very smart of you." Lionel continued to stroke her hair, the picture of patience. His voice was hypnotic and soothing as he went on with, "You've been very brave. Heaven will reward you for your help."

Maude blubbered and sniffed wetly against the shoulder of his expensive coat. "They said something about a China ship, *Nightingale*."

Wrexham instantly gestured toward one of his men. The officer all but sprinted into one of the nearby buildings. Alistair watched the door, his heart thudding in his chest. Joe's entire body was as tense as stone by his side. He caught the quick look Darren sent him before his brother went back to studying Lionel with utter confusion.

"That's exactly what we need to know, darling," Lionel continued to coo to Maude. "Thank you, from the bottom of our hearts. Now, wouldn't you like a nice cuppa and something to eat, love?" Maude nodded and sobbed, clinging to Lionel. "Why don't you go with Officer—"

"Jones, sir," the nearby officer said, as mesmerized by Lionel as Maude was.

"Go with Officer Jones. He'll take you to Lady Clerkenwell's house in Clerkenwell." He spoke to the officer, giving instructions. "Lady Clerkenwell will take good care of you."

"I don't want to go with him. He'll hurt me," Maude squeaked.

"I promise, he won't, love," Lionel said, facing her and taking her face in both hands. He leaned in and whispered something in her ear, then pulled back, kissing her lips softly and holding her gaze for several long seconds before letting her go.

Maude stepped back, her mouth open in awe. Officer Jones moved to rest a hand on her back before leading her off to an alley between the buildings. Maude continued to stare at Lionel as though she'd had a visitation from the Virgin Mary.

"What did you just do to her?" Darren asked with almost as much awe.

"I treated her with humanity," Lionel said, as steady and powerful as a monolith. "It's something you might want to try now and then."

The officer who had dashed into the building came out in just as much of a hurry. "The *Nightingale* is docked just a quarter mile from here, and she hasn't left yet."

His words shattered the spell that Lionel had cast over all of them. Alistair's pulse shot up once more as he glanced to Joe.

"There's no time to lose," Joe said, surging into action.

They didn't bother with carriages. A quarter mile was nothing, and the traffic on the dock would have taken time to get around. They dashed through Batcliff Cross, dodging dockworkers and sailors as they went about their business. Alistair's feeling that they were finally getting somewhere turned to panic for a moment as one of the massive ships began to slowly move, tugging away from its dock. He prayed it wasn't the *Nightingale*.

His prayers were answered.

"It's this one, sir," the officer who had come out of the office shouted to Wrexham as they turned a corner to sprint down a long wharf.

Alistair knew nothing of dockyards and shipping, but he was fairly certain from the way roughly-dressed workers were untying ropes as thick as his arm and gesturing to crew on the deck of the huge ship that the *Nightingale* was getting ready to leave.

"Stop what you're doing at once," Wrexham shouted to the workers. "This ship isn't going anywhere until its searched."

"By whose authority?" a grizzled, older dockworker in a thick, wool coat called from the end of the wharf.

"By her majesty's police," Wrexham called back.

Alistair knew the instant he saw the reaction from the crewmen on the deck above them that they'd guessed right. Panic erupted on the deck. Even though none of them could see it, the ship wasn't so big that Alistair couldn't hear the sudden shouts and thunder of footsteps above them.

"We've got them," Joe whispered by his side. "Thank God, we've finally got them." He grabbed Alistair's hand and held it tight.

It was agony to wait for the ship to be secured and for the crewmen above to be convinced to let down a gangway and to allow Wrexham and the other officers to board. Alistair and Joe charged aboard as well, David and Lionel following. Even Darren moved warily aboard the ship, his eyes wide with expectation and his mouth firmly shut. Darren's face lost all its color at the first, distant sound of a child screaming.

"I'll kill anyone who's harmed so much as a hair on any of their heads," Joe growled as they waited for the officers to appear from below with the children.

"Get in line," Lionel said in a voice as cold as ice, his face a mask of fury.

Alistair nearly burst into tears as the first, bedraggled child in tattered clothes was brought out onto the main deck from below. The terrified little girl's face was streaked with dirt and tears, and she didn't know what to do with herself. Two more girls followed, then a shivering little boy.

"Toby," Joe called, the sound ripped from him, and leapt forward.

The boy jerked his head up. The moment he spotted Joe he burst into tears and ran for him. Joe crouched and opened his arms, wrapping them around Toby with a cry of pure heartache that squeezed Alistair's throat with emotion. A few seconds later, a small girl raced to join them, and Joe enfolded her in his arms along with Toby.

"Emma, thank God," Joe wept.

Alistair wanted to go to him, to join in the moment, but far less tender emotions assailed him. He turned to Darren. "Do you still think we're perverted beasts?" he snapped, shaking with anger. "Are you still proud of yourself for threatening to disown me and standing in our way? Would you have been proud if we'd been just fifteen minutes late?"

Darren met his eyes. His mouth dropped open, but nothing came out. The pain and shock in his expression was everything his brother deserved until he let go of petty prejudices and faced the bigger problems of the world.

"We need to get them off the ship and someplace warm," David said, moving forward to speak to Wrexham. "And we need to get them something to eat."

"Agreed," Wrexham said. He turned to his officers. "Search the ship for Burbage or Chisolm, or anyone connected to them."

His words had a paradoxical effect. The sailors—who had all shrunk to the sides of the ship and sat gloomily, waiting for their punishment—suddenly stirred. Half a dozen dashed from their spots to the edges of the ship and the gangplank. Before the police officers could move in, one escaped and climbed a rope down the side of the ship.

Alistair dashed to the railing and looked over to see where the man disappeared to. He swore under his breath when he spotted the man tearing up the wharf and pushing people aside as he did. "He's gone to warn Burbage," Alistair shouted.

Wrexham shouted orders to his men, and two of them charged down the gangplank to chase after the escaped man.

"Lily!"

Alistair whipped around at the sound of Joe's shout,

hope thundering through him. But that hope was instantly dashed.

"Lily?" Joe stood, Toby and Emma clinging to his sides, searching the children who had come out from below. "Lily, where are you?"

Alistair knew immediately he wouldn't find her. Wrexham's men had a dozen children clustered together to one side of the deck. Lionel and David were with them, repeating the same sort of soothing act Lionel had used with Maude. But all of the children were young, none of them more than ten years old. They wept and shivered, shrinking away from the police officers and sailors. None were even close to being a fourteen-year-old girl.

Alistair pushed away from the side of the ship, striding to Joe's side and resting a hand on his shoulder. "She's not here," he said as carefully as he could.

Joe met his eyes with a look of such pain that tears stung at Alistair's eyes. His mouth worked, but he couldn't bring himself to speak.

"Just because she isn't with these children doesn't mean she isn't still out there to be found," he said. "We'll find her. We'll catch Burbage and pry everything out of him. We will find her."

Joe nodded, but it wasn't enough. Alistair threw his arms around him as best he could with Toby and Emma wedged against him. The children seemed to sense that Alistair was someone who could be trusted too, and Emma hugged his leg. It was strangely endearing.

"Eccles House," Joe said at last, peeling himself away from Alistair. His grief had transformed into vengeance. "That's where we have to go. If someone went to warn Burbage, that's where he'll be."

"You're right," Alistair said, pivoting to search for David. When David glanced up from the children and met Alistair's eyes, Alistair called, "Eccles House. We have to go there to catch Burbage and Chisolm before they can make another move."

"Agreed," David said, breaking away from the children. "Lionel, can you take care of them?"

"Yes," Lionel said, gesturing to some of Wrexham's officers.

David crossed the deck, motioning for Alistair and Joe to follow. Alistair squeezed Joe's shoulder and started after him. A still-stunned Darren came with him.

"Go with Lionel," Joe told Toby and Emma, in spite of their protests, as he freed himself from them. "He'll take you someplace safe, and then I'll come and see you, I promise."

They let him go. By the time Alistair made it down to the wharf, Joe had caught up to his side.

"I'm going to make Burbage pay for this," Joe hissed.

"We both are," Alistair agreed.

CHAPTER 20

*E*very second that it took for the carriages taking Joe and Alistair and the others from the far end of London's dockyards to Eccles House in Mayfair seemed to drag by.

"Can't they go any faster?" Joe hissed, leaning against the window and looking out. "We could run there faster than this."

"We couldn't, and they're going as fast as they can," Alistair assured him, resting a hand on Joe's knee.

Alistair's brother had leapt into the carriage with them. He sat with his arms folded tightly over his chest, studying Joe and Alistair with an unreadable expression. *At least he's stopped raging on about perversion and indecency.* Joe didn't think he could handle any sort of tirade against his personal life at the moment. Not when he was so close to discovering Lily's fate.

He was a breath away from finding his sister, he knew

it. Toby and Emma were in safe hands now, and he clung to his desperate hope that Lily would be in his arms again by the end of the evening. They would catch Burbage and Chisolm and bring them to justice. He knew it as deeply as he knew his own soul.

When the carriage ground to a halt just a block before Mayfair, his patience snapped.

"I'm going the rest of the way on foot," he growled, throwing open the carriage door.

"Then I'm going with you," Alistair said.

The two of them jumped down to the pavement. Alistair's brother followed silently. As the three of them raced past the carriage holding David, Wrexham, and another officer, David stepped down.

"We're going on foot," Alistair told him before he could ask.

"Right," David said, nodding back into the carriage, then following.

Wrexham and his officer launched into motion too. The six of them were an intimidating sight as they charged down the otherwise peaceful and posh street, looking as though they were out for vengeance. Night was beginning to fall, and those residents who were just stepping out for their evening entertainments gasped and dodged out of the way as their group charged on.

Joe ignored them, only one thought on his mind. Burbage would tell him where Lily was, and then he would pay.

"I beg your pardon. What is the meaning of this?"

Mr. Vine demanded as the six of them pushed past him the second he opened Eccles House's front door. He spotted Joe, and his eyes went wide. "You cannot just barge in here. You've been sacked."

"This is a police investigation," Wrexham said, stepping forward, David right behind him.

Mr. Vine's mouth flapped as the full impact of what was happening hit him. His confused gaze landed on Alistair. "Lord Farnham, what is going on here?"

"It is as Officer Wrexham said. This is a police investigation. Where are Chisolm and Burbage?"

The color drained from Mr. Vine's face. "They aren't at home," he snapped, backing up a few paces and searching the hall.

He caught the eye of a footman at the far end of the hall. The young man turned and ran.

"He's going to warn them," Joe shouted, launching into a chase.

Wrexham and his officer immediately followed.

"What is going on?" a female voice sounded from one of the parlors as Joe ran past. He caught a brief glimpse of Lady Matilda before putting his full energy into chasing the footman.

"Stay where you are," Alistair ordered her as he joined the chase.

"Why are you here?" Lady Matilda followed them regardless.

Joe didn't hear his answer. The footman turned a corner, and instantly Joe knew where he was going. "He's in his study," Joe said over his shoulder to Wrexham. "You'll find all the evidence you need to arrest him in there."

He was right. The footman reached the open door to the office and shouted, "My lord, the police—"

He got no further before Wrexham lunged ahead of Joe and into the office. Joe managed to rush in right after him, in time to see Burbage hunched over his desk, his arms full of papers that he appeared to be feeding into the fireplace across from the desk. Burbage recoiled at the sight of them, dropping everything in his arms.

"Don't move," Wrexham shouted. "Stay right where you are."

Burbage's startled look lasted for only as long as it took him to notice Joe. Then his expression pinched into one of hate and revulsion. "What is the meaning of this invasion?"

The others crammed into the room. David shot straight toward the desk, gathering the papers Burbage had dropped.

"A transaction of the vilest nature has been stopped just now at Batcliff Cross Docks," Wrexham explained. "A dozen children were rescued from trafficking. The crew of the ship has been taken in for questioning, and perpetrators have been named."

Joe peeked at Wrexham out of the corner of his eye, wondering if the man was bluffing or if he'd been too occupied with Toby, Emma, and the others to notice questions being asked. Either way, he turned to Burbage and said, "The game is up. You've been discovered and you will be brought to justice."

"I've done nothing." Burbage stood straighter, a calculating look in his eyes as he glanced from Wrexham to Joe, and then on to Alistair. "This is all a blatant lie designed to hide the perversion between these two." He pointed to Joe and Alistair.

"This is everything we need," David said, the light of triumph in his eyes, as he pored over the disorganized papers on Burbage's desk. "There are plenty of details about transactions, dates, and people involved."

"None of that is mine." Burbage changed his tactic, backing away from the desk. "I don't know what any of this is about."

"Is this not your house?" Wrexham demanded. "Your study?"

"It's...it's my father's house," Burbage stammered. "He has been known to allow his friends to keep their things in some of our unused rooms. I've never even been in this room until tonight."

"That's a lie," Joe growled, stepping toward him. "You and I were in this very room not a week ago."

"How dare you?" Burbage rounded on him. "Who do you think you are?" He turned to Wrexham. "This is the man who should be arrested. This filthy sodomite was recently dismissed from my employment. I discovered his sins and couldn't bear the sight of him. He has fabricated all of this as a means of revenge."

Joe wondered if Burbage would sing the same tune if

281

he knew that most of the men surrounding him were members of The Brotherhood.

David seemed utterly nonplussed by the drama unfolding around him. "Gather everything you can here and take it someplace safe," he told the police officer with them. "There's enough evidence here to bring the case to court at least."

The officer glanced hesitantly to Wrexham, but as soon as Wrexham nodded, he began collecting evidence along with David.

"Stop this at once," Burbage shouted. He stood as though he intended to take control of the situation, but his eyes were filled with fear. "You cannot simply burst into the home of a peer and confiscate personal property."

"I thought you said none of this was yours," Alistair said, radiating confidence.

"I—" Burbage stammered for a moment before blurting out, "None of it is mine. I'm not involved in the whole sordid business, I swear."

Joe sucked in a breath at the near confession. They had him. At last, they'd pinned Burbage into a position he wouldn't be able to wheedle out of.

Desperation clicked inside of Joe, and he lunged toward Burbage, grasping his arms and throwing him back against the wall. "Where is Lily?" he demanded. "Where is my sister?"

"Joe," Alistair cautioned him, rushing to lay a hand

on Joe's shoulder. It was a comfort, but not quite enough to calm the rage boiling in Joe's gut.

"I don't know. I swear, I don't know," Burbage said, panic lacing his voice and draining the color from his face.

"You do know. You know where she is just as you knew where Toby and Emma were until we found them," Joe insisted.

"I swear on my life, I don't know anything," Burbage said, his voice raw with fear.

Alistair squeezed Joe's shoulder, and Joe stepped back, breathing heavily. David and Wrexham moved in on either side, keeping Burbage trapped in his corner.

"As a solicitor, I advise you to cooperate with this investigation," David said in a commanding voice.

"You're a solicitor?" Burbage asked, his arms raised protectively in front of him.

"I am." David nodded. "I've been spearheading this investigation, and I can assure you, the only reasonable course of action for you at this point is to tell us what you know and hope the court is lenient with you."

"But I don't know anything, I swear on my life," Burbage insisted.

"Your life isn't worth much," Joe spat.

Burbage managed to glare at him through his fear. Even with his back literally and figuratively against the wall, his hatred was palpable. "Those two are the criminals you should be arresting," he said. "Their sins are many. All I've done is invest in a private investment."

"Children are not an investment," Joe growled. "They are people, precious people, with lives of their own."

"I saw the state those children were in," Alistair seethed, narrowing his eyes at Burbage. "Only a truly evil man could allow that to happen, could *invest* in it."

"I don't know what you're talking about," Burbage said, moving restlessly from foot to foot. "I invested in a company, that was all. I never bothered to investigate all of its facets."

"These papers seem to tell another story," David said, holding up a ledger.

"As I told you, I don't know who those belong to." Burbage raised his voice, but also looked as though he might start hyperventilating. "My father allowed his friends to keep things here."

"Friends involved with your investments?" Alistair asked. He hadn't removed his hand from Joe's shoulder, and his grip was like iron because of his anger.

"Where is your father?" Wrexham asked. "He should be fetched at once."

"He's not here," Burbage said, relief flashing into his expression. "He's...he's away."

Joe didn't believe it for a second. He also noticed for the first time that the footman wasn't in the room with them. "Someone needs to search the house," he said, dashing for the door and glancing out into the hall.

"He's not here, I swear it," Burbage shouted as Wrexham's officer strode out into the hall as well.

"He's probably long gone," Joe sighed, rubbing a hand over his face.

"I'll search the house all the same," the officer said.

Joe stepped back into the study. Wrexham and David still had Burbage cornered. Alistair looked ready to pummel Burbage. Alistair's brother and Lady Matilda stood together near the door, watching the scene unfold with wide eyes and startled faces.

"You can't prove anything," Burbage said, his shoulders dropping in defeat. "Even if you could, no court in England would touch a case against an old and noble family like ours."

"Is that an admission of guilt?" Alistair asked, swaying toward Burbage, fists clenched.

"It is not," Burbage barked. "I am merely pointing out that, should you be foolish enough as to take this matter any further, it will end in humiliation for you. I will be exonerated."

"Will your father?" David asked, scanning through the papers rather than looking at Burbage. "I don't think so." He glanced up, smiling at Burbage in a way that should have chilled the man's blood. He turned to Wrexham. "I trust more of your men will be here soon. We'll also need a wagon to take Lord Chisolm and Lord Burbage—" he glanced to Burbage, "to Newgate Prison."

Burbage recoiled. "How dare you even consider placing me or my father there? It is out of the question. We are peers."

David shrugged. "For a crime like this, nothing is out of the question."

"I told you, I have done nothing wrong," Burbage insisted yet again. "I want you all to leave my house at once."

"The only people leaving this house are you and your father," David said. He handed the documents he'd been studying to Alistair, then took a step toward Burbage. "You can leave this house one of two ways. Either you can be escorted by Officer Wrexham's men and taken to whichever prison they see fit to deposit you in, or—" He paused, letting the tiny word linger in the air.

"Or what?" Burbage asked, his eyes wide with worry.

David shrugged. "Or you can cooperate, tell us everything you know about who is trafficking children, where those children have been taken, and what sort of headquarters the traffickers operate out of."

"But I told you, I know nothing," Burbage shouted, a new sort of fear coming over him, as if he suddenly understood just how trapped he was. "I merely provided money. And occasionally alibis."

"And children?" Joe asked through a clenched jaw. When Burbage gaped at him, he said, "Toby and Emma came from your household. So did Lily. How many others have gone missing from this house over the years?"

"I don't know what you're talking about," Burbage said desperately.

Joe was beginning to wonder if Burbage really didn't

know what he'd gotten involved in. The possibility only aggravated him.

"After what we have seen today," Alistair began in a low voice filled with fury, "for you to deny involvement is not just abhorrent, it is evil."

"And you think you are one to lecture me on evil?" Burbage asked him. "You, who parade around with your valet lover?"

"You don't know half as much as you think you do," Alistair said, shaking his head in disgust. "And what you do know is wrong. Joe and I have worked tirelessly for these last few weeks to bring an end to your sordid business. And we have. That is all you need to know."

"You've brought an end to nothing," Burbage told him. "Do you think this whole enterprise begins and ends with me or my father?"

An uneasy knot formed in Joe's gut.

"I may not understand anything, as you accuse me of, but I am not lying when I say this is not my business." Burbage turned to David, then glanced on to Wrexham. "You would be a fool to arrest me, or anyone in this house, or to make any attempt to pin this crime on us. Your career would be ruined." He glanced back to David. "Your license to practice law would be revoked."

David lowered his head slightly, a wry smile tugging at the corner of his mouth. He took a step closer to Burbage. "My lord, you do not know whom you are dealing with. Your title may protect you from full prose-cution, but I can assure you that there are far worse things for your sort than to be brought before a court or before the House of Lords."

Burbage scoffed. "I doubt it."

David stepped quickly up to him, leaning in close enough to whisper something in Burbage's ear that Joe couldn't hear. He exchanged a glance with Alistair, who evidently couldn't hear what was said either. All Joe knew was that when David stepped back, Burbage was as pale as a ghost and his mouth hung open.

"This is how things will proceed," David went on, glancing to Wrexham, then to Alistair and Joe, then fixing Burbage with a sharp stare. "You will hand over any and all documents pertaining to this investigation within your possession. You will go with Officer Wrexham to wherever he feels he can best interrogate you on the matter to glean what information you do have. When that is finished, you and your father will leave England for an extended holiday in whatever remote corner of the world you choose to explore, the farther the better."

Joe's brow shot up at the unexpected condition. Alistair seemed just as surprised.

"You must give me time to make arrangements," Burbage said in a hoarse voice.

"You will go with Wrexham immediately," David said. "You have until the end of the week to make your arrangements."

"But I—"

"We're finished here." David turned away from

Burbage as Wrexham stepped forward to grasp his arm. As Wrexham led Burbage out of the room—and Joe was shocked at how quietly the man went—David turned a reassuring look to Joe. "We'll find out what happened to your sister, Joe. I truly believe Burbage doesn't know, but someone does. Something in this web of villainy he's a part of must know something."

"Thank you," Joe said, not knowing what else he could say.

As soon as Wrexham marched Burbage out into the hall, it felt as though most of the energy drained from the room. Joe let out a long breath and rubbed a hand over his face. "I wish I felt as though things were settled," he said.

Alistair raised a hand to rub his back. "They will be settled. Soon. I'll make sure of it."

Joe sent him a grateful smile. He didn't have Lily. He still didn't know where she was. But he had Alistair, and everything within him was certain that wasn't going to change.

"Were...were there really children on a ship about to be taken away?" Lady Matilda asked, her voice weak and wavering.

"There were," Alistair's brother answered her, as somber as a priest. "I saw them with my own eyes." He glanced up at his brother. "They were in every bit as wretched a state as Alistair said they were. If he and...and Mr. Logan hadn't worked so hard to rescue them, I shudder to think what would have become of them."

"They're safe now, my lady," Alistair told Lady

Matilda, taking a step toward her, trying to smile. "Rest assured of that."

Lady Matilda nodded, slowly breaking down into tears. Her shoulders shook as the three of them who were left in the study with her looked on. Alistair finally stepped forward, slipping his arm around Lady Matilda and letting her cry against his shoulder.

"It's so frightening," she sobbed. "And to think, my sister is married to that man. If I hadn't said something...." Her words trailed off into a moan.

Joe arched one eyebrow. True, Lady Matilda's well-timed revelation had meant the difference between rescuing the children or losing them, but if she had any thought of taking credit for the whole thing....

"I'm so sorry," she said, suddenly lifting her head from Alistair's shoulder and taking a step back. She glanced from Alistair to Joe. "I don't understand what the two of you...." She swallowed, her face blushing deep pink. "I don't think it's right, but...but I cannot continue believing it is entirely wrong. Not when it has become clear to me that you have put your all into saving these children."

"Thank you, Lady Matilda," Alistair said softly. "My heartfelt advice to you is not to think of it at all. Put it out of your mind for good."

Lady Matilda nodded. Her face pinched into grief again as fresh tears wet her face. "It simply isn't fair. You are the nicest man I have met, Lord Farnham. Why can you not be normal?"

Joe wasn't sure whether to laugh or shake his head in disgust.

"I honestly don't know, my lady," Alistair said, raising Lady Matilda's hand to his lips for a friendly kiss.

"We should go home," Alistair's brother said in a subdued voice. He glanced to Joe with an exhausted frown. "There are things we must discuss in private."

Joe stood straighter, crossing his arms and arching an eyebrow. So he was to be included in the discussion now? "Agreed," he said.

"Then let's go," Alistair said, taking Lady Matilda's arm and leading her out of the room.

CHAPTER 21

The ride home from Eccles House was nearly silent. Alistair was only marginally satisfied with leaving David and Wrexham to finish what they needed to in terms of the investigation. Chisolm truly wasn't at home, which was unsettling, but Burbage was taken into police custody in spite of his protests. Alistair would have stayed behind to make certain every possible measure had been taken to ensure whatever part the Eccles family had played in the trafficking ring had ended. He would have given anything to uncover information about Lily Logan. But his own family matters were far more pressing.

Darren studied Joe with an unreadable expression through the short ride home. Every time they passed a streetlamp, an eerie blend of shadow and light would illuminate both men's faces. Joe met Darren's scrutiny with implacable strength, giving Alistair the feeling that some sort of battle would break out once they were safely tucked away at home. The two men he cared the most about in the world, aside from his father, seemed to be heading toward an explosion.

It was something of a relief when they discovered Father was still awake and tucked in his chair in the parlor once they got home.

"Is something wrong?" Alistair asked, striding forward to see to his father, and possibly to avoid the inevitable confrontation. "Shouldn't you be in bed, Father?"

"I had a feeling in my old bones that I needed to wait up for the two of you to return," his father said, taking Alistair's hand with his frail one and squeezing it. His father's face lit with delight at the sight of Joe. "There you are, young man," he said. "I was wondering what became of you. No one would tell me. But I suppose it must be time consuming to acclimate yourself to a position in a new house."

His smile was so innocent that all Alistair could do was send a knowing smile to Joe, then a sterner look to Darren. "Mr. Logan isn't going anywhere, Father," he said. "He will be on hand to care for you, if you'd like him to, as well as serving my needs."

He hadn't meant the phrase to have a double meaning, but Darren coughed and scowled all the same.

"Are you ready to go up to bed?" Joe asked their father, stepping forward without waiting for someone to issue a command. "I can help, if you'd like."

"Thank you, my boy." Their father took Joe's hand in both of his and patted it. "I am feeling a bit done in. But you can call for Jeffrey. He knows the routine."

Joe took a step back, but before he could launch into action, Darren stepped out of the room to find the footman.

Everything that had happened throughout the day suddenly felt like a heavy burden on Alistair's shoulders that he was ready to remove. "You were right, Father," he said, crouching by his father's chair so that he could look up into his eyes. He took his father's hand. "You were right about everything all along. I'm so sorry we doubted you."

"I'm always right," his father laughed, a vague and cheery smile making him look like a youth trapped in an old and decaying body. He leaned closer to Alistair. "What was I right about this time?"

"The Eccles family has been involved with a slave trade of sorts," Alistair explained. He was careful not to include too many upsetting details as he went on with, "Not just in the eighteenth century, but now. Joe—that is, Mr. Logan—and I have been working hard to investigate their business dealings, and this evening, we finally proved that they have been up to every sort of evil."

"Isn't that what I've told you all along?" his father said, cheeks pink with pleasure. "You've always been such a smart boy. I knew you would crack their nefarious code eventually."

"Burbage has been arrested," Alistair went on.

"Though, as a peer, I'm not sure how much the law can truly do to bring him to justice. It looks as though the best we can hope for is that he and his father will leave the country permanently."

"It's damnably unfair that a title can serve as a broom to sweep all manner of sins under the carpet," his father scoffed. "If I were you, I'd make sure and certain that the Eccles family assets were frozen as quickly as possible and that any outstanding debts were called in. That should provide the justice that the law won't."

Alistair stood, his brow rising as he did. "I hope David has thought of that," he said to Joe.

"I'm sure he has," Joe answered. "I'm beginning to see that nothing gets past the law offices of Dandie & Wirth."

"I'll contact a few of the people I know to whom Burbage and Chisolm owe money," Darren said. Alistair hadn't noticed him return to the room, but he wasn't surprised.

Jeffrey was with him. "Are you ready, my lord?" the young man asked.

"As I'll ever be," their father sighed as the footman came over to help him out of the chair. "And perhaps, if I'm lucky, the good Lord will take me home tonight. I feel as though my work here is done."

The simple statement, delivered with such peace and resignation, chilled Alistair to the bone. "Not yet, Father," he said, throat tight with sadness. He rested a hand on his father's arm as Jeffrey led him past. "Please, not yet. I'm not ready for you to go." Surprise tears stung at his eyes.

His father looked at him with so much affection and pride that it was almost impossible for Alistair to hold himself together. "If you're not ready, I'm not ready either, my boy." He reached for Alistair's hand. "And truly, I receive far too much joy from watching you conquer the world as the man you've become to want to rush off to the hereafter yet. You are the apple of my eye and the spring in my heart." He turned to Darren. "You as well. And that rapscallion sister of yours, whenever she deigns to stay at home for more than a fortnight on end."

Alistair let out his emotion with a laugh and wiped away the rogue tear that escaped from him. "Thank you, Father," he said, watching as Jeffrey led his father on. "You have no idea how much it means to me to hear you say that."

"In that case," his father said over his shoulder as he reached the doorway, "I should say it more often."

Alistair drew in a long, settling breath as his father disappeared around the corner. He felt too much emotion to speak or move. How long had he waited for his father to say something like what he'd just said? To tell him that he was loved and that his father approved of him? His father had said enough for Alistair to know that he was proud of him, that he truly had done his duty to his family, whether he followed the standard path to that duty or not. As Joe stepped up behind him, resting a hand on his shoulder, Alistair felt as though he had, indeed, conquered the world, as his father had said. He'd brought evil men to justice, he'd helped the innocent and helpless, and he'd found love.

"Are you going to be all right?" Joe asked him in a low, voice, leaning into him.

Alistair nodded and reached back to take Joe's hand.

The only thing preventing him from being completely happy was the way Darren stared at the two of them. The heightened emotion in the room bristled into uncertainty.

"I only wonder how long Father knew before we caught on to things," Darren said at last. It wasn't what Alistair expected him to say.

"He's been telling us to keep an eye out for years," Alistair said.

"He must have known all along, then." Darren nodded, taking a step toward them. "But why didn't he tell us when his mind was still clear?"

"Perhaps he thought you weren't ready," Joe said.

Darren paused a few feet in front of Alistair and Joe, a puzzled look coming over him. "I don't understand you," he admitted. "I find you utterly incomprehensible."

"Because I'm nothing but a country valet, standing in front of you like an equal?" Joe asked, a hint of mischief in his eyes.

"You know what I mean," Darren said in a quiet voice. He paused, then said, "But yes, that too." He paused again before saying, "You aren't going to show me the least bit of deference in my own house going forward, are you?"

"None at all," Joe said with a smile. His hand tightened on Alistair's shoulder.

"And you're not going to give this up and return to normal," Darren went on, glancing to Alistair.

"This is my normal," Alistair said, taking Joe's hand.

Darren nodded, then let out an exhausted breath and rubbed a hand over his face. "What sort of arrangements do you suggest we make? Do you intend to live under this roof...as you are?"

Alistair shrugged. "Anything else would be seen as suspicious. And I believe the best course of action in situations like this is to raise as little suspicion as humanly possible."

"You must find a way to keep this hidden from Beth," Darren insisted.

"Beth already knows," Alistair said, smiling at the acceptance she'd given him during their conversation about it. "And, I might add, she approves."

Darren's brow shot up. "She really is a rapscallion."

Alistair was tired of dithering and talking around things. "No one on the outside will so much as raise an eyebrow at my having a valet," he said. "I have some concerns about our servants, but they can be easily navigated as well. And, in all honesty, if it is easier for everyone, I wouldn't mind traveling a bit, seeing the world." He glanced to Joe. "If that's something you'd like."

"I wouldn't mind." Joe smiled, but that smile faded. "As soon as we find Lily."

Alistair's heart ached for Joe. He was more than ready to retire to his room with Joe so he could wrap him in the care and affection Joe clearly needed. "We'll find her," he said.

For the first time in a long time, it felt as though things were settling. Darren continued to look uncomfortable, but at least the disgust and anger was gone from him.

"You realize this means you will be my heir," Alistair told him with a brotherly smile. "So it will be up to you to marry and produce more heirs. I believe Lady Matilda is in the market for a husband."

"Good Lord." Darren's eyes went wide. "In that respect, you were a braver man than me. I think I'll search out a wife in greener pastures than that."

"It's up to you." Alistair let go of Joe and moved to embrace his brother. It was a quick, somewhat awkward embrace, but at least it was a start. "And now, I'm off to bed." He glanced over his shoulder to Joe, who fell into step with him. Whatever Darren thought of that or assumed would happen next was none of Alistair's concern.

By the time he and Joe made it upstairs and behind the closed and locked doors of his bedroom, Alistair was finally starting to feel as though everything that could be resolved had been.

"You won't mind?" he asked Joe as he shrugged out of his jacket and loosened his tie.

"Mind what?" Joe asked as he, too, began undressing.

"Living a life as my valet? Having all the world assume we are simply employer and employee?"

Joe laughed. "You're right when you say it's the safest arrangement we could come to. But you know that rumors will spread over the years when you never marry. Especially if anyone notices your complete devotion to your handsome and charming valet." He tossed his jacket aside, then moved to stand toe-to-toe with Alistair, embracing him.

Alistair laughed, then circled his arms around Joe, leaning in for a kiss. It felt like the most natural thing in the world. It felt like home.

"We won't be able to hide anything," he admitted with a sigh, brushing one hand through Joe's hair, then stroking the side of his face. "Anyone who looks at us will know we're in love."

"I do love you so," Joe said with a burst of emotion that would have been comically maudlin, if it weren't so genuine.

"And I love you." Alistair kissed him again. "I would drop to my knees and ask you to marry me, if I could."

"I'll drop to my knees and do other things," Joe said with a saucy grin, then did just that.

Alistair sucked in a breath as Joe reached for the fastening of his trousers. Things had turned amorous between them so quickly that the feeling of the unexpected heightened every sensation as Joe's hands brushed against his hardening cock. But Joe took his time, unfastening his trousers slowly and tugging his shirttails up before stroking his hands over Alistair's sides and stomach.

"I don't think I will ever grow tired of your body," Joe murmured, lifting Alistair's shirt enough to kiss the flat of his abdomen.

Hot, pulsing need coursed through Alistair, but he joked, "Even if I grow fat and go to seed?"

Joe glanced up at him tantalizingly. "I won't let that happen. I'll take care of you and make sure it doesn't."

The idea of Joe taking care of him for the rest of his life, and of him doing the same for Joe, brought pure joy to Alistair's heart. He threaded his fingers through Joe's hair, wanting to lift him to his feet so that they could kiss and embrace and be as close to each other as possible.

Joe had more carnal things in mind. He raked his hands down Alistair's sides, taking his trousers and drawers down over his hips as he did. Alistair gasped as his prick jumped free. It was already hard enough to stand up, but once exposed, Joe took it in hand and worked it to iron hardness. Every inch of his touch sent hot desire racing through Alistair's veins. His body felt alive with pleasure, especially his cock, as Joe teased and tantalized him.

Alistair somehow managed to unbutton his cuffs and yank his shirt up over his head, dropping it to the floor. The sight of his own, mostly-naked body, his trousers bunched around his thighs as Joe stroked his cock was far more arousing than it should have been. If he wasn't careful, he would come far too soon and spoil what could otherwise be an amazing night. The tip of his prick was already slick with moisture as Joe rubbed his thumb over it, drawing a deep moan from Alistair.

"I think we could establish quite the bedtime routine, you know," Joe teased him, glancing up with a flicker of his eyebrow. "I know just how to tuck a tired nobleman into bed and to make sure he sleeps soundly all night."

"I'm not sure sleep is the first thing on my mind," Alistair said.

Or at least tried to say. Before he could finish, Joe leaned into him, holding his cock upright and closing his lips around his head. Alistair gasped at the pleasure of it, then let out a shaky groan as Joe bore down on him, sinking him deeper and deeper. The way he moved, the way his tongue stroked, and the way his mouth created just the right amount of suction had Alistair's knees so weak that he feared he might collapse. He dug his fingertips into Joe's scalp, grabbing fistfuls of hair as Joe picked up his pace, taking him deeper.

There was no point in fighting it. Alistair knew he was a lost cause as the overwhelming sensuality of the whole thing swallowed him. He couldn't tear his eyes away from the sight of Joe enveloping him, couldn't shut his ears to the desperate sounds of enjoyment Joe made as he did it. The whole thing was too much.

"Oh, God, I'm coming," he gasped, gripping Joe's hair

harder as pleasure rocketed from the base of his spine through his entire body. He cried out with the intensity of the magic Joe had stirred within him as he came, deep in Joe's throat.

Joe's eyes lit with surprise as he swallowed, then rocked gently back, letting Alistair go. "You certainly were ready," he panted.

"I'm sorry." Alistair had a hard time catching his breath as Joe pushed his trousers all the way down his legs and helped him take off his shoes and step out of them. "Now I'll be a useless lump."

"Just the way I want you." The mischief in Joe's eyes was unmistakable as he rose, stroking his hands up Alistair's body as he did.

There was something incredibly erotic in being completely naked when Joe was still fully dressed. Especially as Joe touched and explored him as though he were a coveted prize he'd won. Alistair's warm, post-orgasmic glow only heightened the sensations, and hinted to him that he would be up for another round in no time.

"I'm far from done with you yet," Joe said, the glitter in his eyes downright wicked.

He advanced on Alistair, forcing him to take a few steps back until his legs hit the side of his bed. Once that happened, Joe pushed him, and he fell to his back, splayed across the bed. From there, Joe grabbed his knees and shoved them apart, but then he took a large step back.

"I want you to think about all the ways I'm going to

fuck you while you watch me undress," he said, reaching for the top buttons of his shirt.

Alistair shivered with anticipation as he watched Joe remove his clothes with agonizing slowness. Joe pulled his shirt up over his head and threw it aside, but instead of undoing his trousers, which Alistair practically salivated for, he bent to remove his shoes next. Then he made an agonizingly long show of working loose the fastenings over the distinct bulge in his trousers. It usually took Alistair much longer to recover from orgasm, but he was feeling the surge as intensely as ever as he watched Joe strip.

At last, Joe, finished with his trousers and pushed them down over his hips. Lust pounded through Alistair as Joe's thick cock sprung up in readiness. Joe stepped out of his trousers and kicked them aside, then stalked closer to Alistair. He wedged his legs between Alistair's and bent over him, resting his hands on either side of Alistair's shoulders.

"Now," he said. "I trust you have something to ease this whole process along. I wouldn't want to hurt you as I fuck you until you're calling out my name in prayer."

"In the drawer," Alistair panted, pointing to the table beside the bed.

With a smile wicked enough to turn Alistair's blood to fire, Joe stepped to the side, opening the drawer and taking out a small jar of ointment. He made a devastating show of opening the jar, then spreading its slick contents over his penis. In fact, Joe seemed to be enjoying pleasuring himself so much as he positioned himself between Alistair's legs again that watching him took Alistair's breath away. He wasn't sure which he wanted more—to watch Joe bring himself to climax or to feel him deep within.

He didn't have to make the decision. Breathing heavily, his expression suddenly serious, Joe let go of himself and grasped Alistair's hips. Alistair let out an eager sound of anticipation and offered himself as Joe stretched over him. Without hesitation, Joe guided himself to the right spot, then thrust into Alistair.

It was magnificent. They worked through the slightest bit of resistance before fitting together perfectly. Neither of them could keep quiet as Joe moved faster and harder, holding Alistair's knees and keeping him spread and open. Alistair closed his eyes and arched his head back as Joe worked the spot within him that sent a deeper kind of pleasure swirling through him. It was good, so, so good. He was throbbing again in no time and grasped himself with one hand and Joe's hip with the other, working himself as Joe drove into him.

As intense as the pleasure was, he managed to hold off until Joe came inside of him with a shattering cry. As soon as the intensity of Joe's thrusts slowed, Alistair jerked himself hard, coming with enough force to awaken the heavens. Joe collapsed on top of him, and together they rolled to their sides in a sweaty, sticky, satisfied mass.

"You are everything to me," Alistair panted, caressing

Joe's face and kissing him as they lay tangled up in each other.

"And you are all I've ever wanted," Joe said, kissing him in return. "Ours will be a beautiful life."

Alistair closed his eyes and smiled, knowing that it would be.

EPILOGUE

$\mathcal{D}$avid Wirth sat at the desk in his office, poring over the documents he and Wrexham had taken from Eccles House. There was enough information about the ring of men—and some women—who were trafficking children for every manner of evil to convict an army, and yet none of it was specific enough to condemn specific individuals.

"They're smart, I'll give them credit for that," he murmured as he went through yet another set of cryptic notes about delivery locations and shipments.

"Any criminal not rotting away behind bars is smart," Lionel said, walking into the room and setting a steaming cup of tea on David's desk. "That's why they haven't been caught."

David frowned up at him and reached for the tea. "I hate knowing that men who have evil intentions toward children are so clever. It means they've gotten away with horrendous sins without anyone being able to stop them."

"Without anyone being able to stop them yet," Lionel corrected him. He sat on the corner of the desk and crossed his arms, looking every bit the deadly fashion plate he was. "I was able to question some of those children that we rescued from the *Nightingale*. They all tell the same story. A mannish-looking woman in a colorful, ragged coat offered them sweets if they would help her look for her lost puppy."

"It's the oldest and most effective trick in the book," David sighed, leaning back in his chair and sipping his tea. "And it's on all of our heads that those children are so desperate for affection and special attention that they fall for it instead of running." He took another sip before saying, "Though I'm not sure that explains why an older child, like Lily Logan, would be taken in."

"We don't know what Lily was offered," Lionel argued.

David nodded, then winced. "I hope to God that we are able to find Joe Logan's sister. It eats me up that she wasn't with the others."

"Lily Logan went missing months ago, which means she'll be harder to find," Lionel said.

"You're right. I just wish I knew more about this woman who has lured the children away."

Lionel hummed dangerously, his pretty face knitting into a frown. "What I find interesting is the implication that this Adler person we've been looking for might be a woman."

David nodded. "They're clever to use a woman to do their dirty work. Few people would immediately think that a woman would lure children into slavery."

"And even fewer would think a queer or two would be the ones hot on their trail, so we have the advantage there," Lionel added.

David sent him a stern look. "The idea is not to reveal who we are, so that they have no reason to suspect anything."

"Speak for yourself, darling." Lionel stood and turned to head back to the main part of the office. "I know who I am, and I'd rather use that to my advantage than run from it."

"Obviously," David called after him with a grin. Of course, Lionel had the benefit of power on his side. Far more than anyone in London knew. He's spun that web of power himself, and he was cutthroat enough to use it for his own means when he needed to. Which was probably why David admired the hell out of him.

He was on the verge of returning to his work when he heard the sound of the main office door opening, then shutting.

"Good morning, Mr. Siddel," Lionel greeted their guest in his softest, sweetest voice. "It's nice to see you again. How can I help you?"

"I was told that Dandie & Wirth might be able to

assist with a serious problem I have," the vaguely familiar voice of Stephen Siddel said.

David sat straighter, craning his neck in the hope of getting a glimpse of their new arrival, but without any luck. He'd met Stephen Siddel once at The Chameleon Club and had been impressed with the man's kindness and compassion.

"We are experts in helping people with serious problems," Lionel answered the man. "What is the nature of your problem."

"As you know, I run an orphanage in Limehouse." He didn't sound like he was from that part of the city. "And yesterday, one of our children has gone missing. Two little boys from the home run by the Sisters of Our Lady of Perpetual Sorrow too."

David jumped to his feet and marched around his desk and out of his office, his heart suddenly racing.

"Missing children?" he asked.

Mr. Siddel looked just as David remembered him— young, perhaps thirty. He had a cheerful face, blue eyes, dark, carefully combed hair, and spectacles. His suit was clean and well-made, but simple. And he wore a look of such genuine distress that David instantly wanted to help him.

"Yes," Stephen said. "A little girl from my orphanage and two boys from the Sisters'. I was given the impression in our last conversation that you might know what to do about children that have gone missing."

"Unfortunately, we do," Lionel said, getting up and

crossing the room to fetch Mr. Siddel tea. Leave it to Lionel to make certain that the rules of hospitality and congeniality were always observed, even in the direst of situations.

"When did these children go missing?" David asked, gesturing for Mr. Siddel to have a seat on the sofas.

"Yesterday," Stephen said, looking confused, but taking the offered seat all the same. "My children and the Sisters' performed at a benefit concert that was held at the Bardess mansion. Afterwards, we realized the two were nowhere to be found."

David's pulse shot up. The concert at the Bardess mansion. Alistair Bevan had come from there the day Lady Matilda told him about Burbage. And now more children were missing. There had to be a connection.

"You've come to the right place, Mr. Siddel," David said as Lionel handed the man a cup of tea. "We're already investigating this kidnapping ring, and we won't stop until we bring it down."

❦

I HOPE YOU HAVE ENJOYED ALISTAIR AND JOE'S story! They were lucky to be able to have a perfectly legitimate excuse to build a life together, in spite of the inherent inequality of Joe becoming Alistair's valet. Building a life together was a challenge for gay men in the nineteenth century, but it wasn't impossible. While The Brotherhood organization is my own invention, it has roots in actual underground societies of the time. Support networks were in place for the LGBTQ community of the Victorian era, though none of them were a part of respectable society. But in fact, the first gay rights organization in England, The Order of Chaerona, was formed in 1892, so the need for societies of support and advancement for gay men were definitely a part of the landscape of London.

As twenty-first century people, we tend to misunderstand the way society operated in the nineteenth century. The first and best line of defense for the homosexual community was that far fewer people were even aware of their existence, unlike today. That's not to say life was better or safer for gay men, but they were afforded a certain amount of anonymity that doesn't exist today. And as you'll discover in future books in *The Brotherhood* series, when the majority of people don't understand who or what you are, you can get away with a lot more than most people would suspect.

BUT WHAT ABOUT THE MISSING CHILDREN? WILL Lily Logan ever be found? And what has become of the children Stephen Siddel has reported missing? You can find out more about Stephen—and his admirer, Lord Maxwell Hillsboro—in book two of *The Brotherhood, Just a Little Temptation*, coming soon! Keep clicking to get started reading Chapter One!

. . .

IF YOU ENJOYED THIS BOOK AND WOULD LIKE TO HEAR more from me, please sign up for my newsletter! When you sign up, you'll get a free, full-length novella, *A Passionate Deception*. Victorian identity theft has never been so exciting in this story of hope, tricks, and starting over. Part of my *West Meets East* series, *A Passionate Deception* can be read as a stand-alone. Pick up your free copy today by signing up to receive my newsletter (which I only send out when I have a new release)!

Sign up here: http://eepurl.com/cbaVMH

ARE YOU ON SOCIAL MEDIA? I AM! COME AND JOIN the fun on Facebook: http://www.facebook.com/merryfarmerreaders

I'M ALSO A HUGE FAN OF INSTAGRAM AND POST LOTS of original content there: https://www.instagram.com/merryfarmer/

AND NOW, GET STARTED ON JUST A LITTLE TEMPTATION...

Chapter One

LONDON – APRIL, 1890

STEPHEN SIDDEL HAD HIS HANDS FULL. MORE THAN full.

"Sir! Fanny is hogging all the biscuits!"

"I can't find my other shoe, sir!"

"Jane dipped my braid in ink!"

"No I didn't!"

"Sir, it isn't fair!"

The second Stephen stepped into the great hall of his orphanage, chaos erupted. Without fail. It was no wonder. Two dozen girls between the ages of five and fifteen ran mad in the spacious room, finishing up their breakfasts, attempting to complete last-minute school-work, playing with ragged dolls or roughly-carved wooden animals, chattering up a storm, and generally behaving the way all spritely and contented children did. The pandemonium always made Stephen smile, in spite of the exhaustion it inevitably brought with it.

"Jane, the only things that should be dipped in ink are pens," he said, adjusting his spectacles and walking down the center aisle between two long tables and resting a hand on the shoulder of a ten-year-old with freckles and hair that was still cropped short after an unfortunate bout of lice. "Your hair will grow back in no time, so there's no reason to be envious."

"Yes, sir," the girl said with a sigh, glancing adoringly up at him.

"And Katie, let's work on your tattling, shall we?" he grinned at the girl with the end of her braid blackened.

"She shouldn't have done it," Katie protested. Stephen gave her a frank look and her shoulders sagged. "Yes, sir."

Stephen walked on, "Fanny, one biscuit only until you finish your maths." He plucked the mostly empty bowl of biscuits from the end of the table as he reached a plump eleven-year-old and her coterie of studious friends.

"I was sharing them," Fanny reassured him, peering up at him with moon eyes.

"I know, sweetheart." He rested a hand on her head before carrying the bowl on to the head table.

"Sir, can you help me find my shoe?" a small girl named Ivy asked, tugging on the tails of his coat.

Stephen turned to find he'd developed a small entourage of girls. They looked to him as though he held the answers to every question in the universe in his hands. "When was the last time you had two shoes?" he asked Ivy in a kind voice.

"I don't know." Ivy shrugged.

Her younger sister, Lori, slipped a sticky hand into Stephen's and leaned against him for no apparent reason. The gesture lifted his heart, making him smile in spite of the chaos that still ruled.

"Did you check under the stairs?" he asked. "I've no idea why, but missing things always seem to show up under the stairs."

"We didn't check there," Ivy admitted, filling with energy. "Come on," she said to her friends, turning and dashing off down the aisle between tables.

"No running," Stephen called after them, though he might as well have been telling them not to be young.

A game of tag had popped up on one side of the room, under the windows that beamed with morning sunshine. The sun illuminated the sad state of the great hall. It was large and bright, but half the wallpaper had peeled away months ago, leaving grubby plaster exposed. The wainscoting needed a thorough scrub, and perhaps a coat of paint. The floor was scuffed and worn. It most certainly could have used a polish. The curtains that hung from the windows—or what was left of them after the moths had had their way—were in desperate need of laundering. The entire orphanage had a run-down, drab feel to it. At least, in appearance. Stephen was fiercely proud of the fact that, underneath the wear and tear, his home, the home he'd provided for the unfortunate girls who had been cast off by an uncaring society, was filled with joy and love.

Hard on the heels of that blissful thought came a sigh from Mrs. Ross, who was seated at the head table, several ledgers spread in front of her.

"It's no use, Mr. Siddel," she said, shaking her head and rubbing her temples. "There's far more going out than there is coming in. At this rate, we might have to shut our doors by the end of the year."

"We're not going to shut our doors," Stephen told her,

still maintaining his smile. "These girls have nowhere to go and no one to care for them if not us."

As if to emphasize his point, a thin, towhead girl skipped over to him, silently handing him a drawing of a bird that she'd just finished. Stephen took it, adjusted his spectacles as he glanced at it, and exaggerated his delight as he studied the drawing.

"This is beautiful, Ginny," he told her resting a hand on her head. "You've the makings of a brilliant artist."

Ginny smiled up at him, her two front teeth missing, then wheeled around and darted back to her place at one of the tables.

Mrs. Ross humphed. "The way you let them waste paper is a sin. Are you aware of how much paper costs?"

"It's a price I'm willing to pay to foster creativity," Stephen said, placing Ginny's drawing on the table.

Mrs. Ross glanced at it with a fairly impressed look, and Mrs. Ross wasn't generally free with her praise. She had seen more than most people in her fifty years, which was reflected in her grey hair—which she still managed to style fashionably—and the lines on her face. Stephen had been lucky to find Mrs. Ross, and her daughter, Annie, when he'd inherited the building that housed the orphanage ten years ago, at the tender age of twenty. Few people would even consider hiring a former prostitute and her illegitimate daughter, especially to run an estab-lishment meant to care for children, but Stephen recognized the older woman's sharp mind and savvy busi-ness sense right from the start.

She had recognized a few key things about him as well. Things he desperately needed to keep hidden if he was to maintain his place in what passed for society in East London. She had been willing to keep his secrets right from the beginning, and he had been quick to give her a secure living and a roof over her head.

"You'd better hope the concert at the Bardess Mansion next week brings in a flood of donations," Mrs. Ross warned him. "We're living hand-to-mouth as it is."

"We'll be fine, Mrs. Ross," Stephen told her with a wink. "Something always comes along to rescue us just before we're thrown into the fire."

Mrs. Ross hummed doubtfully, then pulled the largest ledger closer to her. She did have a point, though. They needed to perform outstandingly at the Bardess Mansion concert so that the high and mighty of society opened their purses. The wallpaper and curtains depended on it. Although, if the concert proved to be a disappointment, Stephen had other places to turn for help. He'd already appealed to The Brotherhood and had faith that the organization would come through for him.

Until that happened, God helped those who helped themselves.

"Girls!" He clapped his hands, doing his best to snag the attention of the noisy, busy room. "Girls, it's time for song practice."

Several of his young charges erupted into shouts of excitement. A few raced from one end of the hall to the piano in the front corner. Fanny and her group closed up their schoolbooks, stacking them neatly on the corner of the table. Katie and Jane appeared to be bickering and hadn't paid attention to his announcement. Stephen started toward them, dodging pigtails, skirts, and giggles as the girls made their way toward the piano, where Annie Ross already sat, playing the first notes of a simple hymn. The piano was badly out of tune, but the music of a dozen young voices breaking into song was like heaven.

That slice of heaven burst into the full glow of paradise as Stephen glanced to the doorway and spotted the most handsome gentleman he'd ever seen. He stood a little straighter and touched his spectacles to make certain he was seeing right. The man was clearly a part of the aristocracy. His clothes said as much. They were of fine fabrics and fit exquisitely, though Stephen knew he shouldn't be studying the man's trim waist and broad shoulders. His thoughts refused to settle as he took in the man's dark, curly hair, sparkling, hazel eyes, and shapely lips. If he didn't replace thought with action, he'd be in trouble before he could say "boo".

"Can I help you?" he asked, striding up the aisle between the tables to meet the man.

"Yes, I'm looking for Mr. Stephen Siddel," the gentleman said.

Stephen's heart flipped in his chest. *Thank you, Lord.* Aloud, he said, "I'm Stephen Siddel," and extended a hand.

The gentleman took it with a pleased grin. "Lord Maxwell Hillsboro," he introduced himself.

"My lord." Stephen nodded respectfully.

"Oh, none of that," Lord Hillsboro laughed. "I'm barely a lord at all. Only by default. I'm a younger son, and it was only a stroke of luck that my father had a subsidiary title left over to give me the honorific. In truth, I'm desperate to get as far away from all that as possible." He was rambling, and a charming flush splashed his cheeks.

"I see." Stephen smiled in spite of the voice in his head that told him to behave. Lord Hillsboro's hand felt strong and warm in his as they shook, which made good sense hard to hold onto. The man really did have the most fetching eyes. He hadn't had such a strong reaction to a stranger in years. "How can I help you, Lord Hillsboro?" he managed to ask.

"Actually, I was hoping I could help you," Lord Hillsboro said.

WANT TO READ MORE?
PICK UP JUST A LITTLE TEMPTATION TODAY!

Click here for a complete list of other works by Merry Farmer.

ABOUT THE AUTHOR

I hope you have enjoyed *Just a Little Wickedness*. If you'd like to be the first to learn about when new books in the series come out and more, please sign up for my newsletter here: http://eepurl.com/cbaVMH And remember, Read it, Review it, Share it! For a complete list of works by Merry Farmer with links, please visit http://wp.me/P5ttjb-14F.

Merry Farmer is an award-winning novelist who lives in suburban Philadelphia with her cats, Torpedo, her grumpy old man, and Justine, her hyperactive new baby. She has been writing since she was ten years old and realized one day that she didn't have to wait for the teacher to assign a creative writing project to write something. It was the best day of her life. She then went on to earn not one but two degrees in History so that she would always have something to write about. Her books have reached the Top 100 at Amazon, iBooks, and Barnes & Noble, and have been named finalists in the prestigious RONE and Rom Com Reader's Crown awards.

ACKNOWLEDGMENTS

I owe a huge debt of gratitude to my awesome beta-readers, Caroline Lee and Jolene Stewart, for their suggestions and advice. And double thanks to Julie Tague, for being a truly excellent editor and assistant!

Click here for a complete list of other works by Merry Farmer.

Printed in Great Britain
by Amazon